THE NODE

A Novel by Tito Perdue

NINE-BANDED
BOOKS

The Node

Nine-Banded Books
PO Box 1862
Charleston, WV 25327
www.ninebandedbooks.com

ISBN-10   1616583517
ISBN-13   978-1616583514

Editorial assistance: Ann Sterzinger

Cover art © 2011 Alex Kurtagic

Cover design by Kevin I. Slaughter

For Judy,
Judy always

THE NODE

Our earth is degenerate in these latter days.
There are signs the world is speedily coming
to an end.

—Assyrian tablet

1

It remains only to be told how our hero grew up and died. Let it also be told about his physical person, how he drifted from one career to another and this account can quickly be brought to a close. Of his ancestors and other things, little need be said.

To begin, he was a tall man and except for one particular feature, was reasonably average in a great many ways. His legs hung down on both sides, acuminating in two feet of no particular distinction. His arms were perhaps thinner than he would have wanted, as also his neck, ankles, and his reengineered dog, a honey-colored creature purchased at great expense from a nearby biogenetical laboratory (now shut down). But primarily it was our hero's face (because it was pale and broad and box-shaped) that drew the little bit of attention that sometimes came his way. In fact, it was even worse than that, resembling, as it did, that of a squid, or the flywheel of an old-time escrubilator, those with the several holes that had been designed almost as of set purpose to simulate a nose and shrunken mouth. Seen in full sun, it looked, that face, like a slate that had been wiped clean and then redrawn in a faint blue chalk that had mostly peeled away by now. Worse still was his profile, which had a saurian aspect centered upon a bright red tongue that was forever darting in and out. And then, too, his nostrils were so small, minuscule orifices that manifested a whistling noise when he breathed in and viperous aspirations when he breathed out. Not part of his face properly speaking, his hair appeared to be a bituminous product capable of independent movement and employed primarily for testing the quality of the air. Never again was he to see a face like his own, not till that day he came upon a Devonian Age fossil in his own backyard, and found there the original prototype.

Of careers, he had had about twenty of them before he achieved the age of 28. Remember that in those days, when the average life endured for upward of 120 years, a person could dally for a great while before settling upon his authentic career. Accordingly he wasted a good four of those years in putting up drywall for the neighbors and painting over it in acrylic. He was good at this and oftentimes could be seen grinning as he worked. Which is to say until there came the day when suddenly he grew bored with the whole process and turned around and left it, returning two days later to clean up the mess.

He was too old for college but went there anyway. Torn between Sanskrit and Real Estate, he used to come to class and, his face veiled, used to observe the modern youths who sometimes seemed more interested in each other than in what was inscribed upon the school's armorial crest. Himself, he had hated old people when he was young, just as now he hated his co-students, puerile types always trying to get a look behind his veil. The lesson was unmistakable—that the new generation was just as loathsome as the old one used to be.

He studied mining technology, choosing for his specialty the then-burgeoning kaolin industry. Sickened from inhaling so much particulate matter, he then rotated over with evil intent into the study of ventriloquism and bank management. Linguistics was next, though he soon came to doubt the theory of the Indo-European mother tongue as the prime source of western grammar. No, he had seen better and more elegant formulations among certain contemporary rural individuals with whom he enjoyed a personal familiarity. It was mainly for that reason that he had veered over into the study of Moabite Antiquities and then followed that up with a three-month tutorial in the Schleswig-Holstein Problem.

Exhausted before he was granted a degree, he embraced a long stay in the fog-bound purlieu of Lago Todos Los Santos in South American Chile. Here, rising late, he reveled in the good sleeping the place afforded. And yet, here too, his money soon ran out. Angered by his imperative needs, he hitchhiked back to the residual United States and accepted a profitable assignment enforcing the European Union's universal hate crime laws.

His second stay at the University! Chile notwithstanding, he was tempted by seismology, by Pictish numismatics, blood spatter analysis, and other fields of study including most pleasurably (it was to prove his favorite subject) forensic nematology. Studied meta-chemistry and graphology, hotel administration and resumé construction. Briefly he worked as an oculist, an occultist, a honey producer, trapeze artist, and wrote magazine articles for a journal laudatory of a certain breed of poultry. Briefer still, he tried to be a tin monger and then, finally, set up a rocks and minerals booth in Bryson City.

It was true that he had developed a small library, though nothing certainly like what his grandfather had left. Proudest among his volumes was the variorum edition on calfskin of Cockayne's *Leechdoms, Wortcunning, and Starcraft*, a capacious volume that had served him more than once in dealing with his own diseases.

(Diseases: He suffered from glanders and shingles, from nose bleed and accelerated hair growth. Other inadequacies of his were focused mostly below the waist, including the two or three of them [not mentioned here] that he had inherited from his people.)

He possessed a copy of the *Newe Metamorphosis* of Marston together with a boxed set of the annotated A. A. Milne. *The History of the World Conqueror* by Juvaini was his, as also a medical dictionary, two novels by Jerome Wisdom, *Mother Shipton's Dream Book*, and volume IV (only) of *The Cambridge Medieval History*. He had a dictionary.

By this time he had taken a certificate in Teaching English to English Speakers, thus providing himself with a rich source of money. Between this and drywall and the few hundred-weight of strawberries he was able to produce on his 20 acres, he thrived very happily for about two years, which is to say until he ran into a girl with the sort of figure that spoke to him, not realizing until too late that she had been modernized.

"Why so uppity?" he asked. "And why so loud?"

"Oh? And how would you like it, to be a woman in this testosterone hell?"

" 'Hell?' "

"All I ever wanted was to be a CEO!" she wept.

He had two tomes on scientific matters and in the wake of their divorce used some of his alimony to harvest volumes V and VI of the above-mentioned Cambridge set.

He had other possessions, including most especially a .357 magnum revolver that held eight shells. He used to take this out sometimes at night and play with it, yearning for someone to launch an attack on him. He knew the effect of those cartridges, if not on flesh, on watermelons and cantaloupes at any rate. He had two suits, one of them mildewed and the other obsolete. He had a third that fit real well. Had a frying pan, a pocket knife and an outboard motor. But all these fell away into entire inconsequentiality when compared to his most prominent, most expensive, and proudest article of all.

One final book he had, a thing in golden covers that he had bought for its aesthetic appeal. And although he could read no word of it (being illiterate in Persian), he used to carry this around as well. He had no further books.

His investments, to bring this to an end, were negligible but diversified. Every share of stock was hedged by an option, and every option by some stock. He had invested equally in futures and the past. But mostly he had put his money into the so-called "moral dereliction" coupons, granting certain rights. The wisest thing he had ever done, these had quickly been folded into some of the country's best performing mutual funds.

Funds, alimony, coupons and strawberries, he was able by age of 37 to retire to his remaining acres, seven and a half of them. Here, shut off from the business (and busyness) of the outer world, he shortly lost account of what was happening. Did they still wear trousers, new style girls, and the nineteen petroleum producing nations, had they been subdued by now? He really didn't know.

Followed then six years in silence.

2

To leave home at the time of the rising of the dog star—risky behavior in the extreme. (Later on he said it was because he no longer had access to propane that he had chosen to come to town.) The weather, it is true, had been abnormally awful, and he could not stay warm throughout the winter without indenturing himself to hearth and dwindling hoards of hardwood. And though he had read his books and had accumulated a lot of sleeping time, he hadn't laid eyes upon a woman in all those years. Having eschewed television and periodicals of every sort, he still believed the country to be what once it was. And then, too, owing to those nightly bands of stragglers and southern capitulationists migrating across his and his neighbor's land… It was too much, as finally he admitted.

Originally it had been his intention to seek out a cylinder of propane and have it delivered to his place, a scheme that might have sufficed him until June; instead, after trekking the four miles to town and finding nothing of that kind, neither propane nor occupied cottages nor even anything else, he stepped from the edge of the forest and, treading as noiselessly as he could, began to penetrate the ruined suburbs that had washed up along the southern perimeter of Nelson County, as it was denominated in those days. Anyone watching from a moderate distance or less could have seen that he carried a knapsack on his back and was dressed in a hat of some kind that came to a peak and bent over and pointed to the ground. That person could also have seen that he wore moccasins on one foot and boots on the other, and that he had accustomed himself to spats in place of socks.

But no one could have guessed what he carried in his knapsack, save that whatever it was, it was almost too heavy for an individual man. One waited in frustrated expectation of seeing him finally disburden himself of the thing and open it up to view. One also noticed that he was being trailed by a dog, an animal of commensurate size with a metal collar that made somewhat of a chiming noise as the little links happened to brush against each other in time with the pace adopted by the... It chimed. The animal, yes, was old, a burnt-out case really, but endowed still with good dentition.

He said he saw bats (one of them transporting a toad on its back), circling ever so slowly about the smokestack of one of the downtown factories. It was a period of long nights and short days, a symbiotic combination that still worked out to the usual 24 hours, more or less. Next, he crossed over into a Salvadoran neighborhood where he must tread with utmost care lest he be discovered and chased down and stomped to death or inserted into one of the glowing ovens where even now at three o'clock in the morning the local bakery was readying the next day's wares. Pressing at the glass, he spied in upon a numerous family of a burly wife in a peasant's skirt and some four or five children suffering, apparently, from want of vitamin D. No question about it, the odor that came from that place was praiseworthy in the extreme and included new-made pastries that could be smelt if not, however, seen. Here he lingered, aware at the same time that a lamp had come on in one of the overhead apartments. Far away he heard a radio full of static and bits and pieces of Spanish spoken at exaggerated speed.

They moved past the twice life-size statue of a bearded man who had been the western hemisphere's most admired mass murderer. Never pausing, they crossed over into a Korean district where their safety was fractionally improved, as our narrator believed. But if they were awake and active, these neighborhood people, and going about their business, one could not have detected it by obvious signs. Was he being watched by Asian eyes? Probably. And might they leap out upon him as he wandered by? He thought not, no, or not at least with any effect, not so long as he carried in his vest the .357 caliber heirloom revolver handed down to him by his fathers. And this was not even to mention the some 300 rounds of ammunition that formed so integral a part of the freight that he carried on his back.

He was old and getting older, and his footwear was old, too. In younger days he had tried to avoid the cracks in the sidewalk while at the same time keeping a conscientious score of his failings. But not now, not when such matters seemed somewhat less important than more pressing projects bearing upon his prospects and very survival indeed.

By 3:57 he had come to the heart of the downtown city, an underwater garden, as it seemed, owing to so many stalk-like buildings wavering in the current. Here he halted long enough to twine his scarf more snugly about his neck and then take out a cigarette and ignite it hurriedly for the warmth it might give. The stars meantime were jittering back and forth—until he understood that it was but a deception caused by the motion cited above of the downtown structures listing from side to side. He saw then a light burning yellowly in one of the upper stories and silhouetted against it what either was a human being or item of furniture of some kind. There was no question but that the wind was accelerating as it wended among the buildings and ran off down the streets lined on both sides with commercial buildings. It was 4:07 in the morning and they still had several blocks to go.

"About four more blocks," he said. "But what if they won't let us in?"

He groaned, the dog, and then began searching up and down the avenue for other places in which a person and his dog could escape the wind. A capsized car lay in the intersection, its doors missing and offering no sort of protection. Except for that, neither man nor dog could see any sanctuary soever from the weather.

"Too late to go back now."

"Well hell yeah it's too late!" (He was speaking to himself in two voices.) "Should of thought of that before you started out!"

"I did. I thought about it."

"The devil you did! I don't know, sometimes you just…"

He stopped, distracted by an airplane toiling overhead. Many months had gone by since last he had witnessed any such thing as that, a jet-powered ship with fuel enough to get where it was going. The man marveled and watched, shielding his eyes by habit against the weak light of the moon. But what a poor pilot it was to steer like that, an unselfconfident person who changed his mind at the last moment and opted to keep on going instead of setting down.

"He's not stopping."

"Pretty obvious isn't it? Jeez."

A delicatessen came up, a narrow building squeezed in between two much larger ones. Pressing against the window, our traveler detected an illuminated glassed-in counter holding a selection of meats and cheeses together with a gallon jug of knurled pickles floating in brine. He perceived a sausage in there too, a coiled and pudgy thing half again as long as the longer of his own two arms. They were eating well, were these people!

It was not that he intended to possess himself of any of these products, not at this time and not so long as the place held several CCTV cameras looking down from the corners of the room. The hour was late and there was an iron grating over the window that could by no means have been broken open save by aid of much heavier tools than any possessed by him. Even so, he marked down the location, using for that purpose the gel-point pen that he carried in his vest. Already he had circled a good number of landmarks on his street map, including the police station, the waterworks, and several other designations. Suddenly he ducked back under the awning, surprised that the helicopter had come back and was patrolling almost exactly overhead. In the next block an individual of some sort had stepped from his doorway and was scanning up and down the road, oblivious, as it seemed, to our hero and his dog. He estimated it, the man who gave this narration, as the last day in April, 4:38 in the morning, birds circling overhead.

He arrived at his destination and bent down close to the numerals that provided the address, a four-digit citation (1647) that approximated so closely to a well-known historical date that he knew he'd remember it always. He also knew that he was getting ready to knock on the door, and having done so he took off his glove and rapped a second time with greater vigor and simulated confidence. He was not afraid. A little bit queasy maybe. Meantime the building itself was of four stories with a frontage of perhaps a hundred and twenty-seven feet. Each storey had a row of windows, all of them rendered opaque with soot or some other accumulation that effectively formed "mirrors," as it were, reflecting what was left of the washed-out moon. Peering upward, our man then descried a very long and very narrow pennant unfurling atop the building, a black or possibly deep scarlet streamer that reached out over the street below and possibly a little further. He could not of course decipher the insignia all at one time, though it seemed to bear the likeness of a reptile or something of that kind. That was when the door came open suddenly and he discovered himself squinting from a distance of about six inches into the face of a wizened old man, tall and thin, who wore a pained expression. His face was narrower than it should have been and in the moonlight his glasses looked as if they had been covered over in chartreuse paint. In those lenses our traveler could see himself, the building opposite, and an automobile snuffling down the street.

"Peebles, is it?"

"No, I'm ————," our boy said, giving his real name.

"———— ?"

"Yes."

The usher checked his notebook, an inexpensive little affair with a spiral spine.

"I don't see you on the list."

"No, no. I was recommended."

"Yes? And by whom if I may ask?"

He provided the name, our boy, and waited to see if it would register on the person's face.

"Ah. Are we talking about a long-term stay? Or just for the night?"

"Long."

"And the dog?"

"Please."

"You weren't followed?"

"No, no. I'm sure I wasn't."

The usher stood back, giving entrance to both the animal and man. The door, made of metal, was a good four inches thick and had a peephole in it that our hero had been loath to use when he was still in the outside world. He knew he was going to take off his heavy coat—(he had not been invited to do this)—and hang it on one of the hooks in the vestibule where right away he observed some six or seven pairs of galoshes and shoes arrayed in tidy fashion next to the interior door. The usher stood back now and looked him over with a non-committal expression.

"Let me see if Larry is still awake."

"Right." He began to move into the building proper, which is to say until he was forestalled by the man. His arm was long and thin and extruded incongruously from a sleeve with girth enough for half a dozen men. He noted, our boy, a catheter dangling under the fellow's trouser cuff.

"If you'll wait here."

It gave our narrator time enough to seat himself, take off his boots and moccasins and console his soles, as he liked to say. There were a number of etchings on the wall, most conspicuously of the letter "L" (for Larry?) in Holbein's Alphabet of Death. Our man moved closer, examining in detail the full horror of that scene. Perhaps it represented his own impending fate, should these people refuse him and send him on his way.

He was a troubled-looking human being, this "Larry," as could be seen in his face. Our man rose immediately and after wasting a few seconds trying to shake with him, said:

"I ask for sanctuary." And: "I have money."

"So. Are we speaking of a long-term stay? Or just for the night?"

"Long."

"And the animal?"

"Yes."

There were two facing benches in the vestibule, allowing them to sit across from each other. His interlocutor was an austere sort of person with gray hair rotting from the top and pointing off in all directions. His face meantime looked like the underside of the fibulation plate of a disassembled 2013 Husquevarna snow blower. His mouth was wide and had a better number of teeth in it than might have been expected upon first impression. His eyes appeared to have been made, respectively, of porcelain, jasper, and agate. And in sum he was a representative wall-eyed man, rubicund, pixilated, beetle-browed and beery. His handshake, which he consented at last to grant, was firm in the beginning though he very quickly began struggling to get free. Behaving with conspicuous dignity, he then plucked out his handkerchief, used it, and began very calmly to inspect the needlework. "You come to us from…?"

"Yes. Been living out there in the countryside since 2017."

"I should think you'd have wanted to stay."

"I would, yes, like to stay," our man said. "But it's not possible, not any longer. Can't get propane. And too many strangers moving back and forth."

"Strangers?"

"Flagellants, people like that. Rosicrucians. All sorts."

"I see. Yes, we get them, too. Gilians, most of them," he said, referring to one of the new religions. "Well, not as bad as it used to be of course."

He acknowledged the statement, our man did, and then waited for the dialogue to pick up where it had just now broken off.

"Countryside, you say."

"Yes."

"Wife? Children?"

"No children."

"You left out the part about wives."

"Divorce."

"Now it comes out. How many?"

"How many wives? Or how many divorces?"

"Those two numbers ought to be about the same, no?"

"Not necessarily. For example I might still be hanging on to one of those wives, what?"

The man put on an annoyed expression, and then drew out a pad and pencil and made a notation.

"Brought money, you say?"

He delved deeply, our pilgrim, into his knapsack, but then had to go back and release the combination lock that held together this rather protean piece of luggage that contained some forty-four pounds of highly miscellaneous contents. He had two hundred Yuan and a little more, together with another sixty stowed away in a certain pocket accessible only to someone already knowledgeable about it. The man named Larry took up the bills and, wetting his thumb, proceeded to count the stuff, a slow procedure that seemed to give him a detectable pleasure that made both men blush.

"Two hundred and four Yuan, all in specie."

"Yes, Sir."

"Plus whatever's in that little"—he pointed toward it—"that little compartment there."

"I brought some food, too."

"The devil you say."

"No, I really did! See?" He withdrew one after another some dozen cans of sardines and processed meat, a wedge of cheese and box of substitute water.

"No spirits, I assume."

He smiled, our boy, and then took out a pint of rum and another, not quite full, of a coffee liqueur from the former Brazil.

"Gracious. And you're prepared to donate all of this to us? What else did you bring?"

"Books."

"Books! How many? Or rather, how good?"

He lay them on the table, eight separate volumes, each scarcer than the next. The man applauded his selection.

"Anything further? But no, your little green knapsack is almost empty."

"I still have something else in there," the narrator said. (He took out his .357 caliber revolver and 300 pieces of ordnance, well-organized objects standing, each, in a perfectly-fitting little cubicle of its own.)

"Oh gosh! We can use this certainly! I think I'm going to let you into the great room, where we can talk. "

The room was great indeed, a high-ceilinged area that might

almost have been a cathedral or shopping mall emporium at some period. But mostly his attention was for the fire, a robust affair in one of the largest hearths he ever had seen. They gravitated toward it naturally, man and dog, and stood at attention before the warmth. Suddenly he jumped back, surprised to find there an old man in a leather chair peering pessimistically into the flames. Outside it had begun to sleet, a commonplace occurrence these days. It formed a sound like that of grit being thrown unavailingly against the tall and very narrow windows that reached almost to the ceiling.

He was in an unusual place, an atrium really, notable for the absence of any sort of ornamentation or drapery or art works on the wall. He was however able to make out through the gloom a heavy-laden cabinet holding as many as a hundred volumes stored higgledy-piggledy on the shelves.

"Shall we talk?"

He followed the man to the table and sat across from him. A diesel-fired coffee maker took up the middle of the table, although the traveler waited until invited to do so before siphoning off a cup of the stuff for himself. The chinaware was frail and interesting-looking, and bore the schema on it of subatomic particles in rapid motion. The coffee, too, was of almost the perfect formula and there were good supplies of sugar and cream as well. The supervisor watched closely as our boy lifted the cup and quaffed down the contents in three or four hasty actions. And continued to watch as the boy poured out a second cup without risking to be asked.

"You've come far?"

"Yes, Sir. Peluria County."

"Peluria! I thought that would be the last place. You knew that they've cleared Ringo County already?"

"I've heard about it."

"A few stubborn people still clinging on. They're doomed of course."

"I reckon."

"Nativists!"

"Yes, Sir."

They looked at each other. A woman and child had come into the room and then, seeing two men talking, turned and went out again.

"How do you feel about that?" asked the man called Larry.

"I think some of my people were in Ringo."

"Belike."

"Yes, Sir."

"Odd business, no? We spent a thousand years putting together some advantages for ourselves, and now we're supposed to give them all away."

"Yeah. Everybody's good except us. We're bad."

"Precisely. Entirely appropriate that black people, yea and Asians too, should look to their interests. But don't you try it!"

"Yeah. 'Less you want to get 'wedged.'"

"Just so. Is that why you've come?"

"I guess so."

"To stand against this 'malign titration?'"

"I been wanting to for a long time."

"You're an educated man?"

"Little bit. But I can still do things."

"Escrubilator repair? We can always use that."

"Pretty good bricklayer."

"That's even better. I'm already leaning toward letting you stay. Ever killed anyone?"

The boy looked down. "Not yet." And then: "My granddaddy killed a fellow."

"Yes, but we aren't talking about him. Our grandfathers were a different kind of men."

"Yes, Sir, I agree," our pilgrim said, after raising his hand and waiting to be called upon.

"And so we have to start all over again, no? And learn to be more like them?"

The pilgrim frowned painfully, his mind slowly coming into play. "Look out for our own interests? Instead of other people's?"

"Precisely. Can you do that?"

The conversation proceeded smoothly, right up until the boy began to notice that the sun was coming up behind the stained glass panes in the lower sectors of the elongated windows. It illuminated the picture of a reaper sowing in a field, a blue tableau highlighted in pink. He had been wrong, quite wrong, to imagine that the place was devoid of art.

"Yes," the superintendent said, "one of our people made that."

Together they watched as one by one the dawn uncovered a succession of stain glass scenes showing an ancient ship floundering at sea, unicorns and insects and a diagram of the daytime sky that might or might not replicate the reality that illuminated it from behind.

"We could not have created the Chinese civilization, we 'Cauks,'" the man said. "But nor could they ours."

Came next a portrait of the seated Charlemagne, an aged but yet handsome individual with a staff laying across his lap and a terrestrial globe cupped in one hand.

"Those were the days."

The visitor, knowing little of such matters, nodded obligingly. His attention had meantime been called by the sight of some seven or eight men, middle-aged types who had mustered in the vestibule and were preparing to depart the place. One wore goggles, one carried a canteen, and one had a bowie knife strapped at his side. Embarrassed by it, the chieftain tried to explain:

"We have to have some kind of income after all."

"Oh."

"Try to use volunteers of course, but if that isn't enough... Well! There's always the lottery."

Our boy put on a worried face. He had not come to this place in order to take up a position in the outside world. On the other hand, the seven men seemed to form an experienced group that no doubt was accustomed to coping with things. He even thought he detected a certain repressed excitement as they assisted one another with their paraphernalia. The dog, too, wanted to go, though his owner held him back. Meantime he was giving half his attention to the stain glass portrait of a medieval cavalryman clothed in bright red armor composed of scales.

"No one works for more than seven hours," Larry was saying. "And if they do, why we'll go after 'em and bring 'em back."

"Where do they work actually?" the visitor asked, his mind still partly on the cavalryman etched in glass.

"Oh, the usual thing. Rolo there is in sales. The others are mostly public relations, consultancy, facilitation, etc., etc. That wee fellow there? Grief counselor. But never mind, we don't expect people to participate in our little enterprises during their first few days."

"I could teach."

"Not hardly, not unless your Portuguese is a good deal better than mine."

"I can't speak it at all."

"Ah. No wonder you're here."

The boy reached for the coffee but then changed his mind when he saw how bright the day was threatening to become. Oblivious to the law, he took instead a cigarette and ignited it with one of the wax-protected matches he carried always.

"You're tired," the man observed. "You've come far and you're tired."

He admitted it, whereupon the supervisor arose quickly and, taking his candle with him, conducted our boy down a long narrow hallway that grew yet narrower as it disappeared among the dark. Indeed it tapered so radically, that corridor, it caused the people to turn edgewise as they went on. Here were any number of little cells, mere cubicles really, that abutted upon the hall. Some were shut tight, some open to view, and some had individuals in them occupied with books or escrubilators or, in one case, a hunched man bent over a monitor that glowed a virid green. Here they paused, proctor, pilgrim and dog, and introduced themselves.

"Herb? I want you to meet... By God, I haven't even asked your name!"

"————," our narrator said, choosing a name from his recent readings.

They shook all around, Herb, the dog, and our man. He was a gloomy specimen, was this Herb, and because the computers gave so little warmth, had wrapped himself in a vicuña shawl. The office itself was full of clutter, much of it on the floor, and one's first impression was of a chaos so complicated and interesting-looking that it had come to bewitch the rather unhealthy-looking man at the center of it all. Just now his monitor, clouded over by a fog of some kind, revealed a herd of whales roaming at high speed along the bottom of the sea. One's attention turned then to some of the other screens that filled the wall and in two cases were suspended from the ceiling by what looked like nylon fishing cords. Among other visions, a person could see an unsteady black-and-white image of the very doorway by means of which our man had entered the place.

"No one can sneak up upon us now by God," the rector said. "Not since Hollis here joined our ranks!"

"'Herb,' actually."

Our boy meantime needed very urgently to piss, and if he were not soon given access to a mattress, might have to put himself on the unclean carpet and fall off to sleep in plain open view.

"Fellow needs to piss, I believe. See how he's dancing around like that?"

"Yes, Sir. And sleep, need some of that, too."

"I see! Well you can have one of those, but not both. This is not a charity you understand."

"Yes, Sir; I understood that as soon as I handed my money over."

In the event, his chamber, unclean also, did have bedding in it. He disrobed hurriedly and then arranged himself on a pallet barely thicker than the law required. He didn't care. He had been traveling for forty hours and more and was tired of recycling in his mind all that he had done and seen during that time.

And slept well, too, which is to say until about noon when he stirred and stood up and then, assuming he was allowed to use it from time to time, began searching about for the facility. He passed a senescent-looking man sitting in a cell, a bald sort of person bending over a book bound in membrane. The fellow looked up and smiled.

"You're the new fellow."

"Yes, Sir. I guess so."

"And your homestead? Your cozy little farm? What will happen to that?"

"I don't know." (Gloom came down over him.) "The government's talking about giving it to the Cambodians."

"So! An underrepresented group."

"Yes, Sir." Deferring the need to piss, the boy now stepped into the fellow's rather constricted domain and began to marvel at the array of books that covered three walls entirely and a good part of the fourth. A globe of the world, too, although it reflected a very obsolete notion of countries and continents, including the picture of a bosomy mermaid sitting on the shelf of Argentina.

"O, I see," the man said. "You think I'm trying to escape the present world by retreating into the past."

"I would," the boy said, "if I could."

"Larry doesn't like that. He thinks we still have a chance

to bring back the country we used to have. Before you were born."

"Yes, Sir. I've heard about it."

"You've heard about it, but I was there. Bathroom is down the hall and to the right."

He slept again, this time until twilight came and pressed against the window panes. Leaving his compartment, our "boy" (he was 44 by now), stood for a time trying to understand the arrangement of the stalls and the half-dozen entryways that let in and out of the corridor. He saw a woman and child moving from one room to another and then another person of about his own general type and size carrying an ancient-looking leathern satchel with a hammer and drill sticking out. Outside he could hear cars and buses and the other expectable traffic of the city, even if the noise was muffled somewhat by the apparent density of the building. It was as if he had come to a fortress set up by bad judgment in one of the most dangerous of places, 160 miles outside Nashville, Tennessee. Suddenly just then a tightly focused ray of light broke through the window and loitered a few moments on the opposite wall.

"We need to do something about that," said the man called Larry, who had come up behind and was buttoning the curtains more tightly together. "I had my way," he continued, "and we'd brick up these windows."

"I could do it."

"No, all I need from you just now is that ammunition you've alluded to. And the map."

Agreeing to it, the boy returned to his cell and took out both the ammunition and the hand-drawn map, all of which he passed over to the man who stood waiting for it impatiently. His ears, the newcomer observed, were appreciably bigger than they should have been and resembled a set of little wings designed to fly his mind to higher realms. However he said nothing about it, the boy. Instead he said:

"And I have these antibiotic tablets."

The man took them hastily and spilled them out into his hand, also larger than it ought to be. Having settled into the crux of that cup-like paw, they looked like miniature eggs in a nest of fingers.

"They've expired, these. And this one has mutated."

"Yes, Sir. But if you take a lot of 'em at the same time…"

"All right, that'll be all right. Anything else?"

"No, Sir. Just personal possessions."

"'Personal?'"

"Clothes and so forth. Toothbrush."

"Yes, but don't I see another book"—he pointed to it— "another book in that green and formless pouch of yours?"

The boy drew it out reluctantly and then stood by as the superintendent opened ever so gingerly the faded yellow cover and scrutinized the author's name, the title and imprint information. Continuing with it, he then turned to the text and began to read silently, his two lips fluttering in resonance with the high-grade prose. The boy waited. There was a famous scene in chapter three, if the man desired to read that far.

"Now that's the king's true English!" he said finally, after shutting the book and looking to heaven and then opening it again and going on with it. "And such adjectives! He must have searched the world to find those!" And then, smiling sheepishly, "I've been obsessed forever with the English tongue."

Tongue? And so the man was a pervert, our boy said to himself. He then tried but failed to take the book back into his own possession.

"Glad it was written when it was. Today, of course, it could never be published, not with the English-language quota down to seven percent."

"Sir?"

"Oh yes! And that applies to library collections, too."

Outside a heavy truck had come and parked just next to

the building, an armored personnel carrier as the boy at first believed. It was requisite for both men to edge away from the window lest someone perceive them in the dim. Huddled there, the man now gave back the revolver and most of the ammunition, saying:

"Ah, well; you're just as likely to need this as any of us."

The boy took it gratefully and waited for the book as well.

"Nowadays there're just two sorts of Americans, my man. Those who know they're sick, and those who don't. Have you breakfasted?"

"No, Sir. It's not even dark yet."

"My wife, she keeps us in grits and eggs, everything. Watermelon rind pickles. Fine coffee, really good; you'll be coming back for more all night long."

"Sounds good. I think I'll just put that book back where it was and…"

They fought for it while entering the main room, dodging meantime swatches of moonlight that had leaked through the tattered drapes. He counted, the novice, some two dozen adults up and down the length of that enormous table, not including women and pets. It disturbed him that his own dog had so quickly acclimated to things, diluting the allegiance he owed to one person only. But meantime the coffee was good and brown and the boy permitted himself to splash about in it for the first several minutes, ignoring the questions coming in his direction.

"Yes?" he said finally.

"And left it of your own free will?"

"I didn't have any choice! All those people hanging about. Couldn't get any propane."

"Your ancestors, they had propane?"

"No, no," said the third man, a beetling sort of individual with an incised face whose blue lips at first glance appeared to have been positioned above, as opposed to below, his gingham nose.

Known as Charles Roach, he had come to this place from a failed motel business named after himself.

"No, he had every right to leave. Who are we after all?"

"You don't know?"

"We who have come together to avoid those self-same interlopers who..." The man hushed, aware that he had employed one of the illegal words. Two minutes went by in a general embarrassment in which one could hear almost nothing save for the noise of diners breaking open their colored eggs and/or tossing down bits and pieces of the excessively good bacon. Far away the boy saw a bearded man raise his hand and start to speak before realizing at the final moment that he was about to rub up against the prevailing silence. He had started out to say something about "rights," and the sort, something like:

"No, he has every right in the world!"

"OK, Clay, that'll do it for now." And: "Could I ask you to pass the bacon please? Good stuff, by God."

Never before had the lad had access to as much hot coffee as he had now. Lifting the kettle in both hands, he poured out nearly a full quart of the stuff, resolved to drink all of it before the decision went against him and he was made to quit the place.

"Play chess?" asked the man in the double-pane glasses. His hair was a mess, this man's, and offered the perfect habitat for spiderlings and things like that. Some years ago the boy had read an essay about these creatures, their great variety and sexual habits.

"I play a little bit," said the boy. "But I'm not very good at it."

"Glad you warned me. Nothing more tedious than..." His voice trailed off.

"But if they let me stay, maybe I could become a better player. Well! I couldn't be much worse could I?" He laughed merrily.

"'They?'"

"Sir?"

"No, you said 'they.' If 'they' let me stay, you said. That's what you said."

He drank hurriedly, our hero, from his fourth cup of coffee.

"It's Larry makes these decisions, Larry alone. And of course Milt."

The man named Milt now raised his hand. He was, and no doubt is so still, an atrabilious-looking quantity with some sort of decoration pinned just next to the mandated badge that revealed his genome.

"I used to own this building," he said in a reedy voice somewhere between an oboe and clarinet's. He was shy and his hair was as much of a problem as anyone's there. "But hey, what do I need with a building, right? And then, too, Larry is a very persuasive man."

They all looked to Larry, save only Larry himself who went on eating in the meditative style that seemed to suggest he was disquieted both by the quality of the discourse and the outpouring of vitellus spreading across his plate.

"He's the one with the plan after all," added Milt. "That's what we're counting on anyway."

"That's right Milt, tell this stranger here all our secrets why don't you? Christ."

"Don't worry about it—the way he's going he'll be completely caffeinated in another few minutes anyhow."

It was at this juncture that the boy elected to take no further coffee at the present time. He was still young enough to have observed that the woman across from him was, 1., in a bathrobe, and 2., the robe had fallen open somewhat. How he despised these perceptual interruptions that tied his attention to the female body and its things, he who had set out to seek for guidance and a more ethereal form of life. Draining the last of the coffee, he stood with the others and returned their little bows of courtesy, a nice action that told him the place was as

civilized as could be wanted, and no one could want it more
so.

"Because you're the new boy," the administrator said, drawing
him aside and handing off his own unfinished plate, "you get
to slop the hogs."

He laughed merrily, our boy, until the others also began to
donate their leavings, hash brown potatoes that had not been
entirely consumed and shards of bacon fat. No question about
it, the chess player was enjoying this.

"See? You could just as easily have been playing chess."

It was a primitive sort of arrangement, that which had been
set up for the hogs. Open to the sky, the palings enclosed
perhaps some thousand square feet of space squeezed in
between the barracks, the adjacent suntan salon and second-
hand escrubilator lot. Entering with trepidation, our boy
threaded his way among and between the pigs and dozen
or so chickens cohabiting with them in a state of peace as it
seemed. At first he offered the ladle to each animal individually,
meeting with refusals everywhere. The chickens especially
wanted no part of him and stayed as far away as the enclosure
allowed, eyeing him unsmilingly. That was when he perceived
the wooden trough, a rude structure built of planks that ran
around the interior of the den. "It's here they are wont to feed,"
the newcomer said, taking care not to let the chess player
(watching from the window) see what he was thinking. Truth
was, he was impressed by these animals, their general dignity,
their stance and pertinacity. They knew what they were and
had come to accept it with grace. Coming nearer and bending
low, he testified that the leader of them, a robust creature with
a sawed-off nose with two holes in it, possessed intelligence
of a kind, one that reckoned with the outside world in ways
that he himself could only guess about. The moon above,
how, really, did it look in the eye of a swine? Moving to the
adjoining animal, he saw that its face resembled that of one

of his grammar school teachers of long ago. And here again he witnessed that most adroitly positioned of all the world's noses, a dispensation that allowed the thing to pick up crucial scents a good long time before the rest of him arrived upon the scene.

The hens, for their part, were unable to reach the trough, wherefore our novice began to search about for the assumed bag of grain that could be scattered about on the cold hard ground. The third hog, as he attested now, had ears as thin as palimpsest that had been erased so many times and to such effect that actual perforations had developed in the plasma. However, he preferred not to think about it.

3

Glad to get out of the cold, our man retired to the dormitory and went direct to the hearth where a goodly fire was burning in colors of green and gold. He had believed, mistakenly, that the man sitting next to him in a worn-out armchair was snoring.

"Me sleep? Sleep at night?" the person said. "Not I."

"What are you reading?" our man asked. (He could spy a book that had fallen down between the cushions.)

"This? Quite interesting really. Twentieth-century stuff. Deals with the economy and how our troubles began."

"Oh? But the economy's been pretty good lately."

"Lately? It's been good for two hundred years!"

"Yes."

"Ah, Lord. There was a time, my friend—but you're too young to know about it—when we could have stood against everything. Hurricanes, feminism, dictatorship. But what we could not withstand, and never could, was too much prosperity too much prolonged. That's what did it to us."

Our boy came closer, moving his chair to within about a foot of the older man's.

"Prosperity?"

"Certainly. We had come to the point where even eleven-year-olds could have a closet full of training models. And cars were free. No choice really, we had to pacify the masses lest they tear the cities down."

"Might be better if they had."

The man chortled and then reached over and congratulated the comment with a slap on the knee.

"And weighed 30 stone, some of them. I was there, my man, and saw it happen."

The novice came closer.

"And did you…?

"Certainly. Or rather my father did. In those days it were the boys who were nasty while the girls were sweet. We're talking now about the 1940s and '50s you understand."

"How sweet were they?"

"All right, think of it like this, that they were more interested in love than in careers. Yes, and loved their husbands more than life itself."

The child, accustomed to these hallucinations on the part of the very old, could not but snigger and, finally, laugh out audibly.

"You laugh?"

"No, Sir."

"Fog of prosperity! Separation from life I call it. It leaches the life out of life, a tragedy for those as must endure it. Riveted by small pleasures, they remain oblivious to the great ones." Suddenly he stopped and, blushing, said: "Well yes, perhaps he exaggerated, my father. And of course I've never actually seen a prosperous person myself."

"I read a book one time, said even rich people used to get drafted to the Army."

"Oh?"

"Yeah, and said there weren't all that many facilitators back then either."

"I've heard that."

"Claimed that boys liked girls…"

"More than other boys? That's been documented."

They fell silent, the boy's head drifting back to the Babylonians and other such people whose methods had fallen out of use and could no longer be rightly understood.

"My mother used to bake cookies. Till her therapist made her stop I mean."

"Whew! What did her friends say?"

"They never knew."

Silence again. The older man now picked up his book as if he planned to continue with it but then, having lapsed into depression, slowly let it drop again. Speaking as to himself alone he softly said: "There used to be legislators, presidents even, who were normal men."

The child agreed. Across the way the chess player was playing with himself. Playing chess, the boy had meant to say. They looked at each other warily, even though the newcomer had no intention whatsoever of inflicting upon him his own inferior skills. Further down a comely woman dressed in blue was teaching her child the rudiments of what sounded liked the old-fashioned English of a hundred years before. Was this indeed the tongue that held sway in North America once, the dialect of Wolfe, Faulkner and Perdue? Turning again to the depressed man, our boy asked this:

"I don't know if Larry's going to let me stay."

"You brought that revolver didn't you? He'll let you stay. He likes your attitude. And youth."

"I'm 44."

"Here that passes for extreme youth."

The boy now sat back with more assurance in his uncomfortable chair. "I still don't know what his plans are."

"Victory, that's what his 'plans' are. Victory pure and simple."

"Sounds good."

"All that abandoned space, everything between the Mohawk Valley and Idaho—he plans to seed it with Cauks."

"Good Lord."

"Seed it with Cauks! And then start all over again. As for the coasts... Well New York has 140 million now and is altogether welcome to them. And as for that other coast, the one on the other side..."

They laughed, both.

"He holds, Larry does, that literature and agriculture alone are worthwhile pursuits. And music of course."

Scarcely had that word been mooted than our boy picked up the sound of a cello being very sweetly played by a demure woman in a chlamys of some kind. They watched enchanted as a second musician, a harpist in angel's clothing, came to join her. Thus our man, who found himself in a milieu like that.

"I'm not leaving, not even if he wants me to."

Both men laughed, and the chess player, too.

Come 2:15 there were 20 persons in the room, some of them chatting in small groups, some reading, some taking their mid-afternoon tea. Our man the narrator wandered among them at hazard. Occasionally he might stop and look into their faces, as if in that way he could pinpoint what sort of characters were these. Or, he might spell one or another of the men keeping vigil at door or window. (It was for duties such as these that his revolver had been returned to him, together with 100 loads of shells.) Night vision goggles—he had not previously had experience with these.

"How is it?" asked the astrologer who had come to join him. "See anything?"

"Not really. Couple of kids running past."

"In baseball caps?"

"And a police car. Went by real slowly." He allowed the man to use the goggles, but then realized that he was using it rather for the sky than the street outside.

"Dim tonight, Vega is."

The novice agreed. He had put four chocolate-chip cookies

away in his vest and after offering one to his colleague, began consuming the remainder of them with avidity and his cup of warm tea.

"Just wait till Dwayne gets here," the astrologer told him. "Then we'll see something!"

"Dwayne?"

"Why yes. He's in prison just now."

"Prison!"

"Why yes. He was mugged by some black people."

The boy opened the revolver and replaced one of the cartridges that had gone bad. He wanted nothing to do with attenuated ammunition that might or might not carry out its function. Suddenly he reached for his other weapon, a German product with a forest scene graved on the blade. Together they admired that etching, which displayed as well an outrageous sunset going on behind the hills.

"We used to see sunsets like that."

The boy looked him more nearly in the eye. The things that he had seen, the books, the girls! Truth was, he was intimidated somewhat by the close presence of a person who had missed the 1940s and '50s by just one generation only.

"What was it like?"

"Ah, Lord." And then. "Let me take over here now—you've done enough."

The child moved away, drifting at random through the enormous room. One of the people, a middle-aged type of man who very obviously had assumed the responsibility of doing his own sewing and trimming his own hair and ironing his own pants (they were not ironed), was fiddling with the television, a petite apparatus of about the size of an old-fashioned proto-escrubilator. Suddenly just then a holographic image in purple and gold leapt from the tiny orifice and filled the room. This man, as the novice was often to witness, had a weakness for entering personally the soap operas and advertisements and standing about among the actors who, for their part, remained unaware of him. Came then the news, an enormous production featuring some dozen blonde-headed girls all talking at the same time. Next the President, a healthy man good at waterskiing who allowed that although he had been responsible for somewhere between four and five hundred thousand deaths, nevertheless he had come to terms with that and felt good about himself. He was ready to move on, he revealed. "It's what I do."

An hour before dawn our man retired to his own place and opened in succession the three books he had borrowed from the general hoard. How he loved these old artifacts! Inked pages full of the old days. He even liked the imprint information that told about places and publishers no longer extant. One book had a rose in it, a mummified flower pressed down to a thickness not much greater than if it were but one more page. The boy smelt it, recognizing in imagination the authentic scent of the '40s and '50s, if not indeed the century previous to that. The prose, too, was good, even if void of those neologisms that had contributed so importantly to the current condition of the West. Suddenly he stopped, recognizing that he was damaging the ink with his index finger. He must not read aloud neither, not 'less he wanted to estrange both Walter (his dog) and the gerontic man in the adjoining cell.

The next book was better still, having to do, as it did, with life histories of some of the fauna that used to exist. He dawdled for an especially long time over the representation of a "mule," so called, that once had been in command of so much of the country's agriculture. As to horses, they had wings, some of them, and some had horns in the center of their foreheads, and some of the book was more about mythology than anything else.

He aspired to open the third book as well, which is to say until he espied the first of the sun making its way through weak spots in the curtain. Further, he could hear the five or six wage earners mustering in the vestibule in preparation for the day. Further still a wolf, or mayhap one of the reconstituted Neanderthals, was calling piteously down the length of one of the hollow streets. Soon now would the iceman come, a certain sign that it were time to blow out the candle and so to sleep.

4

He had gone to sleep in mid-paragraph and then, certain hours later, had awoken unto this. At first he was tempted to pull the quilt over his head and try for another half-hour of divine unconsciousness; instead, that was when a young boy of perhaps nine or ten dashed inside his cell and, skidding to a halt, described how much he was needed in the superintendent's office.

It was a low-ceilinged affair illuminated by a single lamp that sat just next to a late model escrubilator with three hatches. The man himself was peevish-looking and sat cradling in his hand a heavy-duty coffee cup holding a thick sediment of cigarette ashes. He had three stand-up photographs (our man assumed they were photographs) and a pile of correspondence (it looked like correspondence) stacked up in a pile that was more tidy by far and stable-looking than one would have credited to such a harried individual with so many projects in hand. His left hand had no decorations on it, whereas his right sustained a massy ring mounted with a bloodstone. It bore, that ring, the intaglio of a woman standing on shore wearing a ring of her own that replicated the same tableau exactly. Waiting to be acknowledged, the novice stood at attention for about three minutes and then sank down into a red leather armchair holding further ashes.

The office had a book collection, a globe of the world (hopelessly misshapen), and a deteriorated carpet wherein the weavers had replicated in a series of panels that good old story of Pyramus and Thisbe. On the wall a copy of the famous 1874 portrait of Wagner in a sumptuous robe. He tried, the newcomer, to see the name of the manufacturer of that reprint but failed to decipher it in such paltry light. He saw then a small-scale model of an Egyptian bust sitting between and among the above-mentioned stand-up photographs that faced the other way. No actual information was provided on the bust itself and when he turned it upside down (having arisen from his chair), a sizable fragment of the sculpture fell out and made a noise upon the desk. That did it—the man now looked up at him, squinting painfully across the brief distance.

There was a subsidiary desk available for a secretary (as our man supposed), together with an array of filing cabinets that filled a plurality of the walls. He saw a golf club in the corner and on the carpet another of those hardy teacups positioned on its side to receive the ball. He had a monitor giving off stock market quotations. A model airplane hung from the ceiling while a two-inch porcelain giraffe loitered at one end of the paper-thin mantelpiece.

That mantel held other objects as well, including a golden trophy representing success in an athletic competition of some kind. Coming nearer, our boy tried to make out what exactly the little golden figurine was doing actually. At this range he could also make out a numerous herd of much smaller girafflings trailing after their parent. The golden figurine, our boy now comprehended, was playing squash. Larry spoke:

"There's a creature in the sea that knows how to bore tiny little holes into oysters and climb inside them."

"I've heard about that," the novice said, trying to distract the man from the broken statuary.

"There, swathed in comfort and darkness, they feast at leisure upon their host. No, that's just one example of the basic nature of things."

Our man waited for the lesson to continue.

"You were keeping watch last night?"

"Yes, Sir. For a little while."

"Little while," the man iterated in dreamy fashion, his eyes misting over. And then: "Want to swap dogs? Naw, you don't have to answer right away."

"All right."

"All right what? You want to swap, or you don't want to answer right away?"

"We've gotten accustomed to one another, Walter and me."

"I see. That means you're not going to, are you? Normally our new members try to do things, things that make me happy."

"Member?"

"Yes, yes, yes; we decided long ago that you could stay. Soon as I laid eyes on that eight-shot Smith and Wesson. And besides, we need young fellows such as you."

"I'm 44."

"Ah? Obviously you need more responsibilities, if you want to look your age."

A third man now entered the room, a kind of tall and spindly sort of type who stood forth unashamedly as the living embodiment of someone's indiscretion of long ago. He also wore a little moustache for some reason. Wanting nothing to do with our hero, the newcomer was about to vacate the place when Larry called him back.

"Yes? You wanted something?"

"No, Sir."

"Very well, carry on." And then, turning back to our man, he uttered the following in a somewhat apologetic manner: "We're so few, we pretty much have to accept anyone who comes to our door."

"Yes, Sir. Besides, I don't think he broke that little statue on purpose anyway."

"Turn the world around! A ludicrous ambition, if led by anyone than me." Suddenly he bent closer, moving his upper body out of sight of the CCTV camera fixed to the ceiling. "He who helps me now," he whispered, "now when he most is needed, that man will enjoy extraordinary benefits later on."

"Yes, Sir. But with me it's just the principle of the thing. What benefits?"

"Turn it around and upside down. In my world it'll be the businessmen who come last and the prophets first."

"Good! And what about those who help you?"

"The thing about catastrophes, don't you see, is that it inspires a man like me to put current fashion off to one side."

"You bet."

"For how else, I ask you, can a man like me make up new fashions, while using nothing but whole cloth?"

"I see what you mean. No wonder there's going to be all those benefits for some people."

"Yes. Because I'm determined to bring freedom to the world. You hear me? Even if I have to slaughter every last living one of 'em!"

From there the novice went upstairs and commenced to familiarize himself with the layout of the place. Not that he very often used so stodgy a word as that—commence—even if sometimes it seemed the most commodious fit. And yet no sooner had he climbed the stairs than he saw that the second storey comprised a nursery for the most part with children running up and down. He made his way through this area without speaking, hurrying quickly past an array of human prototypes lying in their bassinets.

It was the floor above that was to prove by far the most interesting of all, a land of cubicles and workshops and a narrow passageway that ran in higgledy-piggledy fashion from one place to another. Smiling cordially to the people, he entered first the rather constricted quarters of the community's lead xylographer, a gnomelike individual in dense glasses who glanced up with the sort of bitterness that no doubt was habitual with him. Notwithstanding that, the boy pushed his way inside, tried to shake with the person, and then waited about uselessly to be offered a chair.

"You're the new one."

"Yes, Sir. Gosh, you sure do have a lot of…" (He removed one of the woodblocks and, holding it obliquely to the lamplight, tried to decipher what sort of image had been carved into the face of the thing. He saw, he thought, a devil or something like that moving swiftly forward on roller skates. That was when the man took it back, an action he was able to carry out without looking up from his work. The whole place stank of formic acid and pine resin.)

"I don't go into your private place and lift up your objects, do I?"

"I don't have a whole lot of objects actually," our man replied. (He had cleared the spare chair and had beseated himself in spite of the man's sustained unfriendliness.)

"Oh? And how about that Smith and Wesson? And dog?"

Our boy admitted that he had in truth brought along those things, his "admission ticket," as he tried to explain. Having explained, he said:

"Gracious, you also sure do have a lot of woodblock engraving plates with pictures on 'em."

"You're in my light."

The novice moved. He had observed a mounted copy on the wall of another of Holbein's very best Danse scenes, this one showing a pitiful old man being escorted off to death by a grinning skeleton. Impossible not to see the similarity between the xylographer and that ill-fated man. A very similar similarity could be seen in the woodblock print of a great black buzzard that, as one later was to learn, represented the man's personal coat of arms. That was when the craftsman took off his heavy glasses (one lens thicker by far than the other and weighing, our boy guessed, a half-pound or more) and began tampering with the thin of his already thin nose, as if he wished to reposition that organ to a more convenient location.

"You might as well know right now," he said, "that I fundamentally disagree with most of what Larry says."

"Oh?"

"Yes. He wants to repopulate the old America with good people, whereas I want good people to, in short, disappear."

"What!"

"Yes. It's just not fair, to expect so much from such a reduced population. Not fair at all."

"Yeah, but some of us want to…"

"Ah! And so you view yourself as one of the good people then?"

The novice fell silent. The xylographer had picked up his chisel and with his eyepiece in place was bending deeply over the only very partially resolved image of a kangaroo manifesting itself slowly on the face of the approximately four-square-inch block of yellow pine.

"But what will happen if all the good people just simply give up and go away and…"

"You been outside lately?"

The boy hushed. He would have accepted it gladly, had only the man proffered him a cup of the coffee currently warming over the paraffin lamp.

"That's varnish," the man said, "not coffee. Mary Lou keeps me in coffee when I need it."

"Your wife?"

A long silence followed, right up until the man made this utterance:

"Not exactly."

"Is she one of the good people?"

"Hmm. Believe you've got a sarcastic strain in you somewhere.

C'mere, look at this."

The pilgrim followed him back into an even more constricted chamber full of books and prints and curious little bottles of ink and, one supposed, high grade varnishes of various type. But the purpose of this visit was for a massive folio that contained some thirty years of the engraver's work. Our person opened the thing approximately in the middle, inhaling sharply when he found himself in a pornographic section detailing the lives and activities of former Presidents.

"O gosh," he said. "Look at that— giving the poor man a blow job!" Next, he turned to a page divided into four sections where the woodcutter had tried to pursue Holbein's great theme all the way to hell and back. "Sadism pure and simple," he said to himself, adding aloud to the artist:

"That's harsh."

"Well certainly. And it'd be a great deal harsher, if I knew how."

"Whew. And who are these people, the ones being flayed alive?"

"With spikes driven into their heads? Television producers."

"Good Lord." He had decided to close the book and turn his notice instead to the tidy array of tools that lay in a long narrow leather-bound case lined with velvet cushions. Without being asked to do so, he took up one of the little burins and examined it perspicaciously in the paraffin light. Two minutes having gone by, the engraver removed his quartzite glasses and stared down sadly at the grain in the wood of the indeed very wooden table that held his paraphernalia. It could be seen that he was preparing to speak.

"What is your function here really? You'd be surprised how many people have asked. 'Soldier, is he? Wine-maker? Public relations?' I mean it's clear you're not a graver or anything like that."

"Well, I've got a degree, almost, in eighteenth-century

pastoral verse. And I know a bit about carpentry and poultry and so forth."

The man's ears pricked up. "Poultry?"

"Associate director of a commercial chicken operation."

"I see!" (His tone had changed. One could see him softening from one moment to the next.) "Anything else?"

"Well, I spent two years in the Navy."

"Don't stop now."

"Sold fire insurance."

"Worthless. Anything else?"

"I was even a housepainter at one time. Drywall. Landscaping. Well! not for very long."

"And?"

"I've electrified a couple of houses."

"Good. But you didn't pick up that plummy accent of yours without more schooling than you've let on to."

"I did spend a year in London, that's true. Royal Institute of Nematology."

"My goodness."

"Done a little zinc smithing. But that didn't last long."

"More?"

"I was a truck driver. Just briefly. Before the Honduran monopoly got all set up and running."

"I won't ask if you've done anything else."

"Tour guide, book reviewer."

"I've heard enough."

"Lathe as well. And locksmith. Pretty good at it, too."

But the fellow had gone back to work and seemed no longer to be heeding.

The boy's next visitation was with the man who kept the arms, a squat sort of person who, unfortunately, went about at all times in an unclean undershirt. Just now he was sighting down the length of a rifle, a particularly long one that, extruding from the window, would have come close to entering the building next door.

"Yes," he said, "longer the better. Best of all is to target the enemy's vital places with this here four-foot-long telescope, know what I mean?"

"Aim at the fellow's head?"

"And/or gizzard. Genitals is almost as well."

His third interview (with the organization's treasurer) came only after he had threaded his way past the printer, the barber, the cobbler, counterfeiter, veterinarian, and several other useful people, all of them whistling as they worked. Our boy, who once upon a time had dealt in mutual funds, came and peeped over the shoulder of the man. His penmanship was admirable, especially as pertains to numbers, and he wore an eyeshade that glimmered greenly in the granular light emitted by some half-dozen well-positioned candles. Worse still was the very heavy tracking device belted about his neck. (Our man had noticed the chalk marks on the floor that marked off the perimeter within which the law had determined he must forever remain.)

"Ha!" quoted our fellow. "And so you've been shorting molybdenum futures!"

The man jumped back, perturbed to have been so unexpectedly interrupted in this fashion. Apparently it needed a great many seconds for his eyes to adjust to distances greater than twelve inches. Meantime his face was pale—one expected that—and looked like a plate of perfectly white Chinese porcelain decorated with examples of that nation's unfortunate logography.

"You're not supposed to be seeing this. I'll tell Larry."

(His voice had qualities peculiar to itself alone.)

"I knew a man who had good penmanship," our novice said nostalgically. "You should have seen his numbers. Looked almost as if they'd been formed by an escrubilator."

"Molybdenum is bad. No, mostly I've been shorting covered arbitrage swaps on cattle derivatives. Molybdenum? Not likely, not when they've just discovered new deposits in Mexico. Sinaloa, to be precise."

"Then maybe we ought to short sell now, before the news gets out."

"'We?'" He had a great number of newspapers on and under his desk together with other sources of information stored in 13-gallon garbage bags. He had a bird, too, an irritating creature continually flitting back and forth inside its bamboo cage.

"Watch it! She bites."

The pilgrim immediately withdrew his finger and began, as William Gay used to say, to "construct" a cigarette out of the materials in his vest. And if at one time he had used Bible pages for this deed, nowadays he went out of his way not to offend people.

"No, this paper comes from a grocery bag," he said. "See how brown it is?"

"Is that real tobacco you've got there?"

"Why yes."

"That could cost you ten to twenty in the feral pen."

"Have to catch me first."

"They will, they will. They caught Charlie T."

"For tobacco?"

"He refused to tattle on his cousin."

"Truly, I think you might want to short those shorts. That would make us long."

"'Us?'"

"...real long. As long almost as those rifles" (he pointed to them) "back yonder."

"So you've had some experience then?"

"Oh yes. I used to work in New York C ... Martin Luther King."

"And yet you have a southern accent."

"Yes, and had to work very hard to get it back again."

"I see. Well, maybe I could use you in market analysis. If you don't mind wearing one of these 'collars' here—they aren't so bad."

Our boy spent almost no time at all with the florist, preferring instead to go direct to the bookbinder who had set up perhaps the most appealing booth of all, decorated as it was with specimens of his craft. Recruited three years earlier from a Gilian monastery, he had brought with him a collection of inks and enamels, a bottle of egg whites (to "fix" the colors), and a two-kilogram box of gold leaf of the most amazing thinness. Even more impressive was his pile of vellum skins that reached to the ceiling and partway back. And then, too, he had done so much rubricating in his time that his right hand had incarnadined and looked like a ruddleman's.

"This is more in my line," said our man. "Much more so than market analysis."

"Don't be too hard on him. He made 19,000 Yuan for us just last year alone."

"How much did he start with?"

"I try to preserve books actually, insofar as I can. Princeton threw out 12,000 volumes just last year alone, did you know that? English stuff. But mostly I specialize in rare papers don't you see. Not that I would ever think to use them for wrapping cigarettes in."

They looked at each other. Then:

"See that set of books over there, the very old ones? I personally stole them from that warehouse of seized goods down at police headquarters."

"Gosh, I wouldn't have expected them to be interested in such things."

The man guffawed long and bitterly, allowing a drop or two of empoisoned drool to plummet head over heels from his chin before coming altogether elsewhere to rest.

"I'll show you what they're interested in."

The novice came closer and waited as the binder pulled open

one of the very many cabinets that filled his space. There in the darkness he perceived the remains of a charred volume lacking about half its pages.

"The cops get a bounty for these, whenever they track down a 'literary' book—that's what they used to call 'em, literary—and turn 'em in to the Leveling Committee. But not this time. 'Cause I have the evidence right here!" He chortled evilly, an echoing sound that our boy tried to imitate by saying:

"But surely there must be one or two copies left. Stored on an escrubilator perhaps?"

"Ha! Ha, ha. Escrubilator my ass, those things are keyed to shred elitist stuff such as"—he held up the spine—"this."

Our boy felt bad. He was not the most highly-read of all people, but he had developed a taste.

"Well maybe I could help out here some," he submitted. "If you can use me that is. That old man"—(Larry)—"is going to insist that I do something."

"Better than a soldier. And anyway he's not as old as me."

The novice climbed then to the next and final floor, a capacious but unheated area used mostly for storage. Somehow the system had acquired a full truckload of Army rations, a gross or more of bottles holding surrogate water, escrubilator parts, roofing materials, dog food, ammo, and a decorated sachet designed for jewelry but which in fact held a hundred injections of a suicide solution, as our boy came finally to understand. Nonplussed by it, he lay the box aside but then by perverse attraction came back and inspected the very delicate watercolor label showing the yellow moon reflected in a woman's eye. Death, sweet death, gorgeous death, he was ready for it not quite yet.

Still followed by the dog, he managed to climb the unsteady stairs that took him to the roof. He had decided to reveal himself by degree lest someone watching from a roof of his own might have been waiting for just such a target as he presented.

However, with a minute or more having passed, he changed his mind and emerged suddenly, exposing his and his dog's whole persons at one and the same moment. Was this in truth the coldest summer ever in these parts? The puddles, certainly, had congealed over, even if the mercury (the mercury still sometimes seen in old-style thermometers) had failed thus far to turn to outright ice. He could not however say much about the clouds, except perhaps that there were a great many of them and that they appeared to have organized themselves into layers that blocked off any hope of moonlight and/or star sightings. Far away an escrubilator tower was emitting in code, something to do, if our boy was right, with even worse weather coming to the South.

The countryside itself was void and black, nor could anything else have been expected of it in view of the attenuated population. He saw, he thought, one weak light moving irregularly along the ridge where he suspected a human individual was struggling to find his way home again. Indeed the sky, such as it was, had more traffic than the city, and contained far too many dirigibles for weather like this.

More discouraging still were those blighted districts where nothing whatsoever could be found, not even so much as a candle to show where someone at least might be holding out against the tides of progress and time. Bending over the rail, he then looked down into the street below, finding two parked cars and not much else. Moving to the pole, he lowered the largest of the Confederate flags, tried to squeeze it free of rain water, and then hoisted it back up again. He was proud of this building, already he was, and took solace in the tremendous beams and stone-work that qualified it for the fortress that in fact it nearly was. Proud as well of the six royal gargoyles that ran along the lintel, their erections protruding about fourteen inches from the roof itself. Suddenly just then a light came on in one of the empty zones but then almost at once went dark again.

Stepping with care, he worked his way to a corner of the roof that looked down into Cleburn Street. It had begun to snow very lightly, an intermittent precipitation that had no important effect on the bonfire blazing just beneath him where members of an ethnic group were leaping through the flames. Far away he heard a truck laboring up a hill, the noise mixing with that of a kindercopter, so-called, coming in for a landing in the rich part of town. Further still he witnessed what looked like the caricature of a lightning strike, a jagged bolt that sank about fifteen feet into the earth and remained upright there.

"And so you'll be the new fellow," came then a voice from out of the dark.

"Yikes!" our boy announced. "I didn't realize anyone else was up here!"

"He is though."

Our boy moved nearer the man, a reticulated person accompanied by an astronomical telescope so long and feeble that it had needed a splint to keep from collapsing. He had also brought a canteen with something good in it, to judge by how he was continually taking off the cap and swilling from it.

"Your telescope is a long one. What, you making observations or something?"

"I do what Larry says."

"He's the man." (Coming closer still, the bloke touched the long length of the telescope with his hand. He did not however ask to make use of it and was not invited to do so at this time.) "Gosh, I bet I could see all the way to my house in the woods, with a thing like that."

"Has a red tile roof, your house?"

"Why yes."

"Books scattered about in the yard? Living room occupied by Mong?"

He groaned, our man. "And how about the framed portraits of my ancestors?"

"You don't want to know."

"O, O, O. May I see please?"

Keeping his canteen, the man gave over to him. Our bloke could not find his home in the dark however and began instead to train upon the sky. There appeared to be all manner of stars out there, weak and bright, not to mention a newly discovered body that had been much in the news of late, called MLK.

"And that green business between Uranus and Neptune—what on earth is that?"

"'On earth?' I think not. Anyway, it hasn't been christened as yet."

"I didn't know planets could give off light."

"Never mind about that. Instead, focus in on that tiny little thing that sits just off the coast of Silenus. See it? Little sucker not much bigger than a grapefruit? Never achieved fusion, poor thing."

"I do, I see it."

"Good. It proves that Nestor is in the ambit of Genevieve tonight."

"Astrology?"

"Yes indeed. They used to laugh at us, remember?"

He was glad to return to the great room below where a fire was blazing vehemently in the hearth, another good product of the woodcutter's art. Coming nearer, the novice verified that it was of hickory and oak, well-seasoned hardwoods drawn from this year's hoard. It was his intention to go to his place, grab up his pallet, bring it back, and read for a while in the firelight; instead, he was stopped by the computer man.

"Hey! Aren't you going to watch the film?"

"Well, I…"

"Oh, you don't want to miss this one." And then, speaking mysteriously and in low voice: "Black and white."

"Oh?"

"From the 1950s." (His voice during this last comment had

fallen even lower.) "Black and white."

"Maybe I will."

They shook. He should have already noticed, our boy, that a good-size movie screen had been hoisted at the back of the room and that some dozen chairs had been brought forth and set in place. He had no especial dislike of these old-fashioned movie films, so-called, originally produced on a celluloid medium representative of the technology of that day. Popcorn, too, he appreciated, and was pleased that two of the women were preparing a kettle of the stuff over the fire. Began then the film. Embarrassed by it at first, they laughed at the clothes of those times and the exaggerated dignity of the actors.

"What are those, 'suits?'"

"Yeah, that's the way it was."

The film was three minutes old and still no sight of piercings, buccal penetration, nipple enhancers and the like.

"No, it's good to be reminded of these things."

But it were the faces that fascinated most. They seemed to reflect a certain hauteur, as if the people of those times saw themselves as sovereign entities authorized to make decisions on their own. A person did not know whether to be indignant about that, or whether a certain fascination was allowed.

"God. Who did they think they were after all?"

"Look at that one."

"Gail Russell—what kind of name is that?"

"She is good-looking, you have to admit."

"But where's the diversity? I just don't see any."

"Yeah, well you don't have to worry about that now. She died about eighty years ago and there's not a whole lot of her left over by now I don't imagine."

"She is attractive, sort of."

"Just shows how self-concerned she was."

The film, having said nothing about the need for recycling, came finally to its end. By this time the audience had been

joined by another half-dozen novitiates drawn from their cells
by the scent of popcorn. The next film also was black and white
and the clothing styles were just as funny.

"'Here's looking at you, kid.' Now just what in hell is that
supposed to mean?"

"I like her," our boy interjected all of a sudden, blurting it
out. His excitement had been growing betimes and he was
encouraged by the glance that Larry, turning in his chair, had
thrown in his direction.

"I like 'em, too," came a tiny voice from the rear of the room.
"Especially the dead one."

Silence. And then: "Well I never said I didn't like 'em,
exactly."

"Oh? Then I must not have heard you correctly."

"And besides, maybe it's all right for some people, if they
think themselves so fine."

"Want to shut up over there Herb? We're trying to listen."

"That's just so like Larry, always going on about 'autonomous
people,' and so forth."

"He's sitting right over there! Idiot."

"Who?"

"Larry."

"Oh."

They watched the rest of the film in near silence. She was
beautiful, that person, and the male seemed to be a reserved
sort of type who had shaved and wore a tie and looked as if he
could have gone through life with but minimal assistance.

5

He spent the following two days with the binder and on the third was recalled to the supervisor's office. An amateur in gilding fore edges, he had wasted a full day trying to make the group's copy of Theopompus a more perfect article than its condition allowed. And then, too, there were those lost fascicles that had told of matters now in danger of falling forever out of mind and memory.

"You're supposed to mend the book, not read it."

He apologized, did our pilgrim.

"All right, you can read some of it. But try to get some work done, too."

That was the moment he was called to Larry's office.

His face on this day, Larry's, looked like an escrubilator's, a snow-colored hexagon on which the two eyes had approached to such proximity, one to another, that they had begun to coalesce along the puncti. His hair was falling out, which is to say until our man recognized he was wearing a cover of some type. Three books were piled upon his desk, the smallest of them on the bottom; it formed an unsteady arrangement.

"We're going to have to ask you to take part in our little endeavors here. I am sorry. We're just not in a position to retain people who don't contribute."

"No, Sir; actually, I'm working with Simon. Worked yesterday, and worked again today, too!"

"Well that's something. But some of our members go outside during the week. Earn money."

"In daylight? Yes, Sir, I've seen them when they leave."

"You're a young man, comparatively speaking."

"I was."

"I ask myself, is it fair to send Lloyd out there when he's fifty years old? Or Lester? Lester is worse, almost sixty now." (His desk, Larry's, supported the ivory replication of a broken skull with brains in it. Our man could not but reach out and touch them, verifying to his own contentment that it wasn't really organic material after all.) He said:

"You're asking if I would be willing to go out there."

The man blushed deeply, refusing to meet the novice's gaze.

"I suppose that is what I'm asking, yes. You're young. And we're going to have a shortfall this week. And Rodney's sick."

"I can do electrical work, if it's not too complicated. Or construction, things like that."

"Excellent! Actually Rodney's in advertising however. Good at it, too."

"Advertising."

"That's right, yes. He's with a company connected to a public relations outfit that's doing work for one of the big consultancy agglomerates."

"Ah. You don't have anything in the way of carpentry do you? Or brick laying?"

"'Fraid not."

"What does he do actually, Rodney?"

The rector blushed deeply and again refused to look back into the beginner's eyes.

"He performs. Hell, I don't know. It's daytime work, that's all I know."

"Doubt I'd be any good at that."

"Doesn't matter in the least. Gov'mint won't let 'em fire anybody, or not for six months anyway. You'll be sick of it by then."

"I'm sick of it now," our man wanted to say.

"I'm sick of it now," our man said.

"Well certainly. Been a long time since there was anything interesting to do out there." (He waved his left paw to the window, encompassing the whole city with his world-historical gesture.) "That's one of the things we're going to fix by Jove."

"And besides I need to tend to the hogs."

The leader laughed out loud, this time meeting our man's gaze. "Why, I don't think you want to go out into the world at all, do you?"

"No, Sir; I wouldn't of come here in the first place if I'd of thought I'd just have to turn around and…"

"Of course. All right, how about this—hold the position 'till Rodney gets well?"

"What's the problem with him?"

"And if you do this, there'll be something in it for you."

The boy waited for the rest of the promise which, however, he failed to hear. Instead the man poured a cup of coffee and, his eyes misting over, began to speak:

"Long time has gone by, it's true. But does that mean we have to give up and die?" And then: "Toynbee was the one, I believe, who saw that civilizations are mostly responsible for what they do to themselves."

The bloke came nearer, focusing on the insights that fell from the man's vibrating lips.

"Long time. And yet I used to think we might squeeze another hundred years out of it, or even more. Instead, they've prepared a place for us, a sort of nursing home for Cauks, if you take my meaning. I don't know, maybe we should just file inside voluntarily and let 'em shut the door."

"Not me."

"Boys and girls used to fall in love, did you know that? The last time I saw a boy and girl together they were with their lawyers drawing up a proactive intercourse agreement. Oh yes, they copulate like monkeys, a fungible procedure they carry out on each other, more like a joint bowel movement than the thing your fathers experienced." And then: "Go back. Go back and listen to the popular music of a hundred years ago, if you want to know the difference between therapy and romance. Look at some old Jennifer Jones films. They didn't want to be men."

Our boy was listening keenly.

"Yes, somewhere along the line they chose, our women, to be like men. Careers, don't you know. They thought it would be a promotion." Dropping his cigar, he began laughing bitterly, a bleating sound interlarded with a good deal of snorting. "I can understand why you aren't married."

"I never could find anybody who…"

"Well of course not! There aren't any."

Outside a truck, or possibly one of the armored personnel carriers, slowed and stopped and then picked up moving again.

"That's right, they wanted a promotion and ended up forfeiting love. And love, my boy, is a woman's mission. Without it, better she had never been. Oh yes certainly, they can do physics and play the piano and so forth. But remember this, that for them it's purely a mnemonic activity. They had to wait for males to invent pianos and physics, and then and only then might they also take up the practice of it. For originality, my friend, is a prerogative of genius, and genius is a prerogative of the male. Think of Mahler."

"Sir?"

"Yes, he had a wife who liked to think she was a composer, too. There is, of course, no such thing as a composer with ovaries."

"I see."

"And the races, too. Entirely equal, we're told. Strange. Horses aren't equal. Restaurants. Escrubilators. In fact I cannot think of any other category in which all the subcategories are as equal as we. OK, I can't speak for amoebas." Suddenly he held up his hand. "But don't tell anyone I told you so! I don't want to go to jail, not at my age."

"OK, I'll take over for Rodney until he gets well."

"Oh child, we came so near. A Golden Age manqué. A twenty-year interlude 'tween barbarism and decay. 1940-1960, approximately speaking."

"I've heard about it."

"It is said that the people of those days would never go downtown without a tie and suit."

"Suit?"

"The apparel of that time. And this: They used to marry for life, it's claimed. No, I go further—the children, almost all of them, had a father and a mother both. And this: A man could support his wife and all those children on just one salary only."

He laughed, our man, until he saw the statement was supposed to be serious.

"Remember this, that every 'improvement,' improperly so-called, hath an equal opposite effect, as science says. Count the 'improvements' of the past hundred years and you'll see why we're now in such disgrace." He drew on his pipe, an artifact of clay that appeared to have nothing in it. "No, really it's a privilege I suppose—to witness from such close quarters the ruin of the West. So it must have felt at Aegospotami on that day."

"Too many improvements?"

"Those little kids! My father said those little kids used to come home from school and play outside until darkness fell. Can you imagine that? And not a single government person anywhere. No crime in those days. Or very little anyway. Lightning bugs everywhere. Whatever happened to those little things by the way?" And then: "My father had a garden and used to take his wife dancing once a week. Used to sit on their front porch and drink sweet tea. Odd, no, how I sentimentalize over an epoch that had vanished ere I were born? But then, I never saw the Belle Epoque either." And finally: "This modern age! it prefers the feminine virtues, the easy ones, the ones that can be exercised while sitting on a sofa in a darkened room—compassion, diversity, tolerance, empathy. But us, we aspire to the hard virtues, the ones that hurt—courage, integrity, stamina and will."

6

Foregoing sleep, our man spent the next hour borrowing the proper clothing—shorts, T-shirt, and the new fashion of mismatched shoes, in his case blue and gold. (It developed later on that he had put the wrong shoes on the wrong feet, meaning that they were as they should be.) He also carried a vial of synthetic water, ice pick, two vending machine slugs, and a fifty-Yuan note that bore an uncanny resemblance to the real thing.

"Gosh," he said. "I didn't come here just in order to go back out again."

"Somebody has to do it." (This was a tall man, somber-looking, with an Eeyoresque sort of posture that saddened everyone within a certain radius.) "But you'd better... how can I say this? Better change your facial expression. Otherwise you might look as though you've got thoughts going on in your head."

"I don't know the first thing about public consultancy and so forth!"

"No need to worry about that—they can't fire you. Just watch that facial expression, all right?"

They were grouped together in the vestibule, our boy and the five other men. There was no question but that the sun was coming up, a sodden denouement prefigured by the sound of trucks and the calls of a few groggy birds grasping with their talons the appendages of the gargoyles up above. Turning to the man in the leather shorts, the beginner asked:

"Is it dangerous out there?"

All five men turned and looked at him.

"Bet your sweet ass it's dangerous! Why do you think we're carrying our escrubilators after all?"

"Oh."

The five continued to stare.

"Aren't you bringing yours?"

"No, but I have my .357."

"Better than nothing, I suppose."

That was when one of the women, a good-looking quantity wearing an appreciable amount of lipstick and other things, came to them with a bottle of brandy and poured small portions into an equal number of little tumblers decorated with the image of six persons profiled in the sun. Containers like these, they held just the right amount. And the stuff was good, too, and went quickly to the appropriate brain centers of the mind.

"Could I have another?" the tall fellow asked. "It's Monday."

"Sun's coming up."

"Try the peephole, Ed, and see what it's like out there."

"I just don't get it. Why would Larry send a beginner out on a day like this?"

"Needs the money I guess."

"Look at him."

"It's almost up now. Actually I'd say that about 80% of it is above the horizon already."

"Yes, but which 80%?—that's what people want to know."

"Oh, oh, watch it! There's a strong woman walking past! Can't you hear her?"

"Hear? She can be heard in Ethiopia. How else would we know she's so strong?"

"Hmm, looks like one of those newscasters on television."

"Blond, you mean?"

"Well, we can't stay here forever."

"Say, maybe we ought to let the new boy go first."

(They laughed, all save Ed who seemed to have some tincture of pity left in him still.)

"I guess that's the end of the brandy."

"She's up! Well, except maybe for a few threads still holding her to the horizon."

"It were the German Teutons, weren't it, who first imputed femininity to the sun? Must have been insane."

This man moved toward the peephole, peeped, and then returned to the back of the indeed very long and narrow vestibule with its paintings and statuary.

"I didn't see any 'threads,' so-called," he said.

"OK. Ready?"

"Go, go, go!"

They pushed out into the light, our man forming the rear. He hadn't thought to bring sunglasses and at first strode off in the wrong direction. He trained his eyes instead on the litter that had blown into drifts, accumulations of lottery tickets, newspapers, hypodermic needles, a placenta and two depleted vials of serotonin reuptake inhibitors. He had to run to catch up with the others. Already a squad of Cambodian-Americans had come pouring out of the opposite building and stood watching sullenly as the wage earners scurried past.

"Oh shit, Cambodians."

"Don't look at 'em."

"How many are they?"

"Haven't finished counting."

"Sun bright enough for you Ed?"

"Sun? I spit on it."

They moved on. Anyone watching from a distance would have mistaken them for just three persons, as compacted as they were. They passed an obvious Cauk trying to pass as Hispanic and then two bedraggled men employing the "good

philosopher, bad philosopher" ploy. Here the wage earners
halted for a moment and after allowing them to prophesize,
paid them off in small coins. Suddenly an automobile happened
upon them from around the corner, a thirty-foot-long model
with all its windows blackened out.

"What is that, a rock star in there?"

"Or basketball player."

Two other rock stars could be seen loitering at the intersection.
The wage earners could themselves be viewed from hundreds
of windows and myriads of eyes, and yet thus far no one had
actually trained on them with an escrubilator or funder gun.
They were making pretty good progress, the new boy believed.

Thus passed the thirty-five minutes needed to arrive at
the place where Edmund was employed. Availing himself of
the entrance set aside for people of his identity, he vanished
momentarily into the dark, only then to reappear and wave
reassuringly to his colleagues.

"OK, that's one. Four to go. Five, counting the new boy."

"How much do these jobs pay actually?" the new boy
inquired.

"Hm? Depends mostly upon your identity I'd say. And a
chance for a bonus at the end of the year."

"Charlie got a bonus one time. 'Course he had to split it with
his facilitator."

"And sexual harassment counselor. Wasn't a whole lot left
over."

"And diversity committee."

"Yeah. He ended up having to pay, is what he told me."

"Right. Try to keep away from bonuses if you can."

Our new boy agreed to do precisely that.

"Not that you're likely to be offered any such thing."

They entered the blighted zone, zigzagging from one
defensive position to another. It was the safest part of their
journey, providing all manner of shelter, collapsed buildings,

etc., etc., and no few cave-like excavations that extended for a greater or less distance into the cold hard ground. It is true that they had encountered a small entourage of Lithuanian-Americans a few yards back, neither group choosing to say anything. He observed, our new boy, that at least two of them had been wounded recently, and had wrapped themselves in plastic shopping bags in lieu of authentic bandages.

"Maybe we ought to join up with 'em," our novice submitted.

"No, they aren't ready for that yet," said Mordecai. "They've got 'em a real screwed up ideology and won't turn loose of it."

"Yeah, they still think the country can get back together again. 'Peace and harmony' is what they want." And then: "Watch it! He's fixing to throw a rock!"

The rock fell short and in any case they had all taken cover in a former upscale coffee shop where the smell of the beans lingered still. He had nine minutes, none more, our new boy, to get him to his place of work.

"Old Rodney! he used to throw rocks with the best of them."

"I'm going to be late."

"I sure do miss that ole son-of-a-bitch."

Emerging from the "park," as it was called by the county commissioners, they hit the street in bright sun. He had six minutes, the amateur binder, and not one minute more. To be sure, he was grateful to his friends for allowing him to remain in the center of their little crowd where he was best defended from stones and other things. No one spoke about the automobile that, apparently, had crashed several days ago but continued to emit a thin wraith of dark blue smoke spiraling skyward. Instead they detoured around it, still saying nothing about the driver's arm and upper body lying in partial view. A dog had been trapped in the rear of the car and was looking back at them beseechingly.

"Maybe we ought to do something," our new boy mooted. The dog was appealing and might have improved the emotional climate back at the Node.

They laughed out loud at him, all save Mordecai who was too polite to do so.

"Oh for goodness sakes, don't you know a booby trap when you see one? I don't know, I worry about you sometimes. Anyway, here's where you work."

It was an immense building, twenty stories tall, with laundry in the upper windows hanging out to dry. It had always dispirited the boy to find tall buildings in the South where such architecture had never properly belonged. What, they wished to flatter the northern cities with these unnatural imitations? That was when he became cognizant that a businessindividual was waiting for him in the sally port.

Our novice climbed out of the group and went forward with his hand extended. It was an extraordinarily well-dressed human being who stood waiting for him, suntanned, a good square jawbone on him, short pants that fell halfway to the knees, and one of those new collars that hooked, like a set of glasses, to his ears. His left shoe was taupe and the other black. They shook, each man examining the other for the risk he might present.

"G'morning!" our boy enunciated in positive spirit. "Time to get to work!"

"Yes; we've been waiting for you. You might have noticed that I'm standing out here in the cold?"

"Yeah, but I'm not late am I?"

Both men checked their watches.

"OK, you're not late in the legal sense. But I guess we're just used to having our people show more… eagerness."

"I'm eager."

"And that tie—where'd you get that?"

"We had a little trouble in the park."

"And haircut?"

"It *is* chilly out here."

"Here, let me take that tie. Better not to have one at all."

The child stood still for it. His friends, still in a group, were watching silently at the curb. Would they, or not, come to his rescue in case the businessperson should try to strangle him in the coils of his admittedly unfashionable neckwear?

He was relieved to find that he was to be provided with a desk, an oaken affair that must have dated back to the integrity age. Passing his hand over the stressed surface, he found several highly decorative retro valentines inscribed by an industrial laser beam. Pleased, too, that he was provided with a full battery of escrubilators, six of them arrayed in order of the year, or month rather, in which they had been reified. It amused him to see here another example of the early models of twenty years ago, a primitive contraption encased in metal instead of biologic matter. (In those days they had tried, and not always without success, to combine the faculties of paramecia and the Antikythera Mechanism.) A pencil lay on the desk as well, although the point had broken off and was lodged in the skin of the Mollyball, as the newest machines were affectionately named. Our boy then settled his attention upon the stand-up photograph of an exhausted-looking pockmarked lady in a virtual frame.

"Rodney's wife?"

"Yes."

"He's dead, isn't he? Rodney is?"

"Now what we need today is for you to do about three or four hours of public relations, and then an hour or two of consultancy for the Schreken Corporation. OK?"

"Schreken?"

"Yes, yes, that's right. They're the ones that manufacture attitude analyzers for the County Commission. Remember?"

"Them! Sure, now I remember." (He slapped himself on the forehead, jarring loose a bunch of memories.) "They're the ones that…"

"Bonuses, yes. And Rodney was in line for one—before he got sick I mean." And then, bending down close to our boy and scanning him with eyes that had been refitted with gamma screens, said:

"You don't look like a public relations person, do you? Not really."

The pilgrim met his gaze. His own eyes were not to be laughed at and were densely packed with rods and cones of all sorts of description. They glared, which is to say until the businessperson seemed to lose interest in the matter.

"OK, what the hell. Anyway, I don't suppose you could be worse than Rodney was."

He was left alone at his desk. People were smiling at him from all directions, most conspicuously a homosexual queer dressed in an earbob with a ruby that dangled down. Our man refused to look at him. From the ruby there depended a florescent stone of some type that began blinking more and more exponentially the longer the fellow studied our new man. Averting his gaze, our amateur then noticed a tiny person, a child really, standing in front of a vending machine stationed in a corner of the enormous room. Above ran a series of portraits of the American presidents, some of the very earliest ones displaying a certain... *on ne sais quoi*. "Integrity," perhaps, as it was understood in those days.

He proceeded to explore the contents of the desk. It was apparent that the man Rodney had been keeping a diary in a penthulian notebook with the portrait of a rock star on the cover. Useless was it to try to break the code he had been using, a cuneiform-like script with a great many exclamation marks embedded in it. For reasons not understood by our man, his predecessor had also kept a jar of kerosene and a 2% solution of greenwort in his left-hand drawer. The other drawer, the one on the right, held an assortment of business equipment, paste-on smiles, handshake enhancers and the like, including what probably had been a very pricey copy of one of the most up-to-date interrogation devices. His mind drifted back to a saying of the Secretary of Inspection and Control, namely that torture is not torture if in the mind of the torturer it's not. Drifting further (and after casting a nervous glance at a strong woman standing a few yards away with her hands on her hips), he dredged up in memory another saying of that man who had done so much to redress the disproportionate impact of the law on the criminally insane.

But it wasn't until he came to the chief drawer of all, opened it, and then jumped back out of range. He was being laughed at from all sides; however, to show his good nature, our boy laughed also, a long drawn-out hooting sound accompanied by a foot-long tongue that brought the place to silence. The next drawer he ignored, intending never to open the thing for as long as he might live.

The time had come to begin his assignment, a solemn process that consisted mostly in using the telephone, a traditional appliance that allowed a person to speak to another even if at the same time it provided neither eye contact nor biometric verification test. Always it had been his tactic to go about things in a certain way, which is to say to attack an enemy in his strength before proceeding to the rest of the problem. Now, taking up the implement, he telepathied the number into the receptor and stood back. The voice that came to him was servile and weak, and belonged obviously to a male. Only after a number of questions had been answered and his verification ascertained was he allowed to talk to the manager herself. Her voice was loud, incredibly so, and had that note of exasperated impatience that showed how strong she was.

"Mdm. Smegma? Rodney here."

"Yes? What is it?" (She was fiddling with her escrubilator, as he could plainly hear.)

"I'm calling…"

"Obviously."

"…to give you the latest on the Washington and Lincoln account."

"And?" (Gosh that voice was loud.) "I'm waiting."

"Well, I can report that our efforts have really begun to pay off. You wouldn't believe the number of people who have come up to me. 'Washington and Lincoln, Washington and Lincoln,' that's all they want to talk about. I think I can assure you that the sales for next quarter…" (He had momentarily lost his place in the template.) "…amazing."

"You don't sound like Rodney."

"Lots of people think your product is actually good for the environment."

"About time. What about the sulfate count?"

"No Ma'm, you don't have to worry about that. The sensors won't pick it up for another eight months at least."

"Just a minute."

She had left him. In the background one could hear a primitive music that our boy identified with the well-known rock star called Cunt Sucker. He was connected to a location where a Siren was howling, followed eftsoons by the sound of four concatenating rifle shots, as our boy guessed them to be. Came then the voice of the weakling man:

"I have to hang up now."

"What's it like there at just this moment? Where you are, I mean?"

"'Bye."

The novice remained on the instrument, making it appear as if he were still working while in actuality he was eavesdropping upon another conversation taking place on an adjoining channel. Here, two white males were sobbing hysterically, the result of a beating that one of them had taken from his wife. Further still and on yet another station he heard what must have been an archived recording of Billy Eckstine's version of

"My Foolish Heart." Really, had such a time ever truly existed, and truly, were it really too late to bring it back again? Yes it was.

He hit the street in high spirits and conspicuous optimism. There was no question but that the sun was retreating from its orbit, leaving the world cooler each time. Today it was no larger than an Indo-Chinese penny, a mere period really, to use a term taken, not from the cycles of time, but from punctuation science. His briefcase had a lock on it and anyway was but a diversion from the papers that he carried in his vest. His knife was long and reasonably sharp, and formed no giveaway bulge beneath his sock. Suddenly just then he espied a Caucasian man, a "Cauk," or "ghost," as now they were called, moving forward intelligently while also chewing gum.

He crossed in the other direction and then entered an alley where he was able to march for about two hundred yards without meeting anyone. Already very weak, the cooling sun was roosting behind one of the taller buildings; a confluence that argued against the present fashion of short pants. His feet, two, were cold, especially the one ensconced in his cerulean shoe. A woman passed by, her face made up like Nephratiri's, one breast hanging out. The boy grabbed for his escrubilator, finding it intact. He had a wallet with 17 authentic Yuan in it, an identity card with a digitized CAT scan, and three cosigned anti-tobacco pledges validated by three licensed testators. Armed with these, his NRA card and late-model escrubilator, no one could have guessed his membership, tentative as it was, in the society of "The Node," as his new home was known.

He eschewed the elevator, basing that decision upon his appraisal of the people crowded inside. His feet were largely frozen, the blue one particularly, and he had developed the urge to piss. Climbing the stairs two at a time, he hurried past the concierge, an impressive human being with two visible escrubilators in her ankle holsters and God knows how many elsewhere. The novice smiled at her, who moved to block him off.

"Hey! Just where do you think you're going shit-head?"

The child smiled and pointed toward the upstairs floors. "I have an appointment," he said, putting on his most salutary face.

"That right?"

"Why yes."

"Sure you do. Let me see your scan. If you don't mind too terrible much that is."

The binder took out his scan and began unscrolling it in the meager light. Blending their efforts, they traced the esophagus, coming rather quickly upon the quantum signifier that proved that he was he.

"OK, that's OK. OK, now let me ask you this."

"Yes?"

"Who do you want to see up there?"

The boy provided the name, a conjoined appellation that referenced the three several ethnicities claimed by the woman in charge. The concierge paled.

"Oh. Her."

"Right."

"Well heck, I don't see any problem with that, shoot no! You just go right on up. You shouldn't have to explain that to anyone. Makes me mad!" And then, gazing down at the boy's footwear: "Green? We don't do much of that anymore."

The boy thanked her and continued on. The stairs were steeper now, the corridor narrower, and the advertisements more conspicuously florescent to militate against the dark. He had hoped to come out onto the seventh floor and find toilet facilities, a blessing that failed him however. Truth was, he was losing his bright hopes for the day and for his new position, for the city and its dwellers, and indeed for a good many other things as well. Came then yet another woman, this one of about six feet in height and under ninety pounds. The stink of pheromones filled the air.

"Yes?" she said.

"I was looking for…"

She couldn't wait for it. Watching her walk away, he was stunned by her hip amplifications and discontinuous waist. He went by a dentist's office, the placard out front promoting zirconium implants and plastic tongues. Came next a pigmentation center and then a government office functioning as part of the I Love Me network.

"I was looking for…." He gave the name.

"Yes, but is she looking for you?" (It was a male, he thought, who answered. He was shaved, had a tattoo on his forehead of the Venusian landscape, and was puffing on a legalized "cigarette" formed of chocolate.

"She's expecting me I think."

"Oh no, honey, she would have told me. Sorry about that. What's your name?" (He moved closer. The fellow's wrist, apparently, was broken and couldn't support the combined weight of his fingers and rings. Moving with courtesy, our boy backed away somewhat and then turned and hastened toward the following office, an important-looking place with a bank of display windows revealing either real kittens or a kinship group of adorable simulations. Here he entered, half hoping to meet his appointment and the other half still seeking for a toilet or, heck, a hole in the floor.

"Yes?"

It was the receptionist, a woman who had gotten herself down to about seventy pounds. In combination with the person next to her, they weighed an average of about 300 pounds. Of breasts, she didn't have any but was exposing the left one nevertheless.

"Excuse me, is there a restroom here?"

"Restroom? But don't you have an appointment with Dr. —————?" (She gave the name.) "I don't think you want to be in the restroom while Dr. ————" (again) "is waiting. Do you?"

"I suppose not."

"No. Anyway, you should have thought about this before you came."

"I know it. I just…"

"What? What did you say?"

"You're right. I said you're right."

It seemed to relax her. He, on the other hand, was being watched by dozens of eyes, all of them belonging to the pool of secretaries and escrubilatoresses who for the sight of him had left off working.

"Oh my God," he heard one say. "Where do they get them?" And then: "Green shoe!"

The pilgrim smiled. The thought had come to him to urinate in his cupped hands and carry the material to the flower pot in which an opium plant, now picked clean, once had stood. This was the moment the CEO/CFO entered and stood looking him up and down. She was stern-looking, a woman of authority, and one of the very strongest such persons since the end of the previous century.

"You don't look like Rodney."

"I been sick."

"Well come on in if you must; I don't have a lot of time."

He followed into a massive office in which one's footsteps echoed back and forth. Our boy was particularly struck by the giant-sized portrait of Ilsa Koch in which that individual was seen gazing spiritually into the stars. Removing his hat, he waited to be invited to sit, a courtesy he had not deserved, as he soon found. The woman meantime continued to apprise herself of the novice's azurite footwear.

"Yes?" (She was dithering simultaneously with her escrubilator and the medallion she wore about her neck.) "You have something for me?"

"Yes, you'll be pleased to know that the people over at the Schreken Corp. are pretty well convinced that the ad campaign you've put together for them has convinced a lot a people to patronize their, how shall I say, their product, yes."

"And has it? Increased sales?" (That medallion about her neck? Had the image of a Gila monster on it.)

"No. But they won't realize that for another three months at least."

"Three months, three months. Four would be better. Or five."

He wrote it down in the little plasma notebook he had inherited from Rodney, a sloppy affair written in code and with the picture of a supermodel on the cover.

"I shall certainly strive," he said slowly and distinctly while hiding one shoe behind the other, "for four."

"Make it five. Have a nice day."

He stood, almost falling on his face when he recognized that he had not been sitting in the first place. The woman had gone, giving him perhaps ten seconds to relieve himself into one of the most nearly perfect pieces of Olmec pottery that ever he had seen.

He was glad, at first, to come back down to the street below. There were any number of cozy little restaurants with Polynesian themes, arts and crafts shops, stores that specialized in candles, rubber and leather outlets, tropical fish with human genes, velvet Elvises, blow-up dolls simulating forty-pound girls, musical roses, horses engineered down to three inches, antique beer cans and comic books, rare cheeses and hummingbird eggs, and most of the other requirements of a thriving economy. He chose finally a middle-sized cafeteria in which he could espy just four or five customers sitting peacefully in their places. Not waiting to be invited to sit, he proceeded authoritatively to the rear where he took up possession of a booth that offered a full array of salt and pepper shakers and marital aids. Came the waitress, a garden-variety sort of person who drew herself up and began to read:

"My name is Eleutheria and I'll be your friend. You will find on our menu everything that you could plausibly ask for. I want to help. You name it, I'll do it. I have a wonderful little kitten at home, do you? Tell me about it."

"Could I have an English menu?"

She went to get it. Far away he saw an anorexic sipping at a cup of synthetic water and at the table next to her two basketball players from the former Namibia. A young boy, an Australasian he believed, was standing in the center showing off some of the new diseases. He was dressed in a T-shirt that pictured the moment of his own conception and no one who saw it could fail to be amused. Just across from him our pilgrim saw a pretty girl whose skirt covered much of her pubis and in places came down to her garter tops. And then, finally, he saw some other people as well.

He was learning a lot just by looking around, but mostly he was learning that the smaller the dietary portions and the greater the number of greeters and violinists who accompanied it to table, the more expensive the tab was likely to prove. Accordingly he tried to order a Moon Pie and mug of Mountain Dew, a communication that threw the waitress into confusion.

"Mountain…"

"Dew."

"We have Bombay Nectar. And it's been blessed, too."

He took what was offered. Long time had gone by since he'd been able to avail himself of the black-eyed peas and collards that had foddered his ancestors on both sides. Meantime his waitress had reappeared.

"Is everything all right?"

"Everything?"

"Are you enjoying your meal? I'm here to make you happy. I bet your little kitty is just lovely. My only reason for living…"

He held up his hand to stop her. The gruel that he had been

served did have flecks of nectar in it but tasted like cabbage soup. And yet he couldn't fail to see the group, two tables away, of high-paid young businesspeople in thousand-Yuan suits sucking deliriously at the stuff. He was very near to taking up a spoonful himself when he perceived a pair of CCTV cameras pointed at him, one of them lodged in the chandelier and the other mounted on the bust of Pallas over the restaurant door. Quickly he put on a pleasant and wholesome face in which no trace whatsoever of mental speculation was exposed.

"Is everything all right?"

"Excellent."

"And the Nectar?"

He lifted the mug and drained off a linear inch or more. It was plain simple grapefruit juice, nothing more.

"Good!" he said.

"Shall I bring more?"

"No, no; no thanks. Thanks all the same. Whew."

It was then that the music came on, a psychopathetic noise, louder than the world. In older days—and he was able to remember some of this—the people's taste was said to have been "in deficit," but still existed at some level. Suddenly he grabbed up the earplugs provided for people of his kind and wedged them into place. Anyway, it was far too late at this date to protest the resumption of the pre-frontal procedure, an effort on behalf of the intellectual equalization scheme designed to erase the famous education gap that had so bedeviled certain politicians. Sitting peacefully at table, our boy allowed himself to drool somewhat, hoping to show that…

"Is everything all right?"

…hoping to show that he had undergone the operation too. No one could see that he had taken sanctuary—so he believed—among a node of unambiguous Cauks and no one (thus far) had offered to give him trouble. He drooled and then took up his beaker and swilled off another half-inch of the vomitous solution, evidence enough, he thought, that he was exactly like everyone else.

He paid in Yuan, took his change in dollars, and then proceeded hurriedly back toward his own building. A number of people had frozen during the night but these had by now been pushed off into the gutter where they were only intermittently visible. For a moment he thought the sun had come back again, as warmth-giving as in old times, but then corrected himself when he understood it was but an advertising sign. It offered, that sign, a two-weeks' vacation in Bali where children were available. Came next a car dealership where a person could buy five of the things for the price of four. No greater progress had been made than in the construction of automobiles, a new system wherein a delta ray, vaporizing unnecessary material, could sculpt them out of tungsten blocks.

Next he passed a suntan salon, a necessity in these days of poisoned light. Anxious to get out from under the sun, he strode past a fenced area where a mob of discarded escrubilators had joined in a woeful chorus that disturbed the passers-by, but especially the lobotomized. His own building, when he came to it, had greyed during the interval, and had the texture of year-old Pablum. The roof was flat. No features were to be seen on that structure save for the composite flag representing the town's nineteen cultures. Entering with a bland face, he acted as if he actually wanted to get on board the elevator. Instead he raced for the staircase that, except for two homeless persons, was not being used. He had forgotten to bring his earplugs. Somehow an escrubilator with just two pellicles had gotten into this area and was struggling in vain to climb the stairs. Ended thus his first half-day on the job.

7

Weeks went by, days, and still his companions came for him and walked him home again. He had acquired a patent, as it almost seemed, on a position in the center of the group where the stones and arrows that came their way were less likely to affect him negatively.

"How was it?" they asked. "How was your day?" (Everybody laughed.)

"How much longer must I...?

"Till Larry says it's over—that's how long."

"I can't go on with it." His tongue narrowed and his eyes flickered in and out.

"Look, 'our man,' if we can do it, so can you."

"Yeah, but you're used to it!"

"And how did that happen?"

He said no more on this subject, not until he said:

"Can't take it."

"O you'll take it all right! Unless you want to get wedged."

And so this time he really did say no more about it, did not our man. Slowly they hiked past the capsized car in which a living child had been substituted for the very appealing dog that until recently had served to lure the unwary. They began then to cross the university campus, the most pitiable site in the entire city. They saw two expressionless boys tossing a Frisbee, a girl with her mouth hanging open, and a procession of English professors walking on all fours, a state-supported dispensation demonstrating rapport with lycanthropic man. They gave witness to a crowd of foreign students speaking in tongues, and then followed for a short distance an impressive-looking scholar dressed in a turtleneck that provided a list of his publications on the front and the likeness of Betty Boop on the back. A few yards further and the campus began to merge with an alternative lifestyles community housed in a rambling building that went on for about three-quarters of a mile before turning and coming back. Faces could be seen in some of the upper windows, one of them a crazed individual calling out "Hey, like what's happening, man? What, you got a self-esteem problem? Scenario! Hey, like, put it into context, right? I think you been, like, pushing the envelope too much. Denial, you're in denial! Peer pressure—is that your narrative? Prioritize things! Parse 'em, too. Need to get your agenda straight. But watch out for the 'other!' Hey, like, you gotta start thinking outside the box! A whole new syndrome! Watch out for paradigm shifts!"

They hurried. The park was empty, or so they imagined until a crowd of snide-looking boys suddenly came out from behind an advertising sign promoting a brand of biofeedback electrodes for household pets. And yet they were not numerous enough to do real harm and our wage earners had no problem warning them off. The littlest of them wore the most scabrous T-shirts while the oldest were drawing nigh unto the age where they might soon present real danger. It was the man called Arvin, a thin sort of fellow who had been carrying his paychecks back to Larry for the last four months and more, he it was who now picked up a good-sized stone and managed to strike one of the urchins on his tattoo. Soon darkness would be upon them and the Nodists were keen to get them back to barracks again. But none yearned more passionately than our man, who called out mentally for his dog and books, his quilt and long mellow pillow with the embroidery on it.

They arrived at a little before six and quickly drained off the mugs of cider (cinnamon in it) offered by the women. They did not however pull the covers up over their heads, or not immediately anyway. Rather, they lined up in front of Larry's office and one by one counted out their day's wages, an appreciable heap of reformed Yuan both in coin and script.

"Ye shall be remembered in history!" the man said, half in jest and half not. "You who make our project possible. No, I find this a little embarrassing really. I, too, have worked and I know what it is."

"Aw, you don't need to be apologizing all the time. Sir. Besides, we don't have anywhere else to go!"

They laughed, some of them. Some did not. Our hero started to laugh, changed his mind, but then did snort once or twice after all.

"Remember," their leader went on, "we don't do this in order to help people. No, no, no, our purpose is to achieve a spiritual condition. Suppose now that Wagner had lacked ink and paper when the last measures of Parsifal came into his head. He was winning points in heaven whether anyone should ever know of it or not."

It was a profound statement. The Nodists looked at one another and after shaking hands all around started off for their cells, or for mess, or to watch the news on television. The meal tonight was to be sausage and sauerkraut, and for dessert one great chocolate pie as big as the sundial outside. Following routine, our boy sat at the end of the great table whence he could keep his attention both on the television and the chess game going on at the other side. Troops were being forwarded to Kyrgyzstan where new threats were suspected. (Thanks to improvements in military science, field commanders these days could discontinue thousands with their bedroom escrubilators, never having to abandon their robe and slippers.) But it wasn't just television and not just chess; our boy also kept his remaining eye on the outside hogs pressing at the window. They were a tasty-looking bunch, these serving-dish-shaped creatures, and already our man had chosen the one to be sacrificed on Nathan Bedford Forrest Day.

Very soon the sun will have disappeared, leaving the novice with no choice but to get some sleep. How he hated it, this dreadful fashion according to which people had perforce to lie unconscious between the lovely hours of midnight and dawn. He had his way and there'd be no sun at all, or none anyway that showed itself for more than three hours out of the twenty-four. Instead, feeling his way down the corridor, he came in upon the computer man sitting in a blue-green discharge that filled his cell. Dressed in a shawl (his computers gave but little warmth), he had three machines currently in operation, one of them showing Bolivians disintegrating in real time, a product of the improvements cited above in weapons science. Meantime the largest of his monitors had trained in upon weather conditions in the Kerguelens, a snow-and-ice-covered terrain where, apart from a cautionary force of U.S. Special Forces, nothing at all was going on.

"Cold!" our boy said. "No, I wonder just how cold it is."

"Windy, too. See how those boys are being blown about from one place to another?"

"Yes!" And then: "Why are they there?"

"Well! you just never know, do you, when our vital interests might be at risk." And then: "Want to look in on France?"

And did so, a simple maneuver that right away gave a bird's eye view of the Auvergne with all the fields stripped bare. He saw two cattle being shepherded forward by a peasant in a crimson blouse.

"Oh no, wait; no, that's the nineteenth century you see there. I must have dismanipulated the chronos button."

He fuddled with it, quickly bringing the Auvergne into better focus. His was the finest machine in town and weighed upward of seven ounces. Itself, the monitor had been scaled for human eyesight and was far larger than required by the internal workings of the thing.

"And where is that?

"Athens. See that hilltop there? Later on they were to put a famous building there."

Suddenly the scene changed entirely, showing instead a top-down view of two men sitting in a tiny chamber full of computer parts. Never had the boy viewed himself from this angle, nor seen the incipient bald spot that seemed to be taking hold in the area of his most vulnerable location.

"Wonder what Larry is doing?"

The expert did the manipulation, ending up with a sidereal view of the superintendent laboring in his third-floor laboratory.

"Amazing man."

"Indeed."

"He works too hard."

"Yes, but he could never have won so many awards otherwise. You knew that he's considered the top virologist in Tennessee?"

"All I know is that he's working on one of the new diseases. Trying to keep it from spreading," our boy submitted.

"What?"

"Keep it from spreading."

The fellow laughed out loud at him.

"I guess you haven't been listening. His view is that we've been far too numerous for far too long. Nothing but a catastrophe— this is what he says—nothing but a catastrophe can save us now."

The two men looked at each other. A living cockroach, large and purple, appeared just then on the interior surface of the computer screen where the thing had found at last its meed of warmth and security.

"He's not trying to kill that virus?" our man eventually asked, not without a premonition of the dread that he had come to expect in this place.

"The contrary, of course."

"Oh shit."

"Look, you're either with us, or you're not."

"I see."

"Yes."

The sun now was fully down, a benefit that attenuated to some degree our hero's dismay. From the great room he could pick up the whiff of peanuts parching over the fire, a superior odor that mixed well with the Debussy played on a flute. Cold night it promised to be and our man had already decided upon spending it on his personal pallet that will have been placed by him in front of the fire. Not that he was the only one to prefer that location! As to Debussy, he was being performed by the woman called Penelope, a comely sort of thirty-year-old with whom Larry had been urging him to breed.

"I think I'll go," our boy said, "and listen to the music."

"Yes. She'd make a fine mother, too, that one. Wish I were about twenty years younger than I am."

As advertised, our boy opted to spend that night before the fire. Behind him he could hear the desultory sound of conversation coming from the library, trucks passing in the road outside, airplanes crisscrossing overhead, and a far-away dog calling in the valley. A hickory nut (or something of that sort) exploded just then in the hearth and gave off a miniature shower of bright golden sparks. Soon he would be looking at positive coals, which is to say the residue of good hardwoods such as hickory and oak, his grandfather's favorite fuels. But he must not think about these matters too intently however (coals, grandfathers, dogs, etc.) lest he be tempted to go and jump into his friend's magic computer and find himself back in some other century once again.

8

The next day, which in fairness ought to have been better but in truth was worse, followed hard upon. Commuting to work in the midst of his friends, he dared to take out a cigarette, but only then to put it back again when he descried one of the tobacco proctors, a grey-headed woman of advanced years coming down the sidewalk at him with a pair of scissors. Acting with great hurry, he disposed of the cigarette and lifted his hat, saying:

"No, no, I was just testing, that's all. Actually I hate tobacco products."

She didn't believe him. Ahead were hills, smoke rising off the summits, and sixteen-mile-high towers issuing today's health instructions. Ironically (ironical when compared and contrasted with good health), it was that very moment they happened upon an escaped escrubilator going through the last stages of mitosis, an appalling process that caused them to cross to the other side of the highway and hurry forward without speaking.

"Gracious," said our man's favorite friend, a courteous type who had survived into these times. "Damned old nasty things!"

They went on. Itself, the park was being rehabilitated and the places of ambush were in process of being pushed aside by two giant machines navigated by teams of Chinese. The noise was enormous; even so, they could still hear the teleported "music" that reverberated from the hills. As yet they had come upon no dead people that day, excepting only a single individual old man of perhaps ninety years who had been set upon and circumcised against his will.

The business district was crowded at this hour and here and there our boys could spot individual Cauks, shamefaced people wending their way to job and office with heads held down. They crossed, the Nodists, in front of a certain notorious building where hundreds of xenophobes had recently been euthanized, and then continued on in the direction of The American Council for Anal Retentive Narratives, an enormous heap covered with graphics that told about the disrespect that had been visited upon these people in the past. Here our boy paused and read the motto engraved along the architrave, an affecting piece of verse composed by a supermodel whose portrait hung out over the entryway. And yet our man tended to shy away from places like this lest... as you can imagine. Lest they pounce upon him and pull his intestines out.

They had come far but still had several hundred yards to go. The last of the public restrooms had shut down years ago, an unwise development resulting in deleterious social behavior. Separating from his companions, the novice moved past an array of vending machines and then leapt on board the MLK Memorial Funicular and rode to the top of a thousand-foot declivity where a bronze tablet memorialized the achievements of a combined force of Choctaws and Cherokees. Next was a hospital encased in concrete, an attempt to forestall certain invincible bacilli from leaching out. His dog meantime had disappeared. Reengineered in 2016, the creature had been endowed with the mollusk-like ability to merge with his immediate surroundings.

He strode past a tattoo parlor that had been granted a

government bailout, and then edged his way through a soup line where some thousand or more old men had marshaled two abreast with their cups and spoons. The "Pale," so-called, was drawing nigh, a restricted district named for the Cauks who resided there. Drawing up to his own building, our boy began to work his way through a series of facial expressions, settling just in time upon the blandest in his repertoire. The doorman, who detested the sight of him, watched dubiously as our fellow went direct to the entrance but then suddenly drew back again. He could see a talk show host and two rock stars loitering in the darkened corridor where a crowd of girls had gathered, their buttocks lifted high and widely separated by digitized "bustles," as these things were atavistically denominated. His intention was to arrive at the staircase in his usual anonymous way, all of which he was in process of carrying out when he was blocked by a dangerous-looking personality who tried, successfully, to intimidate him into purchasing a magazine subscription devoted to recreational canoeing. Other vendors had also set up in the hallway, including a deranged man selling graphic novels about the most successful of the new religions, a seminal (and sullen) doctrine that had promoted the Gila monster to a central position in its iconography. Glad to find himself on the staircase at last, he threaded his way between the human-sized advertisements that leapt up suddenly in his path and gave off odors congruent with the products being described.

He counted slowly up to fifteen, opened the door, and sped to his desk. It nonplussed him to find his supervisor waiting, a suntanned individual just returned from a six-week stay in Indonesia, an island nation where children lived in poverty and molestation laws were few and seldom enforced. His shoes had built-in toes and today he was using a lavender eyeliner that sorted perfectly with the ring in his nose. The man had taken the liberty to seat himself on our boy's desk, unaware that one of the escrubilators was edging ever so slowly in his direction.

"G'morning," said he in friendly fashion. "Hey, like, by the way, how are you making out with the Thompson account?"

"Real good," the pilgrim lied. "Is that the one over on MLK Avenue? Junior, I mean?"

"I want you to handle this, OK? Like, I got to be at a concert" (rock concert) "in ten minutes from now."

"OK, I'll deal with it."

"Cool."

The man departed, making way for one of the female psychics who recently had contracted a preemptive sexual reassignment procedure lasting six months. At huge cost, she had invested in a government-issue reversal kit that had left her with the experiences of her 78 years together with the physiology of a nineteen-year-old.

"And so you decided to come to work after all!"

"Yes," our boy replied modestly, looking down. "I'm taking over the Thompson account."

"Those Chinks? Awesome. But like, hey, I didn't know you could speak Chinese. Wow."

He smiled, our man. It was true that her reassignment had resulted in a marvelous set of abs, enhanced pecs, and two first-class glutes. Obviously she had gotten over her relationship problem, a lengthy interlude during which she had encountered her man at a facilitators' congress and the two of them had begun escrubilating all at once. A year having gone by more or less happily, they then began to date and after proving themselves compatible in six out of nine federally mandated criteria, affixed their signatures by teleconference to a standard postcoital agreement delineating the responsibilities of each. The divorce, occurring just before Kwanza, was regarded as one of the best-attended in years.

"Hey! Speak some Chinese to me."

He waved it away, our man, and then sought to change the subject over to other things—the weather, sports scores, automobile mileage, the basketball draft, and the attempt by some to resurrect white suffrage. The messenger boy, he noticed, was snuggling up against the vending machine, a networked device where for just two Yuan a person could experience as many orgasms as he had patience for. He saw then, saw our man, a small crowd of tobacco recidivists in saffron jackets fulfilling their public service penalties with mops and pails and long-handled dusting tools that reached to the ceiling and back. They were being careful with the artworks on the wall, refusing even to come near an invaluable canvas with a spot in the corner conveying philosophic meanings of all sorts.

He toiled at his desk for the remainder of that morning and then gathered along with the others for the midday supplements. The man called Gwen, a floss monitor with the Dental Committee, had brought an ivory box full of parti-colored pills and was offering them around to the others. Afflicted by lymph pressure, apnea, and a kidney ailment of some kind, he was drawing double wages from the Corporation along with a government chit that bestowed a temporary suspension of speech code penalties.

"Poor thing," said the woman called Pete, thrusting toward each of them in turn a serving ladle full of pink tablets believed helpful to those suffering from low self-esteem. "I have so much compassion for people like you." Her eyes began to water. "Here, try these."

But the pills were simply too large for the ordinary-gullet, "width-challenged" people who had been taken under the wing of the government.

"No, all you have to do is dissolve them in root beer."

"Seems like there was this traveling salesman," interjected just then a bearded man, famous for his jokes, "and a farmer with a real pretty daughter."

"Already heard it Millard." And then, turning to the man with the gullet: "Just drink those pills right down, you hear?"

"Awesome." And proceeded to do so without spilling any great amount of the liquid. The transmogrified woman had meantime taken out a syringe and was injecting herself in the palm of her hand.

"I have MLP," she explained.

"Oh gosh; what is that?"

"Monolingual provincialism—my brother used to have it, too."

Just then the waiter appeared and poured a smidgen of absinth, as it appeared, into the wine glass of the hermaphrodite who up till now had remained silent.

"Taste it please."

"Hmmm," it said. "Nice."

"It's good for panic attacks."

"So one night he goes and knocks on the door, and the farmer..."

They all held out their glasses. The drink was sweet, but also had a mischievous quality that called up memories of boy-, girl-, and ithood days. Twice our man had made some effort to rise from the table, each time to be shamed into sitting back down again.

"I need to get cracking on that Thompson account."

"Oh balls! We haven't even seen what Matt has for us."

She had brought, Matt, a little paper take-out bag full of iridescent capsules synthesized to militate against hyper-passivity and bad dreams.

"Bad dreams?"

"Why yes."

Our boy took three.

The Thompson account was being managed by a stereotypi-cal Chinese in clothen slippers and a coiffure that included a small caged bird. He spoke English, thank goodness, or any-way a variant of that tongue.

"So. You come." His eyes had that oriental problem but otherwise he was fully Americanized. The boy took note of his short pants, his backward baseball cap, and the lewd tattoo that ran around his neck and continued down into his underwear. Except for that, his face had been plasticized to look like a businessman's. His left slipper was yellow—a mistake—and the other green. Our boy looked about for a seat but, finding nothing of the kind, positioned himself directly in front of the person and proceeded to speak:

"We're making real progress with that asbestos company," he said. "Anyway, those people couldn't count up to three."

The man smiled. Perhaps he was Japanese.

"Can't count."

"Not a bit. And if you look at the dividend they're paying… Hell, they're even more unscrupulous than you or me!"

But here the man's face turned sour.

"More than you, maybe. Not I."

There was a place to sit, but to reach it one had to go back and turn around and climb two steps. It had the untoward effect of placing our man a bare two inches off the ground. On a more positive note, the chair was designed to conform to a person's actual person.

"But what I wanted to ask" (our boy speaking) "is whether you'd like to pay your tab this week, or wait till next. We feel like we've done real well by you and we need the money, the Node and me."

Instead the fellow turned on his television and allowed a football game to fill the room. No question but that this recreation had reached a new level since the genetic reintroduction of the Neanderthal—six colonies of them in and around Los Angeles. But even that would not have sufficed without affirmative drafts.

He arrived back at the dormitory in poor state, aware that the medicine he had been given had wrought certain unwanted effects. And then, too, of course, there was that woman waiting for him, the blonde whom Larry had wanted him to fertilize. She was not a bad sort; her face was lovely, her figure entrancing, and her intelligence geared up to high degree. Demure, energetic, loyal, well-read, generous and kind. He had been expected to fall in love with her a good two weeks before this time. Her barcode was still visible however, even though her hair had mostly grown back by now. She offered him a beaker of methylphenidate synthesized in Larry's laboratory.

"You look tired."

"Tired? Tired? All I have ever wanted was just to curl up and die!"

"It's not fair, making you go out there every day!" She pointed to it. "Let somebody else do it."

"No. No, it's my turn I reckon."

She helped him off with his jacket and then guided him to the great room where some two score of persons were closely watching an antique movie from the 1950s.

"What does contender mean, for Gila's sake?" someone asked. "And look, all the color has bled away! I hate this old two-dimensional crap."

But instead of retorting, our man simply traced his way to his favorite couch and sat next to the girl, saying:

"Larry wants us to reproduce—that's the impression I get."

"I know! He's always going on about it. We don't have enough young people—that's what he thinks."

"How young are you?"

"And I think he wants to start up another Node, too."

"What! That's the first I've heard about it."

"In Kansas, I think."

"Kentucky," someone shouted from across the room.

"Oh, I see. So now we're supposed to waddle on down to Kentucky and set up down there and have all sorts of children. I see."

"Up there," that same person shouted. "Not down. Waddle up to have those babies."

"I see. And so now we're supposed to…" He stopped, dodging just in time before a fistfight broke out on the filmic New York waterfront of circa 1954.

"I've never been to Kentucky."

"Nor I. Anyway they were on the wrong side. Could of won, if they would of helped out just a little bit. What, you want to have babies?"

"We could try."

He thought about it. He knew of several people who were breeding every day even when they had no wish for children, the most futile and counterproductive activity in the world. The methyl meantime was good but turned rather bitter as he got down to the lees.

"Heck, I don't mind trying."

They looked at each other. Her eye was blue and contained the image of a lake under Spanish moss and a massy yellow moon. Here foxes wandered at freedom and grasshoppers, wisest of all insects, stridulated all night long in unpremeditated, as the poet said, art.

"If it'll make Larry happy."

"We should."

"Make him happy?"

"Right."

He retired to his chamber and after sprinkling himself with a good-smelling shaving lotion, waited approximately twenty-five minutes before she came to the door and knocked politely. She was dressed in a nightgown that embarrassed the both of them.

"In those days," he started out, "they used to have boxing matches don't you know, and a 'contender' was someone who…"

"Contended?"

He had a three-person sofa in his room that enabled the two of them to sit at opposite ends and view one another in the barely sufficient light. Her father, he learned, had been a professor of chemistry up until just five years earlier, at which time several members of the humanities faculty had waylaid him in the parking lot. After that, they had traveled widely and then later on broadly as well, giving the girl a store of geographical knowledge more ample by far than any of his.

"In Iceland," she said, "They don't have CCTV cameras."

"What!"

"No, and there's no enhanced punishments for dissing towel heads."

She was exaggerating of course. Even so, he let her go on with it. Her stockings were black and had a seam that ran up the back—had someone been revealing his peculiarities?

"Egad," he declared.

"No, and you can see Cauks almost everywhere. They don't even bother to travel in groups."

Our boy, pushing the dog off to one side, came nearer. Long time had gone by since last he had seen lakes like these in a woman's eyes, placid and blue. Rich in scents and orifices, her lips, both, were red and swollen up with estrogen injections. Accordingly, he drew back to get his first true look at her profile against this particular wallpaper. Her nose, it is true, had the very least little bump on it, enough to say that she had probably gone ice skating before the government had discovered how dangerous it was, and she had fallen, or perhaps had blundered into a door, or been born that way. Never one to allow such a minor thing to get in the way of Larry's wishes, he drove the conversation over onto other topics.

"And England?"

"It was pretty. But there're no Cauks there anywhere!"

"*Triste*. But we do have to have diversity, no?"

"I guess. And it's good for the economy they say."

"That settles it then."

In fact they were both of them still embarrassed by her gown, a wispy thing given Larry's approval. He could see a great deal, our boy, and what he saw led him to form all sorts of conjectures about what he couldn't.

"How about South America?"

"We were there in… 2018, I believe."

"Ah. You're so much closer to the door—why not close it, if you want to?"

And did so. But then right away had to open it again and let out the dog, embarrassed also. He caught, our boy, a brief glimpse of Larry striding past in the hall, his head bent around to see, or not to see, what might or might not be going on in cell 43. With his left eye our man had meantime descried a discrete area of the woman's right thigh, a buttermilk-colored territory so soft-looking it would have defeated even his grandfather's rather pretentious vocabulary. Someday he would take off her entire nightgown, he was sure of it, and gander at the whole of her in one unified glance!

"Denmark, they say, is rotten to the core."

9

But here the recitation breaks off in order to show, when it resumes, that a fair amount of time has gone by. Strapping on his .357 ventilator, he had a full breakfast of sorbet and crullers and then relocated his ten-inch blade from his sock to a position under his vest. As expected, Larry came at the last moment to send him on his way.

"It has to be you," he said. "After all, you found a way to get along with that Chink."

"He hates me."

"And you seem to have those people at the needle exchange completely perplexed."

He could not but smile, our man. Some of what Larry said was true.

"They're fools."

"Yes, we rely upon that. You've already squeezed more than 200 Yuan out of 'em. Without it, we wouldn't have been ready for our project."

This was what the pilgrim hated to hear—reminders of the new plantation he was to establish somewhere in Kansas. How, for example, could one be certain that Penelope would like it there? Absorbed in these worries, he shook with the man and stepped down into the street and moved forward with head bent low. These days he was allowed to cross the street alone and after so many months and weeks of attempts and errors had actually blazed a faint trail in the sidewalk indicated by his escrubilator's exudations. In any case he had soon memorized the route, which drifted this way and that and turned in several places and backtracked before leaping off into the "park," so-called, where today some half-dozen decayed-looking youths were waiting with what appeared to be old-fashioned pruning hooks. He stopped. Nor was he the only one with an escrubilator.

"What do you want?" he called out to the children and then, getting no response, opted to leave the area at once and get him to his appointment at the earliest possible moment.

It was an awe-inspiring building, remembered for the approximately two thousand prisoners who had been rendered here from North Korea. And if the elevator proved rather tight and forced him to stand at 30 degrees, yet was it also very fast. Threatened by the need to vomit, he quickly took two pills and washed them down with the reserves of coffee stashed in that little pocket between the cheek and gums. (Filled with tongue, his mouth was far too crowded to hold more than that.) Here, reading material of all sorts was scattered about, including at least one copy of *Arizona Highways* along with the usual bondage journals. He came forward, his face about as non-expressive as he very well could make it.

"G'morning!" he cited. "Hope I'm not late."

She refused to answer. Angry as a hornet, she turned away at first and then, sighing, signaled him on into a hallway lined on both sides with portraits of some of the pioneers of the movement. He thought he recognized Jasmine Whirl, a large woman celebrated on a recent television series for her ability to tear telephone directories in half. Also a reward poster for the identification of the murderer of O. J. Simpson's wife. Suddenly he jumped back, belatedly aware that he was in front of an open office in which three several women were staring back at him.

"G'morning," he recited. "I have an appointment I believe."

"'Believe?'" (Gosh her voice was loud.) "You mean you don't know?"

Our boy grinned. Truth was, he wasn't absolutely sure about the time or even indeed the building. He now yanked out his date book and went splashing through the pages. The appointment was very clearly listed there, along with a photograph of this same woman bench pressing what must have been at least 400 pounds.

"Yes, I'm pretty sure I have an appointment. Don't I?"

They groaned. One of the women, the tallest, got hurriedly to her feet and left the room in umbrage, an insulting behavior that put a smile on the faces of those remaining. They were both watching him with plain open contempt. Checking his zipper, he then opened his bordereau and attempted to spread the materials out on the one available table, as he imagined it to be.

"Not there! Asshole."

As with any voice like that, he reached by instinct for his revolver and blade. But instead of putting them to use, he began bothering with his necktie, a complicated routine in which he had to reformat the knot and placement of the pin. This required time. The pin had the engraving on it of a male Greek hero and had to be hidden.

"What's he doing now? Oh God."

"I'm trying to…"

"I'm not talking to you!" (This one, by contrast, had chosen to leave her left breast exposed, where a person could see that her nipple had crystallized and the numbra was gilded).

Our man nearly pulled out a cigarette, and very nearly lit it, too. "I wanted to show you what's been happening with your image," he said. (With no table to use, he was working on the floor.) "We've done some polling and your approval rating is up, way up. Look at this—a full 87% of the people have said that they had rather jump into a pool of sharks than to…"

"87? It used to be 90!"

"…meet up with just one of you. Wow."

"Well, at least that's better than that shit head—what's his name?—better than he ever did."

"Rodney?"

"Whatever."

"We think of it as the flip-side of charm. And your numbers just keep going up!"

"Yeah, but what about the patriarchy? Things keep up this way and pretty soon they'll be voting again!"

He smiled understandingly, our boy did. "Would you prefer to pay your tab now? Or next week? It's only 20 Yuan." And then: "Patriarchy? O yuk!"

He managed to get out of the building with half a dozen 2-Yuan notes, a few plastic Zloties, and several pieces of small metal currency, a very decent rate of pay he believed for what had actually been achieved. It occurred to him that spring was coming in, a more hopeful time he hoped, characterized by the return of birds and golden youths with their pellet guns. Instead of directing himself back to the office therefore he continued on to a dilapidated café that must have dated back seventy-five years or better. The place was empty, almost, and he had his choice of six different locations where his back would not be exposed. The table, too, was old, and he could discern ancient carvings just beneath the varnish where people had recorded the names of their beloveds. What would they say about this, these moderns, for whom love was but a therapeutic expression? And then, too, there were those old photographs on the wall that either had been rectified or else really did represent people who had been normal at one time. They brought to mind the memory of his own dear grandfather, an irascible man remembered for having beat to death certain evil persons with his four-foot walking stick. And where was he now, that one, now when he most was needed?

Not in the dining room certainly nor, insofar as one could see, neither was he in the kitchen. Ordering coffee, our boy pushed aside the salt and pepper and chocolate cigarettes to make space for it. Incredibly, someone had put on an ancient recording—Till I Waltz Again With You—a song that must have exercised sway at one time over the golden youths of that day. He had tried it before, putting himself in the mind of earlier times, a useless exercise beyond the scope of even the most accomplished historians. Oh yes, a person might know the names of the courtiers, but that was about the sum of it. What, really, did he know of his infamous grandfather, just to take one example, who had struggled for so long and with so much unavailing effort to hold progress at bay?

He walked back slowly in the general direction of his office building. He had been wrong about spring and instead of birds and the like it had begun to look like snowing once again. And why not? Another inch or two of post-modern snow, a brown material with the consistency of waffle syrup, how, really, could another inch bring about anything that hadn't already been seen so many times before? Suddenly he stopped and slapped himself on the hand, so close had he been to drawing out a true cigarette and exposing it to the eyes of the town. Came then to his attention a bookstore that specialized in Near Eastern cuisine and inside it a crowd of pouting youths with their feet up on the tables. Hurrying past all this, he also averted his gaze from the pet shop where modern science had brought forth creatures never seen before, horses he could hold in his hand, etc. Here, pigs could fly indeed and had to wear leashes attached to their pickled feet.

He judged it at about 10:30 in the morning and was grieved when he saw that he had been too optimistic by a good fifteen minutes. And sometimes he would go for hours, seemingly, but only to learn later on that it had been just minutes. Moving desultorily past a haberdashery, he paused and went inside in search of a walking stick.

"All you need is an escrubilator."

"Got one."

"Have another! They're free."

He had to stoop to take it by the hand—every year these things were getting smaller—and usher it from the store. As foreseen above, it had begun to snow, inspiring our person to take up his new appliance, named Elrod, and shield it under his coat. He had intended to discard the object into the nearest trash, until he saw the bin was spilling over with them already. How they thrashed and fought! reminding him of old-world crabs contending for space in the disappearing oceans.

Unwilling as yet to return to his building, he managed to enter a gated community by hiding in the wake of a car. He could pass unnoticed here, he believed, owing to his bling-bling, his short pants and contrasting shoes. And then, too, his escrubilator was of the most recent manufacture. Putting on an expressionless face, he minced his way past a massive house with a ten-acre pool, delightfully perfumed, in which a pod of trained dolphins was disporting gaily in the waves. These people had invested well, putting their money on the short selling of naked currency hedges, or some similar piece of creative action as he assumed. He met the gaze of a woman coming toward him, an unworried type holding a leash and dog (the dog was missing) and dressed in a mask of solidified suntan lotion that gave off a stink. There was no question but that in surroundings like these the process of evolution had collapsed in upon itself, producing an etiolated species, women without eyelids and children with beards. He stopped, turned, dashed through the gate and ran back toward his office building.

10

"I quit," said he to Larry the next time these encountered one another in the hall. "No, that's enough; I quit."

The man could not but laugh. "But it's only been three months! How are you and Penelope getting along?"

"Let me take care of the hogs; that's something I can do."

"There's only one left."

He inquired as to the identity of the remaining hog. But instead of answering, the superintendant said this:

"I've been thinking of a new assignment for you."

"I can imagine! You want me to go somewhere far away and set up a brand-new Node, yes?"

"Correct. You and Penelope. But how did you know that?"

"Look, I'm just not cut out for administration. Public Relations neither."

"Well of course not. Nor consultancy neither."

"Nor advertising."

"While as to hedge funds, certainly not."

"I could of been a real good bricklayer. My great-great-granddaddy used to manufacture those things."

"Please!" He held up his hand. "Don't remind us of those days."

"The music, the girls."

"Yes, yes, yes, you've said quite enough. Very well, be it so;

I'll let Clarence take over for you here. He's the stupidest one left after all."

Our boy thanked him earnestly. "And I'll be able to stay up all night again?"

"Yes, yes. Moses! And you can help Penelope with her project. No, no, I'm not talking about that. Help her with her day job."

Her day job, as it proved, consisted in putting on little theatrical productions that could be recorded and then played back into the listening devices embedded in the toilets and walls. She was good at this and her choice of dramas, dating back to the Romans, showed an understanding of what the government liked to hear.

"'Torture is not torture,'" she quoted, "'if in the perception of the torturer it's not.'"

Our boy helped her to get the right emphasis.

"'We are a compassionate people and white males have nothing to fear.'"

"Good." He enjoyed sitting across from her and looking into her face. She was a fine-looking woman in some respects, though he tended to inculpate the worth of anyone who could possibly be attracted to *him*. Furthermore her eyes, the only truly visible part of her brain, did not hang down out of her head at the end of stalks, nor were they so deeply set that a person had to strike a match to discover where they were. No indeed, they were normal.

"Larry wants me to…"

"I know."

"…establish a new… Wait a minute, how come you knew about it before I did?"

"I'm going, too. And Hingis."

"Hingis!"

"He's a carpenter. No, we're going to need several of them."

Our boy backed off a few steps, although in order to do so he had at first been made to arise from the chair. "Hingis!"

"And at least one welder."

"Good Lord."

"We'll have a garden, too. And pigs."

But here our boy raised his hand. "That's the part I can do."

"And computers and so forth. Escrubilators. Cameras obscuras. Can you do that?"

"My great-granddaddy had hogs. Well! just one or two I mean. Actually they were more like pets. On the other hand I…"

"And guns and rifles and things. Larry knows how to get them."

"That's good, but you can't beat explosives when it comes to self defense. No, I wish we had…" (He indicated with his arms the size of the cache of explosives he wished they had.) "…good old-fashioned dynamite!" And then: "Hey, what about the paleographer, is he coming, too?"

"Larry will give you whomever you ask for, I imagine."

"Naw, I don't really want to go. Think I'll stay right here. How ever will we get the hardtack we're going to need? And water purification equipment?"

"If you're going to worry, worry about pharmaceuticals."

"I do! And money."

"Well, we have that old suitcase up in the attic."

"Oh good Lord, that old thing doesn't have any value. None."

"It's full of Dutch Marks."

"*Deutsche Marks?*"

"That's it!"

"Obsolete."

"No, Larry says they've come back again."

His mind was reeling. "Deutsche Marks!"

"Right. You say it just the way he does."

(There was no question but that she admired him.)

"Anyway, what do I know of currencies? Nothing."

"Oh! You know a lot!" (She had edged her chair somewhat closer and actually had placed her hand on one of his wrists, the left one he believed.)

"OK, I may know a little bit. My grandfather now, he must have had a thousand books in that old shack of his. We used to joke about it. I remember one time when we were going…"

"And clothes. We'll need all sorts."

(She was a woman.)

"Ah. Maybe we could use some of those Deutsche Marks to get you all fitted out."

"Me? Of course there *is* that real cute suit on sale over at Behemoth's. I sneaked out last night to look at it."

He looked her in the face and then moved off slightly, the better to appraise the shape of her head and the quality of her thinking. She ought to produce good children, pretty good, who might prove to be assets to the nodes of the future.

11

To describe these matters as briefly as possible, he spent the whole of May 22nd getting his things together. It wasn't until after he had packed away his shirts and weapon and a plethora of the restored German currency that he agreed to go. He was to be joined in Kentucky, as he understood it, by four other individuals coming from the Mother Node—a plumber, a glazier, and two women good at needlepoint. Truth was, it consternated him to be put in charge of Node types who might be older than himself, and more experienced, and better. Studying their photographs in advance, he detected that one of them looked very like a northern Yankee, what with his overalls, his slack expression and pouch of chewing tobacco.

"I could do without this one," he explained to Larry. (They were in the laboratory where the master had recently set up a series of flasks, each with a frog in it. Other frogs were enjoying the water in a fifty-five gallon drum that had been split laterally down the middle and set up on sawhorses.)

"Listen, 'my man,' he's the only glazier in the whole franchise! You'll take him and you'll treat him sweetly, too, understand?"

Our boy jumped back. He was a man of earned authority, the superintendent was, and not someone lightly to ignore. "Well maybe I'll just go ahead and take him and try to deal with him sweetly," our traveler said.

"Good. And how are you and that other one getting along?"

"Penelope?"

"She'll need her own suitcase of course."

"Yes, and… Watch it!"

Both men moved at the same moment, both of them grabbing for the same frog trying to effectuate an escape. It was just an hour before moonrise, not too early to make last minute adjustments to the pilgrim's luggage.

"Think I'll take a book. Just one."

"Oh? And which would it be?"

He was reluctant to reply. "*The Bee Master of Warilow*," he said almost too quietly.

"A pudgy book, if I remember. With a typeface in Goudy Old Style."

"Yes, Sir."

"And yet it'll weigh twenty pounds, or will appear to, before you've marched a single mile. No, no, take food."

He took food *and* the book. Or rather he snipped out a single etching that seemed to pertain most materially to the ordeals that lay ahead. He also took a paisley tie that he was unwilling to leave behind. Further, he owned a Byzantine coin that had come down to him from his grandfather. It weighed but little and here, too, he was not prepared wholly to abandon the thing. He had a geodetic positioning device, a rabbit's foot, and a compass, a collector's item last used during combat operations in Costa Rica in 2019. Of vittles, he carried several little cans of inexpensive meats, 300 placebo tablets, and two quarts of powdered water. Twice he hefted up the suitcase (testing it for weight), and then got into his foundation and slipped into his shorts. His abs were in relatively good shape, as also his glutes, his pecker and his pecs. Finally, with but minutes to go, he was taken off into a side room and smeared with a darkening solution that gave him an East Indian complexion.

He was to carry some 200 Yuan together with an almost equal sum entrusted to the woman. As for her, she was bringing an old-fashioned purse as long, almost, as a loaf of bread, a thing much too innocent-looking for the debilitating aerosol it actually contained. Her ointment was not so dark as his, a stratagem on Larry's part to adduce greater seeming diversity in these two. Finally, as a parting gift, the master handed off to him a cured scrotum holding a dozen vending machine tokens wrapped in foil.

The moon was slow to rise and was full of holes when finally it arrived. At first our boy thought he had seen it looming over the gene exchange, but then changed his mind when he recognized that it was but an advertising sign for a brand of cornbread mix. It was as good a time as any for getting to know the man named Hingis, a tall individual freighted down with a canvas backpack that must have weighed forty pounds. They shook.

"Heavy burden you got there! Seen any rock stars lately?"

"Well sure it's heavy! Somebody's got to bring this stuff."

Our boy admitted to that. "And are you bringing money?"

The fellow was taller than originally described, so tall indeed that he must carry his haversack a good three or four feet off the ground where the gravity might, or not, be somewhat attenuated, as one could hope. He had also noticed, had our man, that the fellow hadn't answered about the money.

"Where we going?" he answered instead.

"Well, I can tell you this much—it's going to be one hell of a long voyage."

"But we'll still be in Tennessee won't we? When we get there I mean?"

"Not a chance."

"Oh Lord. What have I let myself in for?"

Penelope watched with amusement as the fellow drew out a little tin of snuff and treated himself to some. Our boy watched too. It was an elaborate procedure during which a general silence was in order.

"'Bout 70 Yuan."

"What?"

"Well that's what you asked ain't it?" He pointed (↑) to the question up above.

"I believe I should be in charge of the money actually," our boy stated in calm voice, holding out his ladle-like hand. "Keep it all in one place."

"The hell. This here is *my* money. And I got it the hard way, too."

"I see. Just hope you don't have any warrants out on you."

"Naw! They like me, the police do. Chief Hendricks, he even called me a person of interest."

They set out, one abreast. It had been raining and the pavement was pitted with acid burns. Our man found himself moving more rapidly than the others, an effect of the dog pulling so strenuously at his elastic leash. (A tenor in spite of his great size, the animal seemed bent on waking the town.) Arriving at the intersection, our boy stopped and ignited a cigarette and never mind that he might have been seen from innumerable places. Keeping a sharp eye out for government ladies with scissors, he retreated then into his usual discretion and held the cigarette on the blind side of his valise. He saw a light come on in one of the overhead apartments and then go off again. He judged that most of the apartments in fact were empty, the dwellers having long before decamped for California or New York. He saw, he thought, a telescope protruding from a fifth-floor apartment, causing him to turn suddenly in such a direction that his face could not easily be seen. But he had been wrong to think that he had memorized the route. Having traveled less than a thousand rods, he took the map from his vest pocket in order to avail himself of the last street lamp that was likely to come their way. The prospective path of march was long but discontinuous, and in some areas was indicated but by a series of dots that grew further and further apart until at last it was clear that he would be free at that point to make his own decisions and go "withersoever he willed," as his grandfather had been wont to express these things.

"What are all those dots?" the girl asked him. Her fingernails were professionally done and in one case bore a Bruegelian painting of harvesters bringing in the crop. She was not a bad-looking sort, not really, and in addition to having bathed recently, she smelled of Sweet William and Love-Lies-Bleeding, some of his favorite names for flowers.

"Unexplored territory," our boy answered soon after.

"Oh God. And what are those blots?"

"Cities."

"OK, that's it, I'm going back," Hingis said, turning and making as if he were actually about to leave the group.

"But we aren't going that way."

Hingis came back. That fifth-floor telescope had meantime drawn back into the apartment and the lights had all been quenched. Further still, at the end of the pavement, they detected a numerous family of Chinese who had been reconfigured to look like Elvis. Smoke, fog, clouds and haze, our boy could no longer discern where one started and the other quit. The dog meantime was in despair, overwhelmed by the avalanche of unfamiliar scents passing through. He much preferred them in small doses, the better to analyze them at leisure.

They turned to the right and marched two blocks at high speed. Already some of the working people had ventured out of doors and were sprinting toward the flat-top office buildings that blocked out the light. Dressed for success, they wore, almost all of them, the satin shorts and contrasting shoes that proved they subscribed to the fashions of the day. Our boy, while avoiding the cracks in the sidewalk, strove to get a glimpse into every third face, a successful stratagem that left him with an increased respect for the abandoned countryside. He met and passed a middle-aged woman not easy to describe.

Very different was the gait and the address of her current husband following thirty feet behind, a washed-out sort of person, largely bald, taller than a breadbox but smaller than a horse. And that, of course, was when the weather began to rain.

"Well," spoke Hingis, "I reckon we might as well go on back. Heck, we could do this some other day."

Our boy recognized this of course as the first real test of his leadership.

"Go back? And you think Larry would let us in?"

The question was followed by an extended silence.

"And besides, we have this awning"—he pointed to it—"to keep off the rain."

"Got holes in it."

"Only because of the acid content."

"That's what worries me."

"And besides, we represent the Node, and have our dignity to be concerned about."

"Actually it's my rear end that concerns me predominantly."

But instead of despairing, our novice now pulled a piece of plastic sheeting from his valise and enveloped himself and Penelope in its warmth. She was in any case the snuggling type, and our man began now more seriously to think about making Larry happy, a project that would have been much easier but for the presence of Hingis and the rain. Bending near her porcelain ear, he whispered:

"Things that start out badly, very often they end up good."

She nodded and emitted a little smile, a pro forma gesture offered in lieu of spoken speech. He realized that Hingis was dithering with the door of the pawnshop just behind them, a narrow cavity that seemed to extend for a great distance into the dark.

They entered as a group. It was reasonably warm in the place and no rainfall, insofar as they could see, had made its way through the faraway ceiling. His first temptation, our boy's, was to appropriate one of the bismuth umbrellas that, however, appeared too weighty for sustained use. He saw a saxophone and accordion, a tray of escrubilator parts, photograph albums dating back a hundred years, also tools and coins, a bolt of paisley, military medals from the Bolivian war, forged documents, a new printing of the American Constitution (from which however the 10th Amendment had been omitted), a sawed-off shotgun with two boxes of ammunition, and a considerable collection of books printed on virtual paper. But mostly our man was interested in practical matters, footwear and the like, anti-spyware tablets, a pint of mint-flavored reflux solution, and a set of brass knuckles for the left hand. Of fluids, he selected a quart of belladonna, peach brandy, escrubilator grease, a small tube of sniffing glue, luminal and lanolin, a half-gallon of pink ouzo from the Peloponnese, aqua regia, muriatic acid, rosewater, Astyptodyne, two pounds of dehydrogenated gluten, a tube of valerian and capsule of spackling paste. He did not know what Hingis was taking. Suddenly a cat scampered by, a tangerine-colored animal chased by a small mechanical dog.

"How are we going to pay for all this?" our boy asked the room at large.

"Well," Hingis submitted, "we could leave a few dollars."

Impossible not to laugh. They had taken fifteen Yuan worth at the least. Indeed the woman alone had purloined a good half-Yuan's worth of facial creams. Reluctant to depart from so well-provided a place, they retrieved a jar of aloe and a cellophane envelope holding six grams of cupric oxide in gelatinized form. Hingis stole a mild astringent and a set of little silver teaspoons for administering the stuff. A 40-proof bottle of halogenized calomel and a fifth of corn liquor that had turned to wine. Bromide salts and a famous purgative composed from ambergris. A connoisseur of the new chemistry, our boy reached for and succeeded in taking a transparent box in which a dozen or more catalpa worms, crowded to extremes, had turned against each other. Saltpeter—he scooped up a pound and a half and funneled it off into the canteen he was also stealing. And green teas, said to be good for some of the new diseases. Next, prying open a keg of gunpowder and finding it swarming with roaches, he decided to leave it alone. There was a terrific array of vitamins, some of them in such colorful capsules that he took a great many. Quinine—in the whole course of their thievery they never found any. Oils, on the other hand, were plentiful, including most interestingly those of flax and teak. (Maple syrup played no part in their confiscations, nor salt, nor pepper, nor any of a lot of other things.) Finally he seized up a bottle of buttermilk, satisfied to see that it did have a virtual fly in it, latest fashion of the very rich.

"We could leave a note," she said. "and tell them how sorry we are."

They settled upon that solution, as also upon a used sleeping bag, a snakebite kit, a quart of turpentine, and two pair of satin-lined boots with orthotics in them.

But they had been wrong to believe that the rain had quit; on the contrary, it had coalesced into even greater droplets, pear-sized precipitation that exploded on the sidewalk like glass and dissolved a person's shoe polish. Ought he, or not, go back for the galvanized umbrella that he had opted to leave behind?

"The weather," he said, "and the climate, too, they just get continually worse it seems."

"Oh hell, 'our boy,' everybody knows that. But what you don't seem to understand is that it provides a lot of jobs. What, you want these people to be unemployed?"

That ended the argument. Our boy blushed and looked down, just as he had always looked down and had blushed when economics was discussed.

"Still raining. Maybe we could just stay here for the night,"

"No, we need to borrow someone's car."

"Hmm. Better, certainly, than waiting on the goddamn sun to come up."

"Much better."

"For example you take that blue car over yonder, the double-decker job with all those antennae sticking out. Shoot, it ought to be lots of fun to drive something like that. Shoot yeah."

"Maybe so," our man said. "OK, I'll give it some consideration."

The car was locked of course, and it needed a good five or six seconds for the escrubilator to unscramble the combination. Meantime the woman had taken a raindrop directly on her crown and was trying to steady herself against the nearest traffic sign. It was a robust vehicle, this one, and yet not so very robust as to resist the indentations left by the rain. The car was full of personal possessions, including a much-annotated edition of one of his grandfather's books.

"O dear me, lookie here what we got!" Hingis said.

They marveled at it, a .60 caliber "blow gun," so-called, with a laser pack. A thing like that could advance an explosive dart for a full mile or more, if not indeed a great deal further still. But where was the ammunition?

In answer, the ammunition was in a lockbox disguised as the refrigerator. Rummaging about in the cavity, which is to say after they had used Penelope's miniature escrubilator to open the thing, they uncovered just four pieces of ammunition, one of which proved merely to be a tube of lipstick. Rummaging further, they uncovered a six-pack of beer buried in the ice. And there were some other things, too. Hingis meantime had begun programming the vehicle, setting it on course toward the East-southeast, a route that should carry them over and across the "MLK River," lately so-renamed. Here warmer weather awaited, agricultural fields, villages with people in them, and in short a retrograde society lapped at both edges by great valleys filled to the top with forty-proof oceans full of salt.

"I'm going to build our node on a mountaintop," our boy explained, speaking mostly to himself. Sitting forward, he gazed dreamily in the direction in which they already had begun to move. The primary engine was powerful enough certainly, but the pedals had frozen and contributed in no significant way to the vehicle's speed.

"Seems like we could have left a note," Penelope offered again, "and told 'em how sorry we were."

Weaving in and out of the litter, the vending machines, the dead cats and burnt automobiles, they advanced along the street. A human corpse, or more probably a booby trap, lay in the middle of the road with money spread out around it. Our boy calculated it must be almost two o'clock in the morning, the coldest as also the breeziest minute in the night. But mostly it was the sun that worried him, and never mind that it might have bogged down on the wrong side of the earth. Inexorable, large and yellow, squandering fuel at a very high rate, it continued minute by minute toward its unremitting destination.

"Should be up pretty soon," our child said. "And then we'll be able to see the city in full light."

They adjusted the car, making it faster. There was only the smallest chance they'd be able to break out into the countryside before too late, and no assurance that it (the countryside), still subsisted on the other side of the tall buildings that fenced them in.

"I wonder, do they still have those level places?" the girl asked innocently.

"Fields, you mean?"

"Yes, and…" (She fumbled for the word.)

"Cows?"

"Yes!"

"Doubt it. I saw one in a zoo one time. You can always buy a mock-up of course."

"If you don't mind the mess." (Hingis speaking.)

Up front a man dashed suddenly into the road, stopped, turned and then headed off down the sidewalk at top speed. Soaked in glowing rain, he could have no real hope of enduring till morning came.

"Poor son of a bitch."

Came next a suntan salon, a video rental, a strong woman with an impatient face—they refused to look at it—and then a federal center distributing bottles of champagne to offended people. Reduced to this, our protagonists sat staring straight ahead into the one-time South, a literary place now gone probably to seed. Overhead a satellite had picked them out and was illuminating the way ahead. Two blocks further a three-deck vehicle loaded down with a mixed crowd of skin jobs and businesspeople passed them by and continued on in the direction in which the economy was reputed best. Was it possible they didn't know, all these ambitious types, that the swelling Atlantic had overspread Long Island already and was up to Canarsie by now?

12

Accordingly, they drove on through the night. Candles could be seen in the upper stories of some of the buildings, proof enough, in the absence of reliable elevators, that some people were willing to climb the several hundred steps to find security in high places. Itself, the rain had somewhat waned, though it threatened from time to time to start up again. Entranced by the flashing blue and green indicators on the dashboard, our boy said nothing for a long while. They revealed, those colored lights, what the car was thinking as it maneuvered among the burning cars, the trash and tumuli of masonry that lay at hazard along the route.

Making use of his authority, our boy had assigned Hingis to the rumble seat where soon after he could be heard speaking to himself in a delirium of red-hot anger. It left our pilgrim all alone at last with his as yet unconsummated "bride," as he tended to think of her. Suddenly he reached out and separated the two escrubilators behaving inappropriately in the backseat.

"Well now," uttered our boy, stretching and yawning and in other ways pretending to be more confident than he was. "We've got a long ride in front of us."

"I know." (Her face was the shade of milk, an affect of the moon which tonight had taken up an analogous position in the color spectrum. It was her ear that could not be seen at all, the fault of her black beret that covered almost all of that particular region. He compared her to a summer day, or anyway to summer days as he remembered them to have been —sunlight, bees, bluebells flecking the newly awakened hillsides, etc. He compared her to other things as well, for instance to the scientifically so-called aereoglopogus asianomone, a deep-water anemone drifting languidly down mid-Pacific rifts.) Working gingerly, he raised his front arm and strove to hold her with it, but then immediately brought it back again when he saw it hadn't the needed length.

"No, really," he said, "I'm absolutely determined to put our node on top a hill."

"If that's what you want."

He was liking her better with every day.

"But I'm going to need all the help I can get."

"Well of course." (Her upturned face not only looked like summer; it looked like June.)

"For example, I can't repopulate the American heartland by myself alone."

She said nothing. Her hips were broad enough and she was in possession, he felt sure, of a birthing canal of just the right dimension. Her bosoms were in their places, too, and had a quality that caused him to refer visually to them from one moment to another. Here now was a woman who with but little effort could nurture one set of twins after another until the end of all. He even believed that he could perceive her nipples, appurtenances of about 4/10 an inch in length and as big around, almost, as an old-fashioned Chesterfield cigarette. He smiled at her in friendly fashion. They were passing just then an extensive structure called "The Wedge," a containment center for people of ethnocentric tendencies. One glimpse at those towers and razor wire, the facilitators marching back and forth carrying blowguns over their shoulders… He preferred not to think about it.

They had been moving forward in a more or less straight line; now, without warning, they coasted to a stop and waited while the car adjusted its program and strove to accommodate itself to a suburban landscape that seemed to continue on for as far as they could see. There was no question but that some of the houses had people in them, and in one case indeed a large black modified dog with gossamer wings standing at the edge of his property. A minute went by as the two animals, our boy's and theirs, yelped at each other in an ambiguous manner, as if they couldn't conclude whether they wanted more to fight or get to know each other. A light came on in the house. Using his night vision goggles, our traveler discerned an ornamental yard jockey bending over the curb, a life-size sculpture simulating an anxiety-ridden Cauk in a business suit. He noticed then, our boy, a figure on the roof, a spindly-looking sort of person with night goggles of his own. They decided to continue moving forward.

The business district was in disrepair. Proceeding stealthily, they moved past a fast-food outlet in which a robbery was taking place. Came next a benefits office, two suntan salons, a pedicurist, wig manufacturer, a piercings workshop and leg waxing boutique. Truth was, they had stumbled into a blue light district where prostitutes were hard to find. They passed a notorious massage parlor where massages were given. It was beginning to seem as if this were rather a puritanical sort of place, a supposition that had only slightly to be modified when they halted just next to a late model vending machine painted green. As if by instinct, Hingis came suddenly awake and began inconveniencing our boy for a loan.

"Just two Yuan, OK?"

The novice handed it over. His colleague had had no orgasms in 48 hours, an indisposition that weighed heavily upon a fellow whose preeminent mission was to go about sticking his dick into people. Devoid of mechanical skill, it needed him a good two minutes to hitch himself to the machine and turn the power on. He was at least courteous enough to avert his face.

"That's one," our boy said, noting the moment. "See that spastic movement he made?"

She agreed.

"And now that's two. How many does he have to have for Christ's sakes? Ten is lethal."

(At that time the male required just 35 seconds, and the female an hour and forty-five minutes. This, of course, before recent improvements that finally brought the institution of marriage to its end. [He was reminded of the hideous case of a man in Connecticut when an early model vending machine had slipped into "overdrive," as they explained it. {And yet not even this was as awful as what took place in the former Oregon when the door had jammed during an aromatherapy session}]).

"That's three. Sun'll be up soon."

"Four," noted Penelope, counting them off on her fingers.

"And you?" our hero discretely inquired. "Would you like to use this machine?"

She blushed. "No, I'll wait."

"Just look at that pig. He'll be here till morning comes!" He cursed, our novice, and then had perforce to gather up Penelope's tiny escrubilator, the one with the rhinestones on it, and aim it at the man.

The suburbs never ended, not till they burst suddenly into a much larger but also much more dilapidated town that at one time must have contained as many as a hundred thousand constituents, bourgeois elements, and sports fans. Even the cartographers had overlooked this spot, according to the gazetteer our man carried in his baggage.

"This is the worst I've seen."

"Oh? You ought to see Chicago. They used to have all sorts of people."

"What happened to 'em I wonder?"

"Dead. Or gone to California."

"Same thing."

Up front, the Bob Dylan millennial colossus now moved into view, a gold and granite structure, half a mile in height, showing the subject plucking flowers from the stars. Awed by the sight, our party worked its way among the 80 or 90 little statuettes of some of the man's apostles, an austere people surrounded, each, by yet smaller figurines wearing beatified expressions. Indeed they actually came close enough at one moment to read the inscription, a noble stanza plagiarized from Simonides.

Dawn was overdue by several minutes when all of a sudden the sun-wheel hove into view before any of them had been able to prepare for it. Times like this, one could almost be grateful for the chlorides and sulfates that diffracted the light and, as it were, ameliorated the impact of a reality brought all too quickly into view. To Penelope, dawn looked like an arrangement of peacock feathers, whereas for our boy it resembled either a finger painting by a disturbed child or, more scientifically, a cosmological omelet splashed against the sky. Yet once again it brought to mind the embarrassing comparison and contrast between poor human beings and the ineffable landscape they had been tolerated to occupy.

"We've got about fifteen minutes to find a place in which to hide," Hingis reminded them, offering his most rational statement since starting out.

"We could go to a hotel."

Our boy had to laugh. "Hotel? That's the first place they'd look!"

"Oh. Well how about"—(she pointed toward a large home of three stories and what appeared to be an iced-over swimming pool out back)—"how about that big place with the iced-over swimming pool out back?"

"I don't think so. Besides, someone's looking out the window at us."

His night vision goggles were worthless in morning light. Reverting over to an ordinary pair of binoculars he studied the face at some length, finding it imprinted with one of the most disingenuous smiles he had ever seen. Other faces, reconfigured to look like Elvis's, began to show up in other places.

They inched forward, stealing past an opaline structure with an array of Hellenistic statuary dancing on the roof. He had decided, our protagonist, to keep away from rich places where they were likely to run into members of the elite traumatized by falling stock prices. A 1950s house—that was what he wanted, a home no bigger than it needed to be and holding souvenirs, as it were, of the good years.

"Two bedrooms," he said aloud, "and fifteen hundred square feet. Nobody would bother us there."

"Hey, what about that place? All those newspapers on the porch—nobody's been living there for quite a while."

"Booby trap," our man said.

"Well shit, we got to find someplace to stay."

This, too, was rational.

"All right, how about that condominium over yonder? Looks like the sort of place that has a private gym and hair salon."

"Yeah! And a coffee shop in the basement?"

"Why not? Heck, there might even be a little arts and crafts shop, too, a boutique, don't you see. Cozy and quaint."

"Collectibles and hot tubs. French instruction and a pottery-making club."

"Handmade candles and ice cream sculptures."

"Shoot yeah. And all sorts of arty people milling about."

"Yes, they might be arty. But that don't mean they can't be prosperous, too. See how prosperous that one looks?"

They laughed. No doubt about it, she was both an arty and a prosperous woman, the person they were talking about. Her suntan was of just the hue, her eldritch boots of separate colors, and in spite of the temperature her left breast was hanging out.

Immune to worn-out values, she could be rich and liberal, arty, compassionate and immoral all at the same time!

"Kill her."

But it was too late to do that. Already the sun had lifted a good two inches from the horizon and as the autophagous thing it was, had begun to devour itself to produce the warmth for which above all else it had been famous through time and personal experience alike. The mean temperature had meantime arisen to perhaps 25 degrees or thereabouts, warm enough to calm the escrubilators and turn the thoughts of our heroes to dreams of even further warmth, not to mention meals and sleep.

By 7:15 they had left the city behind, but then shortly turned back again when they perceived no other buildings for a great distance up ahead. The sun now seemed to have a skin on it, or "scab," to be more candid about it. Just that moment they caught sight of an individual darting from one home to another, his hand held aloft to ward away the ultragamma rays. No doubt he was heading off to join the "Fun Through Pain Community," judging from the fruit-size cancer on the back of his neck. It was then that Penelope spotted a modest-looking home that seemed to accord with the novice's desire.

"Is that a 1950s house?"

They circled twice and then came to a stop beneath the ruin of what must have been a tree house all those years ago. It put our boy in mind of things he had heard about the lives of children in that epoch.

"They used to spend most of the time out-of-doors," he said. "Children did. Anyway, that's what I've heard."

"Out-of-doors!"

The residence was open, leaves on the floor, and yet it still possessed the scent that associated itself with the period under consideration—the smell of cookies baked by the woman of the place. Summoning her up in imagination, our man experienced a surge of envy for her and everyone else sleeping blessedly in the ground these past ninety years and more.

The house, as reported, had leaves on the floor and the windows all were broken. They stepped over a scattering of children's crayons exemplifying the usual colors. Congruent to that, several art works had been fixed to the wall, including most curiously a family portrait in which the father was revealed to have been a mild-looking man with a medal of some kind affixed to his lapel. Our hero searched the portrait for a dog, finding it rather in the form of a small white cat. It was also apparent that the son had possessed an erector set, a toy that had quite other meanings in the pre-modern age. Two model airplanes, well-built, dangled by threads from the ceiling. But mostly he was impressed by the child's library, fifteen volumes from The Hardy Boys series along with an illustrated copy of *The Swiss Family Robinson*.

"Golly," Penelope said, coming up alongside him. "They must have been real smart back then."

"No question about it. They could read, many of them, before they were twelve."

She didn't believe him. Her attention strayed to the bed with its antique quilt, a much faded artifact with eight panels telling the fate of Montcalm at Quebec.

There were other things in that child's room, and indeed another room just next to it that apparently had held yet another child. Penelope went automatically to the little dresser with its mirror and set of combs and the half-dozen little miniature bottles of scents and unguents, all long since evaporated. A doll sat in the corner, a Pinocchio with a telescopic nose. Our traveler paid but small attention to these matters, preferring to go down into the basement and hunt for tools and such other materiel as might prove beneficial to them in days to come. However, it turned out to be real fetid down there and the floor held half an inch of standing water in which one could see a frenzy of larvae dogpaddling back and forth. No tools, wherefore he came back up again to find Hingis crouching at the parlor window.

"Somebody out there," he said.

At once our man scrunched down out of view and crawled toward his colleague. It is an accepted feature of sunlight that it tends to illuminate everything, a peculiarity best demonstrated in certain overexposed cinematic films of the 1920s. Promiscuous, hard upon the eyes, it behaves somewhat like water did, obtruding equally into private and public places alike. Meantime it was still the case that someone was out there, a man in a hat who appeared to be searching in tall grass with the aid of an automated golf club. Going for his revolver, our man rested it on the window sill and drew a bead that, if true, would have sent a .357 bullet into the fellow's left ear. Holding his aim for perhaps ten seconds, our novice then took down his weapon, saying:

"Maybe we ought to give him a warning."

"You're the boss. Might not get another shot like this."

"Anyway, what's he looking for over there?"

"I'll tell you what he's looking for, just as soon as you tell me how on earth I could possibly know."

"What is that—an escrubilator sticking out of his back pocket?"

"Yeah. One of those new jobs."

"Oh, oh, I think it's detected us."

They got down lower. The house had been constructed of brick, an earth-based material much in use at one time. It offered, they hoped, some defense against the new-style sensors. It was at that exact moment, of course, that Penelope strode innocently into the room, setting off an enormous Siren just across the road. He fired twice, our boy, hoping to shoo the man and his machine from the vicinity.

They found no foodstuffs anywhere in the house, save only

for a 90-year-old box of Kellogg PEP cereal in which our boy located a premium pinback bearing the portrait of "Snuffy Smith," an authority figure dressed in the modern style. He found next a television guide, a two-dimensional volume promoting programs and personalities of whom he, certainly, had never heard. Money—he found a trove of it in one of the dresser drawers, which is to say until Hingis explained that the stuff had been used in parlor games and had no application in the present world. They found a bottle of wine, they thought, an astringent-smelling stuff that, apparently, had been left to tempt intruders and bring about their deaths. As to the panic-stricken message scrawled on the living room wall, they paid no serious attention to that, knowing what it was worth. All three of them were tired and needed, all three, to register a few hours' sleep before the moon turned up again.

"I'll take the first watch," one of them said.

"That's all right with me. I'm damned tired."

"Me, too. But I'll take the first watch anyway, since someone has to do it."

"Good."

"Boy howdy, are you one lucky fellow."

"Hmm?"

"That someone else has volunteered to take the first watch."

"I suppose so, yes."

"And what about her? Is she going to take a watch, or is she lucky, too?"

The girl raised her hand. "I don't mind."

"No, no; she doesn't have any experience with guns."

"See? Everybody's lucky except me."

"Well let me just ask you this—how ever did you convince Larry to let you join the Node? I've been wondering about that."

"Long time ago. They were desperate back then."

"Ah." That was when his tongue dropped out. Hingis

looked at it, saying:

"Is it true, my pilgrim, that you can catch flies at twenty feet?"

Remaining silent, our boy reeled it part way in, pausing only when he came to a purple place.

"Boy howdy, I sure hope you don't never decide to give me a tongue lashing with that thing."

He endured it, our man, and then exunted off to the boy's little bedroom where it were impossible to take up a posture on the bed without one or more of the model airplanes bumping every now and again into his head. Consonant with that, Penelope went to the girl's little room and set about taking off her shoes which she organized side by side on the floor in the same relationship to each other as if she were wearing them still. He was glad to see that, our boy, who all too many times had borne witness to people who did it the other way around. Would she, or not, draw her dress up over her head and... That was when she closed the door.

He slept well, our boy, until just past noon. His escrubilator had also been sleeping, wherefore our man felt doubly refreshed as he got up to piss. Nothing surprised him anymore, and it especially failed to surprise him to find Hingis snoring in the kitchen with five voided cans of beer—and where, pray, had he found them?—five empties rolling about on the floor. Looking down upon him, our man picked up where he had left off with his plan to rid himself of this person before they reached Virginia.

"I don't suppose you left a beer for me."

"Say what?" (He jumped up.) "Beer?"

"Yes, and I don't suppose you've been keeping watch either."

He grinned. The sun was bright and brilliant and had turned the icicles into prisms that, depending upon where a person actually stood, displayed all the acknowledged colors from lavender to blue. Officially, it was midsummer now and soon the children would be dialing to warm weather programs on their hologram sets. Drawing his revolver and checking it twice, our boy remanded Hingis to the other room and then squandered several moments searching for any overlooked bottles of Mexican beer that would have served so well at this stage in their progress. Finding nothing of that kind, he cuddled up in the leathern sofa and, to his embarrassment, very nearly fell off into yet another sleep that would have enabled his colleague to do as he willed.

He never slept. Using his binary scope, he had found a world of things to look at, including most dismayingly a former golf course about four hundred yards away where a squad of youths on horseback was chasing high quality droids engineered to look like former presidents. That was when a silhouette passed between himself and the scene, blocking off the moment of the kill. Changing hastily into his ordinary glasses, he was surprised to see a suburban woman in short pants strolling down the street in full light. Either she knew nothing about delta beams, or else was infected already and no longer cared. Nor was the boy able to stop his own dog from barking out loud at the vision and in this way putting the lot of them in peril.

He saw other things, saw an armored personnel carrier disguised as an ice cream truck, an armadillo lurking in the gutter, and a long black sedan with the insignia on it of The Wedge. Twice he refused to let Penelope spell him, a generous type of behavior that had characterized western males in general before the onset of the gendered age.

"You're like somebody from out of the past," she mentioned, taking up a position at the adjoining window.

Embarrassed by the compliment, he waved it away. She was dressed in lipstick and had put herself in a gown of some type. And then, too, there was not much question but that she had arrogated to herself a drop or two of the household perfume.

"Hingis is sleeping."

Outside, the "Wedge" truck had returned, this time almost coming to a halt in front of the house. He discerned two rifles and a steel umbrella in the window rack. They lay without breathing, our man and woman, each searching the other's eyes for an escape route. Better to die at once, or thirty years ago, than be transported down to the headquarters of this particular organization. And where was Hingis when he most was needed, a better man with an escrubilator than either of them?

The moment passed, the vehicle picked up moving again, the armadillo had disappeared. The sun meanwhile had run past the moment of 1:00—would night never come?—and all three of them were in need of better food than that offered by a ninety-year-old PEP cereal container.

Hingis: "Maybe we ought to open one of those cans of Vienna Sausages?"

"No, no, no. Just no. We can't afford to get into our reserves this early in the game."

"OK, I'll wait till two o'clock. And then I'm going to that place"—he pointed to it—"that place, as I was saying, right over yonder."

The clock was slow and it did not hit two o'clock until they had taken their coffee, had gone outside, and then had raced across the erstwhile golf course with its flags and sand traps and waist-high grass. He harvested, our boy, one single golf ball, lost there perhaps fifty years ago. He had been accustomed to selling these things back to the golfers when he was young, but had no hope of doing so now, not since droids had taken over that occupation. And then, too, there always was the danger that he might be understood as a droid himself.

The building was unlocked and all the windows broken out. They entered in single file, escrubilators at the ready, and began to search the rooms while ignoring for the nonce the many file cabinets and bundled documents stacked almost to the ceiling in what appeared to be the central office. They circled around the computer, a bulky device dating back to the period when a famous genius had developed a program that paralyzed, not the machine itself, but anyone chancing to gaze uninvited at the screen. Our boy then halted beneath the portrait of Conchita ("The Pussy") Esterhazy, the country's penultimate president, a much beloved transvestite who had made his reputation as the lead singer in one of the bands of that day. It dawned on the boy that they had come into a government building of some sort, a branch office, no doubt, of the Compassion Commission, to judge from the display on the wall of so many blood-red valentines drawn by the children of the officials. One could learn a great deal from these drawings and file cabinets, had one but the time for it. Opening one such drawer at random, he focused on a folder pertaining to "The Cauk Problem," as it was labeled. But where were the people, the clerks and secretaries, the factotums and skin jobs that would have been needed to staff the place? This was the question he addressed to Hingis.

"The people! What, are they all dead or something?"

"Hm? Naw, they're in Florida probably. Or out there chasing droids."

Suddenly, as if to confirm those words, two loud explosions could be heard from far away. He knew that noise, our man, and knew that it proceeded from a shotgun and nothing else.

"Well. As long as they're just shooting synthetic people."

"Some of 'em are syns. Anyway, there's not one can of beer in the whole place."

The following room also had nothing in it, save for a new-style calendar on the wall displaying the 26 "months," each dedicated to its own bacterium. And then there was a narrow doorway that, as soon as he opened it, presented a staircase that led down into the dark.

"I wouldn't go down there if I was you."

"Got a candle?"

Instead, using his escrubilator, our pilgrim made his way slowly to the bottom with its earthen floor. He thought at first this place also was empty, which is to say until his goggles allowed him to make out the chains and waterboarding equipment situated among the other utilities—the 200 horsepower shredder for instance and old-fashioned furnace that still held the charred remains of documents too blackened to be read. No beer.

"Let's get out of here."

"Yes."

"Just look at that goddamn dog. What's he trying to dig up there?"

"Looks like a femur to me."

They emerged in single file, the animal coming away only reluctantly. It was not yet three o'clock in the afternoon, a half hour too early for the annealing darkness that came each day a little sooner. He used the time, our boy, for shaving off his incipient beard, for changing socks, for refreshing his revolver, etc., etc., and for seeing that the girl was given the privacy traditionally afforded to the members of her caste. A good decision—she had used the time to reapply her makeup and emerged looking more like a 24-year-old than the 26 he knew her to be.

"Can we open those sausages now?" our second-in-command respectfully inquired.

"We can not."

"You're hard. Real hard!"

"He is not!" (Girl speaking.)

"But I will grant you this—that just as soon as it's dark, we'll pay us a little visit to one of these high-class restaurants they seem to have so many of."

"Oh, I got it—you want to end up in The Wedge."

"We'll disguise ourselves."

"Good, good. What, you going to pretend you're a Chink or something?"

"No, we'll simply make ourselves… Ambiguous."

"Ambiguous. That ought to do it."

"Someplace where there's not much light."

"Agreed."

"Someplace where they still take dollars."

"Not in your lifetime."

(It was falling dark, an insidious procedure that, first, obliterated the outside features and then, secondarily, the inside people. They reached out to each other, the dog especially. Counting in unison, they got no higher than six before the last of the light dropped through a hole in the floor as it almost seemed, and they could actually feel the texture of this black night between their thumbs and fingers. Using his night scope, the pilgrim could make out the lesser Magellanic Cloud in its glory. A long time had gone by since the "expanding universe" theory had been exploded, he punned, and wise people been made to admit the Cloud in fact was drawing closer.)

"Look at all those stars!"

"Yes. They used to think they were light years away, remember? They didn't realize it was just the way the brain works that made them think that way."

"Light years my ass."

"The Greeks were better. They figured the stars were holes in the tarpaulin of the sky."

"Oh good. You know, I'm getting kind of tired of you, our man."

The car was close to where they had left it, though it was clear someone had tried, all quite in vain, to penetrate the self-regenerating windows on the lower deck. Having programmed the vehicle toward a series of nearby restaurants listed in inverse correlation of cost, the girl almost immediately fell off into a slumber in which our boy could scrutinize her face in much better detail than at any time therebefore. He would have said she derived from North European ancestry, the most endangered of all ethnoses, save only for outright Norwegians. Could he, or not, get from her a renewal of that species, the West made new, a numerous people inhabiting everything between the Rockies and Appalachian mountain chains? He knew that he could not. The resumption of fine literature, star travel, Wagnerian opera houses? Not a chance of that.

They approached the neon-lit café and waited to see the sort of people coming in and out. First appeared a swart individual with pink hair and a nose held on by a string.

"Hmm. Not as bad as I expected."

"No? Look at that one."

They continued on. The next place had been designed to look like The White House in the city at one time known to us as "Washington, D. C."

"Hey, I thought we were in a blue light district."

The third establishment was the one they chose, after witnessing a woman who, apart from her bald head and iridescent lipstick, looked to be some eighty or eight-five per-cent normal. Even so, they drove twice more about the block and then came to rest about eighty or eighty-five yards from the establishment itself. Penelope, freshly awake, had come out with a broad-brimmed hat that hid much of her admittedly North European face.

"You go first," the two men recommended. "But keep your escrubilator handy."

The door was of metal and the woman had to knock several times before the spy hole opened up. It gave our boy time enough to verify that he still carried his own escrubilator, an article of about two pounds avoirdupois with two supernumerary pellicles. His knife was sharp and fit snugly beneath the band of his knee-high socks. Certainly he had his revolver, too, and in addition had retained a high degree of confidence in his right-hand fist. That fist wore a ring that in turn had a protuberance on it that in some measure substituted for the brass knuckles he no longer possessed. Hingis was similarly outfitted, or so our boy assumed.

"Have your weapons with you?" he asked.

"More than you know."

"Good. Very good." And then: "What is it I don't know about?"

The spy hole closed, remained that way, and then the door opened up to admit the girl. They could not hear what words she was addressing to the person.

It was an ornate establishment, this eatery, much taller than it was wide but wider than any possible diagonal. This last-mentioned dimension was indeed quite short. Short also was the waiter who came promptly to their table and then wasted a deal of time trying to get a glimpse beneath the girl's broad-rim hat.

"Coffee," our boy iterated, hoping to call the fellow's attention back to his duties. He was wearing his Snuffy Smith pin and had allowed one of the tethers of his escrubilator to float about in midair.

"Yes, Sir!" the man responded, his face taking on the submissive expression that people like to see.

"And green tea for the girl."

"We have…"

Our boy looked at him severely.

"Green tea, yes Sir! I'm writing it down. It doesn't bother me, not at all, having to go across town to get some."

"And for the rest, we'll take…" (He enunciated what they would take, a traditional list of meats and vegetables that ought to keep them foddered for the next three days. It included sweet potatoes and black-eyed peas with the honey needed to hold them to the knife.)

"Ahhh," spoke the waiter. "I don't believe we have any of that."

"And across town?"

He wrote it down. It was hard for them to understand one another owing to the music, an exceptionally loud composition having to do with fucking. The dialect here had numerous Spanish and Portuguese elements and had liberated itself from several erstwhile English consonants. They looked for, and identified, three pock-marked adolescents, their eyes squeezed tight in a sort of musical ecstasy. Our man actually experienced a certain pity for them, knowing that in time they'd be made to utter words and wipe themselves without federal assistance.

They consumed their meals hurriedly, finishing it before the wine arrived. The charge was high, nor was Hingis able to interpose a few dollar bills among the Yuan. The car remained within a few rods of where they had left it and the striations on the rear window had mostly healed by now.

13

The open road! He loved to go up on deck and stick his head, as it were, among the permutations of the stars! Instead, that was exactly when a federal official came up out of nowhere and forced them off the road. Our boy had just time enough to gather up his switchblade and hide it in his vest. He believed that he could draw the thing out in short order and use it, if he must.

"Now just what do we got here I wonder?" the patrolman asked, probing the cabin with his oxide beam. "Man and two girls?"

"Approximately."

"And one old dog. I like dogs." (He called the animal and began to scratch it in that little sunken spot midway between the nostrils and the eyes.) "Oh wait, two mans and one girl."

"Right. I hope we weren't speeding."

"Hmm; I never even considered that. Were you? Speeding?"

"No, Sir!"

"Just a little," the girl said.

"No, I was noticing all that smoke coming out your exhaust. Whew!"

"Yeah, we're going to get that fixed."

"Says here…" (He had produced a government pamphlet from somewhere and had begun to read in the halting and semi-literate fashion familiar to them from the world. "… says here that when you got smoke like that, says it increases wear and tear on the treadle."

"Maybe so, but it's not our car anyway."

"And says here, says it increases the chance of ionization by—listen to this—sixteen per-cent."

"Sixteen! We just got to get that fixed. Isn't that what I've been saying?"

"He's been saying it all day."

"Well, I could, like, maybe let you off with a warning this time. Haven't seen any Cauks, have you? Hey! I don't suppose you want to buy a couple of tickets to the Patrolmen's Bash, do you?"

"Yes we do. Been wanting to do that for a long time. We'll take two."

"How about the girl?"

"OK, three. How much are they?"

The man, who must have been six and a half feet tall and who wore a kepi with the Federal scorpion on it, began searching about for the price.

"Can you take dollars?" Hingis foolishly asked.

"What's that you said just now? Dang! And I thought we were getting along just fine."

"We are, we are. He's just horsing around with you. Pulling your leg, and so forth."

The man, his face now darkened, peeled off three tickets and held out his hand for payment in modern currency. It needed him a full minute to examine the bills by holding them to the moon and counting the encryptions embedded in the D string of Dylan's guitar. Meantime up ahead a raccoon or some equivalent animal had stepped out onto the highway and was firing back at them with golden eyes.

The following forty-minutes proceeded without anything exceptional taking place. Penelope had gathered up her knitting while the dog, normally imperturbable, seemed to be embroiled in a nightmare in which he was being chased by a number of things. Working gingerly, our boy opened his satchel, took out two helium-based psychomachia tablets of 40 mg each, and inserted them between the creature's thin black lips. As to the ambient landscape, he could see virtually nothing apart from the faraway hills with smoke coming off the summits. The blood moon had meanwhile changed position, boding great bale for boys and girls like them. That was when he witnessed a dust devil wheeling across the plain, an intimidating vision followed shortly after by a stampede of armadillos—he thought the earth itself was shifting—melancholy creatures with their eyes close to the ground.

Stars? He could now make out only the most powerful of them together with a myriad of advertising signs. He thought at one moment that those were cows grazing in nightly pastures, as indeed they were. Here a person could stop and very easily drain off into his hat a good half-gallon of the freshest kind of milk, if only he but would. But he wouldn't. Much too intent upon his night vision goggles, he was occupied with spying into the homes and farmsteads that appeared momentarily (very momentarily indeed at 300 miles the hour) along their route. He did catch sight of a painting on someone's wall, a sentimental landscape beneath which a living farmer was levitating in his armchair. And was that a windmill in the yard, a dog sleeping under the porch, a 1940s child reading bedtime stories?

He snorted at the very thought of it. Children, if any there still were, would be on the computer at this hour studying rectal intercourse. As was her wont, Penelope had gone into her late night "molten" state, a lassitudinous condition in which a glass of wine and piece of music would make her available for almost anything. And besides, it had never been Larry's intention to repopulate the world solely from the nation's semen bank, not after he had downloaded the names of the contributors.

No, he wanted southern lads as could handle a pitchfork and escrubilator alike, immune to fear, blood on their hands.

There was a bad moment at about 3:15 when the vehicle jumped the tracks and had to be returned to them by hand. Radio signals were feeble in such a wrinkled terrain; even so, he selected this moment for putting the transmitter into contact with Larry. Immediately they picked up an intermittent noise arriving from far away, a voice possibly, or the sound of interference owing to the congestion of beta waves crisscrossing overhead. If voice, it belonged to someone experiencing a high degree of panic, but if not, it belonged then to the interference noted just above.

"My God, they're under attack!"

(He had meant to use the machine in English but by error had punched Estonian instead. Nor could he return to his own language without providing instructions in that Baltic tongue of which he understood not any.)

"No, that's Sybil! I know her voice!"

Other voices now began to expose themselves, including that of the paleographer, one of our boy's favorite persons. They heard then what might have been gunfire, or doors slamming, or of trucks and automobiles backfiring in the street outside. Followed then six minutes of silence which itself was followed by Larry's voice:

"Where are you?" he asked. "Still in Tennessee?"

"My gosh, Sir, we thought we heard a commotion going on! What's happening back there?"

He laughed. "No, no, just a couple of the girls. Everything's calm again. Why are you speaking in Estonian?"

Our boy at last succeeded in rotating over to their common tongue and then, to mystify the federal eavesdroppers, began to speak in formal English.

"We were stopped by the highway patrol."

"County or state?"

"Federal."

"Oh Christ."

"But I bought three tickets and he let us go. Also, he likes dogs."

"And the car that you seem to be using—where'd you get that?"

"Borrowed it."

"Ah! And are you still being followed?"

They turned and inspected the road behind.

"Don't think so." And then: "No, wait!" And then a moment later: "No, it's clear back there."

"Good, good. Where are you now?"

"'Patrolman's Bash,' he called it. Shoot, I didn't even know they used that word anymore."

"Where are you?"

(This was the question our man wanted more than any other to ignore.)

"We still have two bricks of fuel. Treadle's working fine."

"Where are you?"

"I can't say, Sir. The maps don't work."

"What? Those maps are only six months old!"

"I know it. But they aren't any good anymore."

"Baal! So how do you know where you're going?"

"Dead reckoning, Sir. Hingis is good at that. And besides, we have the stars."

"Ah? Well don't confuse them with advertising lights."

It was too late for that. Even so, our boy answered confidently and with good intentions made manifest: "I'll contact you again tomorrow. Sir."

Ahead, an injured cow was resting in the roadbed. They had to force it aside, a parlous procedure with lamentable results at 314 miles an hour. It was a strange truth that old-fashioned telephone poles still deprecated the landscape in this region, as also occasional xenophobes dangling from the cross beams.

A dying crow was perched astride one of the wires, the last member, very likely, of its species. They passed then a ranch-style home striving very obviously to hide itself amid a copse of escrubilator towers. They saw a stone structure interfering with the horizon, and then a "field of bones," as they were tempted to call it, owing to the number of bones.

They saw other things—an upside-down automobile with the usual puppy and then, next, a roadside sign inscribed in one of the Hamitic languages. Twice they found themselves caught for a moment in the focus of a searchlight that issued, as it seemed, from a place in the sky, a powerful beam that could have engendered round holes in normal persons and done significant harm even to very large ones. They halted briefly at a roadside vegetable stand, saddened to find the produce fossilized by age. Here an early model escrubilator had broken down and had rotted in the grass, drawing a crowd of other escrubilators from far and near. They passed an outdoor theater that had exhibited *Casablanca* for 10,000 successive nights. Next they encountered and then hurried on past an oncoming passenger vehicle that wasn't able quickly enough to train its analyzers on them at their conjoined 600 miles per hour.

Soon now the sun would have crossed the meridian on the blind side of the huge round world. They might even outpace the thing (sun) if their transport could go just 700 miles faster than it could, an impossible demand when they were using the sort of low-grade fuel that they were. Very soon they ought to draw in sight of the delegation from the Mother Node, assuming the map was even partway reliable. He tried to foretell the sort of disguises they might be using—assuming they hadn't the folly to stand in plain open view in the middle of the night.

"I'm thinking," he said, "they'll be dressed like peasants. Yes, and wearing straw hats and the like."

"Doubt it. We haven't had any real peasants for a long, long time."

"Or migrants."

"Maybe so. At least then the federals will leave them alone."

"Or minstrels wandering from town to town. Seers willing to prognosticate for small coins." (He knew he was hypothecating wildly, an old-time weakness of his.) "Or maybe they won't wear any disguises at all!"

"They aren't that reckless."

But now had come time to replenish the fuel, a perilous operation that needed special gloves and quick movements lest the hydrogenated halogens eat into the flesh.

"I'll do it," the girl said.

Both men laughed out loud at her.

"Look, just because things are the way they are, that doesn't mean we can't still be gentlemen."

In the end it was Hingis who lifted the lid and the other man who ventured to grasp the exhausted brick in his thorium glove and toss it a short distance away where they could observe energy changing into time even as they gazed upon it. It was the woman (the males wanted no more to do with it), who then snatched it up in her right hand and flushed it away through the hole in the floor called, self-explanatorily, "the hole" (in the floor). And if someday a child might come along and gather it up… But they hoped it wouldn't happen.

They had left Kentucky behind, a fact made all too obvious by the color of the grass. They passed a hitchhiker in the form of a scraggly man with his thumb up in the air. Far away to the east they could vaguely make out the towering silhouette of the gigantic apartment complex known as "Nietzsche's Head," and further yet, the dull glow, purple and red, of old Epsilon, largest entry in the ever-changing northeast Alabama volcano field. The better to see it, our boy resorted to his escrubilator and zoomed the view up to within about a quarter-mile, the optimal distance for observing lava flows. He saw, he thought, ruined houses tumbling downstream in the stuff and birds making a large detour around spumes of smoke lifting to the sky. Further still they saw other things, including a three-day-old nova in the one-star constellation known sometimes as Sylenus and sometimes by other names. Finally, and this was his last observation of the night, he found in the extreme distance the world-famous "Taos" glacier inching up from Mexico. Training on it with the most powerful of his devices, he perceived several dozens of persons suspended helplessly in the ice.

They were absolutely determined, Hingis and him, to find the Mother Node people before night had finished; accordingly, our fellow posted himself at starboard and scanned the countryside fore and aft. No one could say what he was seeing, not until he called out "City up ahead! Big one, too!" or words to that effect.

They put on speed, hurrying past it at above 342 miles the hour, too quick for the smell, the people, and the irradiation to take much effect. Came next a lake of recycled toluene, a good fifty acres of the stuff sparkling in the crimson night. Obviously their colleagues of the Mother Node would never choose to meet them in a place like this, populated as it was by mosquitoes and myriads of adaptive crabs that had penetrated so far inland.

"Maybe they were discovered," Hingis mooted, referring not to crabs but the individuals they were assigned to collect.

"Maybe they got lost," someone said.

"Or perhaps decided not to come at all!"

"Or maybe…"

They stopped talking. There were dozens of possibilities and no one wished to explore them all. And then, too, there was an all-night cafeteria up ahead in the twilight zone.

They stopped and pulled over and exited the vehicle. The place was full of truck drivers and throngs in thongs who grew irritated if anyone looked at them. Our man meantime sauntered to the pinball machine and stood there doing nothing, as if he had grown bored even before investing his hundred-dollar coin. He had no wish to get into a conflict with these people in their boots and jackets and belt buckles and for that reason had left his escrubilator dangling from his belt. The waitress was a mediocre-looking woman of about forty years, her face showing the effects of a wasted life.

"Water," our leader said, taking out a two-Yuan piece with the unified bust of Brad and Angelina on it. As a new customer he was given a choice between two kinds of water, one of them holding just six or fewer parts per hundred of hydrocarbons and the other some other kind of stuff. He lifted the tumbler with a rugged expression and threw it down with aplomb, his eye coming into contact with a Mayan calendar predicting the winner of next year's Super Bowl.

"Water," Penelope said, choosing the same contamination levels as our boy.

"What's it like out there?" the waitress inquired.

"Chilly. And getting chillier, I believe."

"Everybody says that."

"Oh?"

"Yeah. And I'm getting sick of hearing it, too."

Across the way one of the motorcyclists had arisen and was looking at them with menace.

"Nice place you got here," our pilgrim ventured.

"Again with that? I guess I've heard that ten million times."

"Cozy, too."

"Oh God almighty!"

The motorcyclist was a large sort of individual, as big as our own boy multiplied by almost twice his actual weight and size. He rose, approached, and said this:

"You come in here. They bothering you, Mary Ann?"

"Well heck yeah they're bothering me! Look at 'em."

"Now just you hold on a minute!" (Hingis talking.) "She's the one that said 'what's it like out there?'"

The cyclist turned to Mary Ann. "Is that true?"

She looked down. Her bib had grease on it and her bosoms, inasmuch as she had any, had lost every bit of their one-time impertinence and self-substantiating quality. Small but heavy, they made the impression of belonging to an older person.

"More water," Hingis said. "The six-parts kind."

"And blueberry pie." (Our boy.)

"Yeah, me too." (The cyclist.) "Pie."

The place *was* cozy, Hingis hadn't lied. They actually preferred a down-and-out sort of establishment with obsolete calendars and congealed pies with flies hiking about on top. He did not precisely need to use the restroom, our man, but remained curious about it all the same. Would it still have those puddles of urine and condom machines redolent of old days? Telephone numbers on the wall? Dispensing devices devoid of paper towels? He decided to learn the truth.

"May I use your restroom?" he courteously inquired.

"Same old thing. Weather, water, restroom. Aren't you going to ask me out?"

She did however turn over the key, a wooden manufacture tethered to a chain that he, certainly, could never have broken in twain. Next, he had to walk a good hundred yards in the rain and chilly air only to find the chamber occupied already. Meanwhile back at the restaurant his two friends had ordered further water and appeared to be settling in for a longer stay. They were tired, tired and peeved for having to travel so far at such mediocre speed.

Meantime, reverting to the outdoor restroom, our man had begun to cough and kick up the gravel in hopes of stimulating the man inside to leave. Finally, exasperated beyond patience, he drew out his member and micturated gratuitously in the litter in which he had detected a number of things. He could have availed himself of a bowel movement as well, but believed he could still postpone it for another few days.

The restroom proved to be very like what he had supposed, the converter not flushed and the paper towels completely gone. Sneaking a cigarette, he tried to read some of the inscriptions, but gave it up finally when he had to confess how weak his Spanish was. The ceiling fan, clogged with wasp nests, functioned no longer. All in all it was an unpleasant place, but had at least one high-grade drawing on the wall. As an act of altruism he tried to flush the processor, but then had instead to exit the place as hurriedly as he could. For some time he had been wanting to spy upon his two friends, apprehensive that Hingis might actually be trying to insinuate himself with the girl.

The window was unclean and fly-blown with, naturally, blow flies. As to his friends, they were simply conversing in an amiable but by no means passionate manner. She was bored and he was bored, too, and now our boy began also to feel bored, a superior emotion to the one he was prepared for. She had a bracelet with charms on it, hollow contrivances for transporting private messages. Her eyes were blood-shot and her hair was uncoiling, but she was still a better-looking person than dozens he could have named. Well-shod in pretty good shoes, she wore stockings that sorted oddly with the requisite shorts. Soon he would be getting children on her, although in truth the children had become a secondary consideration insofar as he was presently concerned.

So how far had they actually traveled by this time? Hard to say, due to the fallibility of the maps and quality of fuel they were using, a diluted stuff that gave off popping sounds that interfered with reading. Glancing up from the map, our boy observed that they were passing "Fair Meadows," the state's largest reeducation camp for culture snobs. Came next the former headquarters of the MESI project, a government-financed search for extraterrestrial life that had been made to shut down two years earlier by some outside force. They were cruising at almost 400 miles the hour and time, as if to substantiate an old theory, was slowing down. And was the girl younger than she used to be, and the vehicle, was it rejuvenating even as they went on reading desultorily in their books and celebrity magazines? Indisputably. And were those the Mother Node people huddled by the freeway (beggars they almost seemed), was it them?

They drove past at high speed, slowed, and then turned and came back. Bedraggled, rain-drenched, complaining non-stop, our man was tempted to wheel about and resume his former course.

"Do we have to pick them up?"

"Yep. Goddamn it."

Slowly, cautiously, Hingis opened the front door and spoke to them through the screen.

"Are you…?"

"Well hell yeah we are! What, you think we came out here just to stand about in the rain? It's killing us!"

"…the Mother Node people?"

"You can call us that, but it's not what we call us. What, you think the Greeks called themselves 'Greeks?' They did not."

He was a middle-aged person, seemingly a male but with a fulgent powder of some sort in his hair. It was only much later on that our man learned about him, namely that his embryologist, a jocund personality, had mixed him with some 150 butterfly genes.

"Called themselves Hellenes, I believe."

"All right, so you read a book once. Do we get to come in? Or not?"

"Let me ask Larry."

"Sure, you can talk to Larry. And I'll talk to Harry. Harry has lots more authority than Larry."

"But not as much as Barry."

"Barry my ass! He'll do whatever Cary asks."

That did it. Standing aside, they permitted the four wanderers to enter one by one, a slow process that allowed the three originals to inspect them as individuals in all the defects that individuals have. In second place there came a woman of about 5'4" carrying approximately 132 pounds. Our man, who always had preferred your well-fleshed women, compared her to the other two females before then mentally discarding the one that would have been discarded by almost anyone. He smiled nevertheless and relieved her of her rather heavy suitcase held together in coils of old-fashioned string.

"Let me help you," he said.

"No, no, go ahead and help Lisa. I know you want to."

She was more to the point, and her shorts, Lisa's, really were extraordinarily short. She had no suitcase however.

"Let me help you," he said.

"How?"

"Well! We have water."

No, she had a flask of her own.

And then there was this fourth person, an aggrieved-looking sort of type with all manner of mannerisms about him. Not until later on was it revealed how this person had made his fortune, specifically by demonstrating to the government how much cheaper it was to maintain lists of normal people than of sexual offenders.

"G'morning," our pilgrim said.

"Morning?"

"Yes, it's just past four."

"What day?"

Our man cited the day, or night rather, and then watched with fascination the surprise that registered on his face.

"July, you say?"

"Why yes."

"Not according to our calendar."

The last our person wanted was to get into a quarrel over new-, middle-, and old-style calendars. Instead, he flagged the fellow to the best chair and passed him a bowl of reprocessed chocolate candies wrapped in bright red foils with symbols on them. They were moving at about 150 miles per hour and would require a long time to get, in both senses, up to speed. One thing was immediately clear, that the two girls, Lisa and Lynn, had so far failed to develop admiring opinions of each other. By now they were moving at about 210 MPH and the two groups had pretty well settled in and had begun interrogating each other about their aspirations and other quiddities.

"You were an educator, I believe?" Hingis asked, aiming his remark at the man with the powdery hair.

"I was. Briefly. Before I got fired. And now I'm as you see me to be."

"Fired, you say?"

"I was too severe—this is what they said—too severe upon the students. The final straw, I suppose, was when I began to curtail access to the vending machines." He lifted his canteen and drank, never allowing a single drop to escape. He had a moustache that turned up and seemed to be smiling; otherwise his face was like a mirror that reflected his interlocutor's image back upon itself. It could be seen that his tongue was as thin as a spaniel's and that his original teeth had been replaced with a material too nacrous to be real. His hair, of course, was a problem, and never mind how little he had. As for the nose, our boy refused even to report about a thing like that.

"Yes," he went on, speaking in the insouciant tones of a northeastern professor, "I made my name in fugitive poetry of the Kwarezmian Period."

"Interesting!"

"Yes. Well of course it is true that I had to … recapitulate some of the material myself. Creative recompositions, far better than the original stuff."

"I'd like to see some of them repositions," Hingis said, raising his hand in classroom fashion. He had not been in the presence of the professor for more than a minute and already he was giving more regard to him than to the one he should. The teacher still went on:

"Cultural studies. My partner and me, we were…"

"'Partner?' Oh God."

"…regendering the *Iliad*—a famous old book— some of you may have heard of it—regendering it for the rising generation."

"And getting paid for it, I presume."

"Post-cultural reassignations. My next project will focus on Tarot Cards with patriarchal themes."

Fascinated by this sort of talk, the Nodists, all but one, gathered around to hear him talk. Wishing to break up this sort of conversation, our boy then asked, "How long, I say how long have you four people been waiting at the edge of the highway?"

Lisa tried to answer but was cut short by the transmitter that came on each night at this time, wished for or not. They were moving at 294 miles the hour while auditing the music of an adorable band of youths lauded by The New York Times. Instead, our novice turned his attention to the entrepreneur, a gentlemanly sort of person who had earned his second fortune in refereed journals for tenure seekers. Refereed by his wife and daughter, he had made good money by putting the stuff into print.

"And you," our pilgrim demanded, "how did you manage to become a Node person?"

"Harry. It was him what recruited me."

"Ah."

"Yes, he had submitted a long article and I was able to…"

"Get it into print."

"Precisely. However, there's more to me than just that. I can weld large pieces of metal together. I can butcher cows."

"You thought those were cows?"

"I've never met Harry myself," the narrator admitted.

"Oh, he's a lot like Cary. Prone to tarry."

"If only he would marry."

"Marry? Thought he was a fairy."

Etc.

By 4:45 they had come up to 315 mph and with but little dark left to them they spotted an advertisement that closed off further progress. It needed a long time to bring the conveyance to a stop, at the end of which period the billionaire leapt out and went forward and illuminated the obstacle with his book of matches.

"Hmm," said he. "Seems to be inscribed in a 14-point Times New Roman font."

"That text? Or this?"

Followed by one of the three girls, our boy also left the car and went forward to read the ad:

"Ichthyological exhibit up ahead! Two miles! See!"

"We could bust right through that old sign," Hingis said. "It ain't nothing but reprocessed something or another."

"No, I want to see the ichthyo… The exhibit."

"Oh boy, here we go."

"Me, too, I'd like to see it, too," said Penelope, expressing herself to our boy's displeasure. He had wanted to keep on running forward.

"Don't have time," he said. "No, that ole sun'll be up before you can…"

"You don't have to go. We'll go. And we'll take our umbrellas anyway."

He passed out the umbrellas, our man, and then at the last instant grabbed one for himself.

It was a small building, perhaps a leftover gasoline refilling station from the old days. With one eye on the impending sun, the Node people strode up in a group to the impresario, a man in a hat standing just before the open door. He was vile-looking and his face about like what they expected.

"Seven tickets, please," they asked of him.

"Yeah?" Suddenly he reached out and probed the breast pocket of the butterfly man, as if tobacco products might be hiding there.

"You wired?"

"No, no. Just the usual stuff."

"OK, come on in, you think you have to."

They entered on tiptoes, feeling their ways into the dark with outstretched hands.

"Can't see!" one of the girls reacted.

"Hey! A little patience maybe? Just a little bit? Sure would appreciate it."

They quieted. Penelope had come to stand by our man's side, as if consternated by what she might see once the lights came on. They were all of them troubled to some degree. Perhaps the man had taken their fees and run away. Or, they were to be shut up in that building and themselves turned into an exhibit. Or, the sun would come up during their distraction and set the countryside on fire. That was when the lights came on.

They were in a forest, a two-tree manifestation with blooms along the bough.

"Gosh!"

"I saw a tree once. But it weren't like this."

"How was it?"

He described how it was, a ten-foot-high job but no blooms along the bough. Only belatedly did they realize that a narrow stream, perfectly clear, ran between the two arboreal simulations while giving off a water-like noise.

"This is where the ichthyological part comes in," Hingis said, pointing to the stream. "Right down there in all that water."

"Water? You want water, go to Greenland." (He seemed not

to realize, this man, that Greenland had been reduced to a minuscule iceberg and at last report had bogged down off the shelf of Argentina.) "This here is reprocessed naphthalene, pure and simple. We used water, we'd have to charge six times as much."

"Yes, and now that you mention it, it doesn't really smell like water at all."

"When does the ichthyological part come in? No, I'm just wondering."

"Don't believe I've ever seen so many impatient people before. OK, here we go, just keep your eye on that little flue down there—see it?—she'll be coming out of that."

Together they bent over the flue. But if they had expected a salmon or a trout... No, they were being shown a perch of about five inches in net length, a speedy creature, quite plausible-looking, that came bursting into view and began at once to swim about in shrinking circles. The girls jumped back in amazement and even the men gave signs of being surprised.

"Damn!"

"Looks like a little... I don't know what."

"Like a perch—that's what it's supposed to look like."

"And scales! How do they make them I wonder?"

"You have to give it to them, those science people. Is there anything they can't do?"

"Wonder what they use as a power source?"

"Don't ask," the showman replied. "Unless you want to ruin the illusion. Well, your two minutes is just about over."

Indeed, the animal was moving slower and appeared to be in danger of drowning if they continued to gape at it much longer.

"Two more Yuan" (each) "and I'll wind her up again."

"No, no. Thanks anyway."

They watched the little creature return to the outlet and then, reluctantly as it seemed, pass out of sight.

"My God."

The lights came on.

"Who made him?"

"Her."

"Who made her?"

"Laboratory out in Montana. Actually, they're doing some pretty terrific things out there. They've got 'em a supply of water and they're dumping all kinds of chemicals into it. Figure they'll recombine, don't you know, and we'll get us some real fish someday. Fish, oysters, the whole ten yards. 'Course we might have to wait a while."

"Like about a billion years?"

"Maybe. But I'll still be here, trying to entertain you folks."

They laughed and shook hands all around. Undoubtedly he was the most loathsome person they had encountered during the whole trip. Meantime he was aware, our man, of something telling him that the sun already was peeping over the edge. Hurriedly he hoisted his parasol, an unwieldy model left over from last October, and then tried to assist one of the new girls, who wanted no help.

"Help Lisa, you're so crazy about her."

"Think she'd let me?"

"Oh God."

The sun was up, albeit roosting just now behind a toluene cloud. Running back to the vehicle in single file, Lisa was allowed to climb in first. Her shorts were not that short and instead of following immediately hard upon, our boy made way also for Penelope and one or two others.

The open highway! it cheered them all. There was a signpost up ahead, a laughable effort to send them astray. Jesting about it, they opened a sealed package of chocolate chip cookies and turned on the television, only slightly surprised to find that the bombing campaign against Bolivia was already under way. It was a good show, they had to admit, with no dearth of holographic casualties cumulating in the streets.

"This ought to be good for the next election."

"My God, look at that one! A man would have to be a fool to underrate American air power."

"We gave them every chance after all."

That was when the program was interrupted by a third-quarter basketball score just now coming in from Delaware. Our man was trying to grasp the significance of it when this in turn was interrupted by the news that the country's second-most admired superstarlet had just last night been fertilized by her analyst. They listened with attention to the congratulations arriving from far and near. The sun had by now fully arisen, making it possible to discern a small boy on a bicycle caught in their slipstream.

"We need to find a place to pass the day."

"Absolutely. How about that farm house over yonder?"

They slowed, but then sped away when they detected a capsized car with a puppy in it. There were other such houses, most of them in awful condition indeed. They saw, they thought, an actual farmer poised on board a tractor, only belatedly realizing that he had been dead these many years. Meantime sunbeams were threatening to come through the windows of the vehicle, too many for the filters properly to depolarize. They ran then over a culvert that might have offered some protection, assuming they were willing to shelter there and squat for hours in rivulets of naphtha passing under the highway. Far, very far ahead they saw what had been a city at one time, a place remembered for its shopping riots.

"Maybe we could take sanctuary in that city up ahead."

No, our boy vetoed it at once.

"What, you get to make all the decisions, is that how it is?"

"Yes."

"Why, because of Larry?"

"Yes, that. And Cary."

"Cary? Cary retired two years ago! Living in New York, is what I hear."

They passed an old-time grain elevator that had split apart, its contents providing a feast for some of the local people wading up to their waists. They were now moving through a flat region that, while it might be easy on the automobile's suspension system, had been aesthetically impoverished ever since the locusts came.

"Wouldn't be half bad here, if we still had trees."

The Nodists were falling to sleep all around him—this is how it seemed to the one in charge. Still listening inattentively to the news, he was advised that cattle futures were down. Next, reaching for the implement, our man attempted again to put himself into contact with Larry, but then hurriedly put it away when he saw that the sun had fully detached from the horizon. There was no question but that the rays were beginning to have a deleterious effect upon the seat covers and Penelope's face. Finally, willing to risk these things no longer, he pulled off onto a subsidiary road that, however, almost immediately began to peter out into a discontinuous series of shallow puddles of human shape.

"Where are we?" (Penelope)

"Arkansas. Or Alabama maybe."

"Alabama? All those racists?"

"We could take cover in that old barn."

They edged closer to the building. Not for a very long time had cattle inhabited the place, nor horses nor ewes nor other things. And then, too, the entrance was broad enough, and high, they could drive into the place wholesale and look about before opening the car.

"Oh gosh, what is that?"

"Hay."

"Oh." And then: "What do you do with it?"

It offered good bedding, no question about that. A man could curl up in stuff like that and reserve the whole of next week for dealing with his redbug bites.

14

He slept well for about six hours and then, speculating on how he might make himself even more comfortable, jumped up and urinated at length. Thereafter two more hours of pretty good sleep followed hard upon. Sun down, moon up, stars shining, he lay for a time in a hypnoidal state, watching bemusedly as two of the overhead CCTV devices went on swiveling and twisting in a perpetual effort to monitor each other's behavior.

The moon, ushered onstage by a mob of corybantic moths, was resting like a golf ball on top of an old style industrial smokestack that might not unreasonably have been likened to a "tee." He knew of course that he was getting ready to get up, bringing closure to lying down. Next, calling his will power into play, he really did arise and wash and was on the verge of eliminating when it occurred to him that he might still be able to defer it to another day. He spent a long time on his teeth, aware that his toothbrush was embedded with a "snitch," popularly-called, that reported back to the authorities on his dental habits. Finally he went to rouse the others, disturbed to find Lisa in the arms of the onetime scholar whose chigger bites were visible in the little bit of light.

"Time to rise!" he said, addressing particularly Lisa. It was no doubt true, as claimed by her, that she had been reformatted a decade or more ago and her well-formed legs cloned and prototyped for use by others. Neither was her face all that unpleasant either. "Moon's up!"

They set out at 20 mph and headed off in the direction mandated by the road itself. Not three minutes had gone by before they encountered another vehicle as large as their own, a double-wide copper-colored Dreadmobile with faces in all the windows. Both cars slowed, making it possible for Lisa to catch a glimpse of her husband, a burly man who bore the angriest expression imaginable.

"Faster," she said, "couldn't we go a little faster?"

They could and did (go a little faster). They had penetrated into an alien sort of terrain where things might be lurking behind the hills. He saw, he thought, a rollicking face, larger than the moon's, peeping merrily over the ridge. Hingis meantime had taken three chicken wings from their lunch bucket and after smearing them with mustard, was smacking his sizeable lips over the enjoyment they apparently afforded. Beer—they had none of that. Water neither, forcing them to use a placebo instead. Banana cream pie also was lacking and yet they continued moving forward all the time. Classic, it seemed to our boy, that Penelope was knitting studiously just now, but then from time to time unraveling what she had done. She was a more domestic sort of person (lissome and neat, juicy and sweet), than the even better-looking woman with her right breast hanging out. It was this latter person however who had the dimple just above her knee, not to mention the possibility of yet further dimples in still other places. Turning from her, our man tried to think about philosophy and history and things like that. As if the place between her labia were the world's best address! He snorted at the thought of it.

Toward midnight they espied a gang of kangaroos leaping down the horizon, the work of young malefactors who some twenty years previously had broken down the gates of one of the nation's premier zoos. In this calm time, our boy took out his tobacco pouch and assembled a long thin cigarette that would have vouchsafed him a good fifteen years in prison had anyone caught him at it. The weed, of course, was of inferior quality, and gave off little popping sounds that put one in mind of the violent country it was imported from.

"Got hisself a cigarette!" Hingis said. "Wish I had one."

He built another one, our boy, this one thinner yet and louder still, and handed it off to his fellow passenger. There were far better addresses than the girl's and he hoped shortly to come upon such a place for the implantation of their node. It occurred to him then that, really, it was time to confer with the leader of them all.

The lines were busy, requiring him to wade through three several streams of unspeakable "music" before he could connect to Tennessee. And even then the sound was far away and he could only with much attention hear the sound of traffic in the road outside the rector's office.

"Is that you?" the man asked. "Moses! Where the devil you been?"

"Marching through Georgia," our man replied half amusingly. "No, we're in Alabama I think. Or Arkansas."

"Alabama? All those racists?"

"Naw, they haven't given us any trouble."

"OK, what does it look like there? Where you are I mean."

"Behind us are hills, smoke coming off the summits, and fields of a yellowness that makes a person want to moan out loud."

"Oh, good. What else do you see?"

"Kangaroos and..."

"That was a serious question my man."

"Well, there're some pretty good mountains off to the north-northeast, about six or seven thousand feet high I would say, along with... Hold it. Just a minute. My gosh, those are volcanoes, looks to me. They got that real bright ooze coming out!"

"Good! And is one of them shaped like a camel, more or less?"

"Camel with two humps? Why yes."

"Three humps!" Hingis yelled, calling loudly enough to be heard 800 miles away.

"Was that Hingis?"

"Yes, Sir."

"So he's still with you then."

"Yes, Sir."

"Well, I guess you can let him stay for a few more nights. Now about this volcano, it's called Epsilon. To distinguish it from Alpha and so on."

"Vowels only?"

"And there's a small village just on the other side, if it's still there. Great view. I always thought it would make a perfect site for one of our little communities, what?"

Our boy wrote it down: "View."

"Yes. Now how many people do you have with you exactly, roughly speaking?"

"Ah…" (He counted.) "I got six."

"Six. And do you have that girl, the one with the…"

"Yes, Sir."

"Good material, that one."

"Yes, Sir. But she's already committed, so to speak. Her name is Lisa, but I call her Eve."

"Droll. And what about that butterfly fellow? You don't want to underestimate that one. Speaks five languages."

"Yes, Sir. I got a woman here doesn't speak any."

They were interrupted by music, an aggressive noise laudatory of the cunnilingus community. Long time went by before the two Nodists were in communication again.

"Can you, I say can you hear me?"

"Yes, Sir."

"Now that other fellow, the rich one, he's accustomed to

being rich. I just don't know how long he can get by feeding on armadillo feet. He used to own an apartment complex in Catalonia and two pieces of JFK's underwear. And so be patient with him if you can."

"I can."

"Say what?"

"Can."

"Can't hear you."

"Says he can!" yelled Hingis in that direction.

"And then we have that other person, too," our boy went on saying.

"Yes." (The man's voice had come back!) "There's not much to be said about her."

"My impression, too."

"Even so, you don't want her wandering off. She couldn't take much 'wedging,' if that's what they chose to do."

"Agreed."

"Well, I guess that's about it. I might be able to send another 2,000 Yuan pretty soon, assuming the shuttle" (overhead shuttle traveling on gamma beams) "is functioning."

"Yes, Sir. Any progress in the O. J. Simpson case?"

"Not yet. Well, I got to run. You take care, hear?"

"Yes, Sir."

"And so I'll say goodbye."

So that was it, a final word, a caution, and a promise of Yuan. Never had our little man been faced with so many composite responsibilities piled up so high.

The site chosen by Larry was apt enough and the view quite good; our man however much preferred the emptied village that lay about four stone throws further downstream. It offered a perspective even more vertical than the foregoing, as well as a site that was more defendable withal. They parked and, after searching the vacant homes with their night probes, began to argue about the best placement for their current and future weapons. They wanted overlapping fields of fire capable of sweeping the valley down below. Surely this was the best address in the world, where no one could come within a furlong of the place without setting off the dog, the half-dozen escrubilators, Hingis's Lewis Gun, and the tripwire our man had baited with a flask of apparent water.

Having secured the place, they returned to the largest of the five homes that comprised the onetime settlement. It contained, that building, an atrium and hot tub, and in the corner a cuspidor with a broken cusp. Meantime the man with the languages had been attracted to the "library," a voluminous collection dating back, some of the texts, to several decades earlier.

"Oh dear me," said he. (No one was listening.) "I could have enjoyed these, were I but younger." (He was 38.) "Especially this large tome on Seljukian fabric design. And this: Neanderthalic Grammar, Praxis and Style. Whew. Wonder what sort of person used to live here?"

"Kook."

"Context and Gender in the Phlogiston Narrative!"

"Want to give us a hand over here? The window won't close."

Together they managed it. There was a fairly good supply of firewood and ashes enough in the hearth to show that someone at least had tried to cope with the hard winters that these days continued throughout the year. On the mantelpiece he espied, our man, a bottle of preserves in a Mason jar; however he was far too experienced by now actually to take off the lid and sample the stuff. One might just as well go to the rescue of an upside down puppy in a booby-trapped car. Or jump into a fire, or die for Israel, or succor billionaires.

Truth was, the sun was soon to be coming up. In view of that, our boy now planted himself in the middle of the room whence he would be able to observe the sleeping arrangements of the people—whether, for example, the man with the five languages would lie with Lisa or someone else. And would they all sleep together in the same big room where they could defend each other against the as-yet-undiscovered dangers in this region of Alabama or Arkansas?

"Well," declared the nondescript woman (she could speak!), "reckon I'll retire off to bed now."

They watched. She was adept at unfolding her pallet, puffing up her pillow and making it fat. Fascinated by it, they esteemed the way she was able to disrobe beneath the sheets and then take up her book and read a paragraph or two before blowing out the light and reciting in soft voice a short prayer of which they could hear almost nothing. Left in darkness, our boy still did not understand where Lisa had chosen to place herself, nor Penelope either for that matter. Neither were lying with him. Hingis he was easily able to place, based upon the snoring that came from that direction. They were seven adult beings and a pooch, each of them thinking one's own thoughts while stretched out on a hardwood floor with crown moldings overhead. Far and near they could hear the cicadas and the crickets still slugging it out in their thousand-year-old song contest, the season notwithstanding.

"I could have flipped this house," said the man who previously had been so rich. "If there were any suckers hereabouts."

"Why yes, you could have put up curtains and so on. Give it a paint job."

"Paint? Paint is six Yen a bucket these days. Naw, I'd have just put in a bunch of wet bars and hot tubs. They go for shit like that."

"Good. Well I'm going to call it a day. Night, I mean. And now I'm just going to roll over—I'm doing it now—and see if I can get some rest."

"Stick a couple of virtual trees in the front yard. Magnolias maybe."

"Good. We'll discuss it tomorrow."

"Imitation countertops."

He woke once, did our boy, during the long dry day that followed, but only to see that the three women had taken up in the remotest corner of the room where one could not get at them without a lot of trouble. The crickets meanwhile had fallen silent, leaving one sole individual to represent his genus by himself alone. It gave our narrator a chance to view the valley in full light, a grainy-looking panorama reminiscent of nineteenth-century Hungarian postage stamps. It were old down there (unless it was a booby trap), and he half-expected to see peasants wending homeward with their few poor head of livestock while harkening to the piping of the flute-like tunes that in those times hung in the air. With nothing else to do, he summoned the dog and, after pulling up a stool, began feeding him slowly out of a big iron spoon. He was sincere, that animal, his eyes grateful, and his interest in food about as well developed as anything very well could be. That was when the indescribable woman rose up on one elbow, saying:

"What time is it?

"Almost six," he replied, checking his escrubilator.

She slumped back down. She was a graceless human being and in that area had failed in her first duty as a woman female. It made him mad, seeing her without make-up or piercings, needing a shave. It had required thousands of years for these people to invent the illusion of beauty and here now was one of them ready to spit upon that whole effort.

She was not alone. Hingis, in sleep, looked like an orangutan with his toe in his mouth. Continuing on, the boy noted that the intellectual man, him with the genes and the languages, had extruded a layer of mauve-colored particulates, a dust-like stuff, over both his pillow and the adjacent hardwood flooring. Addressing himself alone, our man said: "Ah well, maybe it's just as well." (Just as well that the human species was dying out.) "Look at 'em."

Someone had tried, but failed, to hijack the automobile. And then, too, the hand crank was recalcitrant and it needed the collective effort both of Hingis and the uninteresting woman to turn it over. Soon enough they were breezing down the highway at about 40 miles the hour, which was not too fast to stop but also not slow enough for them to lose all interest in the outside scenery scrolling past. They passed a weight reduction emergency camp where perhaps 200 souls were standing about in a field of exercise equipment. He was almost tempted to stop, our boy, and give assistance to the person who had bent over for some reason and frozen into position. There was enough protoplasm out there to traduce the orbit of the world.

"Look at that one!"

"Don't look. It's not nice."

"Can't help it."

"How very fortunate" (someone said, probably the five-language man), "so fortunate that we are prosperous enough to offer such treatments!"

"Yea, and prosperous enough to have created the need."

"Oh, I see. Can we expect you to be ironical all the time? Or just occasionally?"

"Once a day."

"Very good, and I'll slam you over the head with this book just once a day, too—OK?"

Our man made haste to put a stop to it. "Book? Maybe you should read out loud so's we can all enjoy it."

They were moving just then through a synthetic forest full of mechanical larks that were perhaps *too* happy, all of it followed by a gated community with 30-storey cottages for supermodels and hockey stars. Penelope had meantime returned to him and gone to sleep with her head on his shoulder, a surrender, as it were, to their mutual promise to be fruitful to each other. Slowly and tenderly he stroked her nose and left cheek with his long bright tongue. All his life he had enjoyed women's heads on his shoulder, especially when, as now, he could peer up through a transparent glass roof at the comets and nebulae going through their evolutions. He settled upon a "green dwarf," improperly so-called, a bilious-looking presence whose light, we are told, had started out from its source very long ago. There was a good deal of litter up there, too, not excluding a plethora of large-scale advertising signs that had been hoisted to the outer perimeter of one of the atmospheric belts mentioned in university texts before the truth had become known.

In fact they were moving rather too quickly now and were forced at last to use the handbrakes before coming to a stop in a parking facility where all sorts of aspiring carjackers were standing about gazing innocently into the distance. In the store itself they discerned perhaps fifty women, all of them obese and loaded down, all, with redundant merchandise carried by light-skinned porters.

"See how they cling to their purchases!" the previously rich man said. (His name, by common agreement, was "Smith.") "Heck, a fellow could make good money in a place like this."

"What other kind is there?"

"And see the expressions on their faces! Afraid someone will take their packages before they can get to their cars."

"And someone will. Look at that one."

Smith went back to reading, an affecting and highly persuasive stuff having to do with the disorders of white males. A male himself, and white, this "Smith" had many years ago been licensed by central government to Sire a child, the result of his poor showing on an intelligence test. (With so many stupid white males, the country's equalization project was swiftly moving ahead.) Exiting the car, this man, still reading out loud, strode confidently toward the store. His tie bore the image on it of a talk show host together with a software implant that authorized him to buy groceries. The seven adults now lined up at the entrance where they would have had to undergo an inspection, had not our man at the last moment thrown back his lapel to reveal his Snuffy Smith credential.

"Oh!"

The shop was long and half that much again and had so many aisles and overhead displays, so many shelves and other places that a person must needs be given a map as soon as he came in. Appropriating one of the carts, they pushed slowly down a corridor lined on both sides with 100-Yuan female prototypes with perfect shapes. Continuing past all this, they arrived at a fruit stand supplied with papayas and plantains and in one case a traditional vegetable claimed to be a product of the U.S.A. The avocados were largely rotten but he knew he would take one anyway. He chose a fresh-smelling homemade apple pie imported just yesterday from a place in Southeast Asia. The others now began to choose their own favorites, including such newly-fashionable delicacies as chitterlings and black-eyed peas. It was possible to acquire two bottles of ale for the price of just one, a bargain that reminded our man of when an ancestor of his had invested in a slave who owned a slave of his own. Pork was cheap. They chose four pounds of the stuff, including two that had been certified by a well-known rock star whose signature was appended in blue ink. Suddenly that moment they recognized that Penelope had strayed off into the cosmetics section, a labyrinthine adjunct where she could have been lost forever.

Smith kept on reading. He had come to that part wherein the western hemisphere, formerly a paradise on earth, had been deconstructed by explorers in wooden ships. That was when a youth, an unlikely-looking lad of European provenance, stopped them in mid-passage and spoke up loud and clear:

"Hey, y'all aren't ... Node people, are you?"

"Possibly." (Jones reached for his escrubilator.) "How could you tell?"

"Book."

"No, no. Ha! No, no, it's not ours, that book. We just…"

"I ain't going to tell nobody! What, did you swipe it?"

"Possibly."

The boy's dog, and the Node's, were critiquing each other worriedly. Indeed, the boy's dog had gone direct to the Node's and was slowly mangling its right ear between his sharp front teeth.

"Your dog…"

"He ain't going to hurt nobody! 'Less I want him to. Say, where y'all staying?"

They didn't like to answer questions like that. Smith then tried to pat the boy on the head who, however, jumped back out of the way.

"Staying up there on Chowder Hill, ain't you? Naw, I seen that big old yeller car up there. Looks a whole lot like that one"—he nodded toward it—"out in the parking lot."

"Shouldn't you be in school?"

"Naw. I had an infusion a couple of years back."

Jones spoke: "You know, it kind of surprises me that you even want to talk to us. Old people, like us."

"I've seen worse."

"After all, there's lots of yellow cars in the world. I saw one yesterday."

"Naw, yours is different. I can do carpentry, roofing, stuff like that. Mostly I do painting."

He was definitely an urchin and his hair was red. Gathering about in a circle, the Node people looked him over, a personality that had come into the world at about age fifteen and had elected to stay that way.

"Anyway, I don't think we could afford you."

"Cook! I can cook beans, different kinds of meat. You name it, I'll fix it."

They moved on. The store offered all different kinds of beans and meats and they chose three of them derived, each, from a different kind of plant or beast. Milk was plentiful, but they lacked the machinery to separate it from its naphtha coefficient. Moving studiously up and down the aisle, sometimes taking off his glasses to get a better look, the former scholar was looking for bargains and in fact finding a good many of them in unexpected places. Already he had seized upon a can of tuna with an acceptable expiration date. Came next the hams and the cheeses, including a notable array from the former Italy. Here our man always tended to get bogged down, entranced as much by the little artistic labels and trademarks as by the actual product. He was weighing a cake of provolone when a gaunt fellow with a suspicious smile came and stood next to him. What his smile was suspicious of, no one could say.

"Been a long time I expect, since you've had a real cigarette."

"Yes, it has," our man replied, smiling right back.

"Years and years."

"At least that."

(Something was fixing to happen and our fellow had a pretty good idea what it was.)

"You can't do better than this," the man said, opening suddenly his long black coat to show a package of Camel cigarettes pinned to the fabric.

Our boy jumped back. The last he wanted at this stage was to be sent off to jail in California, or some such place as that.

"Good Lord!"

"Ssssh! You want 'em? Or not?"

"You take dollars?"

"Wise ass. I come here in all sincerity, trying to be nice."

He paid in Yuan and after inspecting the dromedary-and-pyramid trademark, hied the fellow on his way. Worrisome to him was it that the place was filling with other shoppers, a representative sample of someone's constituents including two homosexual queers, an illegal, a celebrity, three rock stars, a crime scene investigator, an iconic loner, a commercial traveler, a pundit, numerous strong women, a man in denial, and a boy in a thong and tie, all of them monstrously overweight. Watching with a noncommittal expression, our novice was minded of the first time he had taken off the lid and peeped into an escrubilator, and then had rushed outside to vomit on the ground.

Their next stop was at the tavern just across the way, a gaudy place lit up brilliantly with jukeboxes and last year's Christmas tree. And yet hardly had they entered before they began to wish that they had never come, based upon the rough-looking individuals—once, just once, he hoped to go into a place patronized in majority fashion by people like himself—glowering back from the tables. Pretending also to be rough, our boy bellied up to the bar and growled out the one word—"water"—that seemed to satisfy those as might wish to test his manliness. He had left his escrubilator behind; on the other hand he was smoking an original cigarette that proved he had no fear of the law or anything else. The tobacco was old however, and burned all too quickly, right down to the nub.

There was a calendar on the wall, three years premature, with the picture of a celebrity on it.

"Who's that?" he asked the bartender, a bald man, rather obsequious, wearing an apron.

"Celebrity!"

"What's her name?"

He supplied the name.

"Never heard of her," our boy confessed.

"Nobody has."

The water was good and had a bouquet with a mischievous quality, like unto that of elves dancing in a beam of light. But he was annoyed, our man, to see that the urchin and his dog had both followed inside and were standing quietly by. Did they, or not, expect to be furnished with a drink? And that, of course, was when one of the rough men rose and sauntered over and began running his hand through the powder in Jones' hair.

"Well oh my goodness," he said, "lookie here what we got. What, somebody get you all mixed up with some butterfly genes?"

"Moths, actually," the man replied, not without dignity.

"Moths!" (This from the bartender.) "We don't serve your sort here. Sorry." And then more gently: "But you could try across the street."

He reddened, the moth man, and, moving with his characteristic flutter, stepped toward the exit and disappeared. And yet there were other customers in there whose biologic inheritance appeared even more problematic than his. Our narrator fixed upon a heavy person with a snout, and then a woman, as he believed her to be, whose day job very obviously was as a prototype.

The night was young and the Nodists in pretty good spirits as they left the bar. They had cigarettes, they had vittles, and they each had had their daily ration at the bar. Jostling their way down the road, they passed a theatre in which some old two-dimensional films were being shown. How strange they were! these old-time actors, most of them under 300 pounds and dressed in the shoes of that day. And trousers! bifurcated garments that came down to the floor. With his attention fixed on the placards, our boy scarcely noticed it when a police car came rolling past—once, just once, our boy would have liked to evade the notice of these types—slowed, turned, and then came back again. The night was dark and the officer wore smoked glasses that looked like insect eyes. Too large to leave the car, he rolled down the glass and spoke, saying:

"Howdy."

They responded in analogous language.

"Having yourself a real fine evening! Walking around. Two dogs." And then, suddenly very serious: "I believe I'll have a look at your papers, if you don't mind too terrible much."

The urchin's papers were in good order, Smith's much less so. As for our narrator, he handed over the only document he had, an expired laminated library card that had come down to him from his grandfather. The patrolman had a device attached to his glasses, a jeweler's eyepiece as it appeared to be. Availing himself of it, he looked long and hard at the library card, continually comparing the photograph to the person standing just in front of him.

"Well," he said finally, becoming visibly more friendly. "It's OK, I guess."

Our boy took it back, at the same time inadvertently exposing his League of the South membership card. It was time for someone to say something, either that or the whole lot of them were likely to end up in silent embarrassment.

"How'd the team do this year?" our boy hurriedly asked.

"Good, real good. Won all but three."

"Three! That's wonderful. And next year they'll do even better."

"They might. They got that Riley boy now you know. Early draft. Shit, he can do a hundred yards in 10.2."

"All right!"

"Had sixteen tackles last year. Nine assists."

"Well damn!"

(The clouds were exiguous but even so it looked like bad weather coming in. Happily, they had brought their umbrellas; unhappily they were not built for rain. He observed, our central character, that Penelope and one or two others were edging back toward the vehicle that had fetched them to this place.)

"That's not even to mention all them interceptions; I'm not even talking about that."

"No, no. Me neither. Well, I guess we better get on back."

"Just don't let him punt. Don't let him punt and we'll be all right."

They laughed, all.

"He shouldn't be let to punt?"

"Hell no! I just know we lost that North Carolina game on account of that."

"Nothing surprises me, not these days. Well, you take it easy now."

"But you know, I think sometimes ole Sammie is even worse at it than him."

"Naw, I wouldn't go that far."

"Well. Maybe not."

"Anyway, you take it easy now; I need to get on back and see what's happening."

"Best goddamn receiver we ever had."

That was when, in his supreme folly, our boy attempted to light a cigarette, a piece of bad judgment that he was able to set right by very quickly dropping the thing to the pavement and squishing the life out of it.

"Four interceptions. Shit, he must have been coked up that night."

"That would explain it."

Etc.

They arrived home at 3:15 and after throwing a few sticks in the fireplace and setting them alight, divided themselves into eight individuals and began to work cooperatively on the mail that had arrived in their absence.

"Says here," Hingis said, "says Social Security is under threat."

"Social what?"

"A thing they used to have."

"Look at this, they want us to contribute to the wounded war veterans. Hey, I thought the government did that."

"Not since that mess in Bolivia. It's hard, carrying on all these wars at the same time."

"Wants us to subscribe to some magazines. Which ones you want, Smith, the one about mushrooms, or building scale model aircraft carriers?"

"Look at this, the government is offering a new benefit and you can go to jail if you don't apply."

Lisa was going through a mail-order catalog.

"Want to buy a .75 caliber revolver with nitro shells? Got plutonian points and a five-gram payload of cottonmouth venom."

"Says here they've developed some hydroponic tulip bulbs. You can grow 'em in midair."

They splashed through the celebrity magazines, the pornography, the steak knife bargains, Navaho pottery from Thailand, simulated books with luxury bindings, diesel-powered vibrators and a blueprint (very costly) on how to build a hydrogen bomb. All this they added to the fire, save only the newspapers and the material on bombs.

"Ha," our fellow said, citing from the Gadsden Sheet. "Congress went into night session and agreed to everything the Five Families demanded."

"Good! Maybe that will put an end to all these assassinations and suchlike."

(They had long ago perceived the CCTV cameras pointing at them from the mounted moose's head, as also a mousetrap beneath the counter with a toe bone in it.) It would be light in under three hours, just time enough to hear Jones reciting from his books; instead, that was when he (Smith) and she (Lisa) rose up and stretched languorously and then headed off in single file toward one of the far rooms in order to get a start on things.

15

With just a short time before dark, they were awakened violently by the smell of coffee and bacon and hot buttermilk biscuits with several kinds of jam.

"Where on earth," they asked him, "did you get the jam?"

He said nothing, the urchin, nor would he sample anything himself until invited to it by the man called Jones. Invited, he then sampled everything in sight with an extreme display of gustatory delight, he was that hungry. It was chill weather outside and from the last look of things, just before the sun went down, it was evident they had endured a considerable dust storm during the daylight hours.

"Don't think of it as snow. For that would be a mistake."

"Silicates," Smith said, pronouncing the word with the finality that one expected from a person of his kind. "And phosphates. More of the latter however than the foregoing."

"Oh, Christ."

"Yes, and someday soon the whole wide world"—he extended his arms to embrace it—"will be the same."

"Coffee," our man requested. "And more of that toast with the real good jelly."

He was served immediately, the urchin actually putting aside his own meal in order to fetch it.

"By the way," the foregoing went on, "we've decided to let you stay."

It was an arbitrary conclusion and yet he was applauded for it by the rest. And then, too, it was obvious that certain repairs would have to be carried out on the roof where some of the silicates were leaching through.

"And phosphates, too," he was amended.

And thus the three of them, Hingis, the kid, and our own person. The roof was steep and a surplus of dead leaves had filled and overflowed the chimney. It was true that they had the tools—hammer and tacks, a roll of felt and two squares of matching shingles, all of it taken from the little workshop out back that also held two gross of antique bottles holding a transparent fluid with dark red sediment on the bottom. He would have liked, our boy, to have come upon a diary, or heap of newspapers, or anything to tell the story of what had transpired in this place. Finding nothing of that kind, all three men climbed the ladder and set to work.

It was a goodly moon tonight and shortly they could make out the profiles of two or three of the local people who had gathered just on the other side of the property line. Our man waved to them and drew his gun and, although it couldn't be seen, smiled cordially in their direction.

"G'morning!" he called. (He believed that he could hear an answer, a small voice that seemed to come from far away.) "Trying to get this old roof fixed."

"Otis will be pleased."

"Why don't y'all come on in, have some coffee?"

"Coffee?"

"The real stuff."

They stepped over the property line. If he hurried, he could leave the roof and greet them at the door, especially the very tall one whose silhouette included what appeared to be a beard and a hammer of his own.

They chatted for the better part of an hour. The tall man, seated just across from Lisa, seemed to be drawing out the conversation, which is to say until he had finished off two full cups of what had been served to him and had smoked down, in full view, a handmade cigarette that acuminated to a point. The other men were just as rustic, even if not yet as tall as he.

"I brung my boys," he said.

"Yes!"

"We ort to get that old roof fixed up pretty quick."

"That would be wonderful."

"I don't know why we're doing it though, seeing as how y'all probably won't be staying." And then: "We been needing a critical mass, you understand, if we're ever going to have us a decent economy. Critical mass of people. Anyhow, I don't reckon Otis is ever coming back." And then: "Dog of yours sure likes to smell people, don't he?"

They pulled him off, forcing the animal to abandon the man's crotch.

"Where'd Otis go?" someone asked.

"New York City! Yes, Siree. Took his wading boots with him."

They laughed. The floods were up to Brooklyn Heights by now and the waves, seventy feet tall some of them, had dislodged a great deal of wine and brie, leaving it in incongruous places. Meantime the residents were still living on top of one another, just as they always had—such was the news they had of that city.

"Your boys don't talk very much, do they?" someone noted. "No, I'm not saying there's anything wrong with that."

"No, Sir, they don't. 'Course now, if you don't got a critical mass of people…"

"Ah. Need to put these things into perspective, I guess."

"Yes, Sir. Put 'em into context, like the fellow says."

"Prioritize things. Change the whole scenario."

"Yep. And parse it, too."

"Peer pressure."

"They think we're the other."

"Yeah, I get kind of tired of being dissed all the time."

"It's part of their agenda."

"They're so transgressive."

"Need a new paradigm."

"Completely new."

They laughed. The two boys had completed their coffee, had vacated the place, and one could very shortly hear them scrambling about on the roof with an alacrity and efficiency that put to shame the people who had proceeded them up there. After harkening to them for a moment, the man named Smith spoke up loud and clear:

"It's a sick situation we got here. The country, and all."

"Well heck yeah it's sick! I could see it coming when they took *Gunsmoke* off the air."

Smith went on: "Yes. And as a consequence of all that, it has become our intention, all things being equal, which of course they aren't, our intention, as I was saying…"

He was pushed aside by our man who, after all, was in charge of the leadership of this group, putatively speaking. "Our intention," he said, "is to start over again from the very beginning—that's what Larry wants anyway. A new society altogether, one not very different from the original Jamestown, and so forth."

"Don't know much about that place."

"What do you need to know?"

"Don't know."

The noise on the roof had stopped. Was it possible that the work had already been accomplished? Our boy went on:

"A new society, very like the first. We provide the critical mass and you, you provide the labor and skills, that sort of thing. We'll grow our own food! Put a wall around the place."

"That's hard, what you're talking about now. Growing stuff when it's so cold."

"Generate our own power. Any rivers hereabouts?"

"Yes Sir, there is. Frozen."

"And repopulate the nation. Or repopulate, anyway, the acreage between Nevada and The Hudson River Basin. Hopefully the rest will soon be under water anyway."

"I see." He rubbed his whiskers, the old man, and gazed thoughtfully in Lisa's direction. "Repopulate."

"Combine our forces."

"Combine."

"So what do you say?" our fellow asked. "We've got eight people—nine, counting me—and that's not even to speak about the dogs. How many you got?"

They counted. The oldest boy was better at math and soon he came up with a number that was very near the limit that our boy believed he could successfully command.

"Seventeen! Well hell, that's a start. But you'll have to do just as I say."

"Knew I would, soon as I seen you up there on that roof."

"For example our little Penelope here"—(he made her stand and turn around)—"used to be a nurse. We'll need that. Good width on her, too, no?"

"Sure. But how about that one?"

They turned to the nondescript woman who in her steadfast silence and indifferent dress seemed almost to be laughing at them. No one knew what went on inside that person.

"Leave her alone; she's alright."

"You say that?"

It appeared that a renewed dust storm had just moved in, evidenced by the sound of grit impinging on the panes. Give it two more days and the weight on the roof would be as great as ever.

"My God, that stuff is bad."

"Sure. But good for the economy they say."

"I've been meaning to ask—how many women, actually, do y'all have here?"

The old man rubbed his whiskers. One had the impression that they (his whiskers) had ceased to grow at some date and had fossilized at just that length, about a quarter of an inch. "Well, we was raided a couple months ago and they took two of 'em. We still got Ann of course. But she's not in season. And Betty, we got her."

Listening to that, our boy tried to get a mental profile of the population and its abilities. The coffee itself had run out and they were being given a dark and viscous syrup that tasted like the cough medicine of seventy years ago. The women were good at that, finding things in abandoned houses.

They talked deep into the night, at which time Penelope came and sat next to him. There were 13 people present on this occasion, far short of the 77 claimed in later accounts. He speculated that perhaps they should sign a compact of some nature, a constitution almost, or even just a brief paragraph that later on would constrain anyone trying to worm out of it. But neither pen nor paper was anywhere to be found throughout the house.

"And who else? Besides Betty and Ann I mean?"

"Well, we got Clara Sue. But she's mine."

"And cattle, got any cattle?"

"Used to," he said wistfully, thinking back upon it. "Dust got 'em."

"Ah. Well what about goats and chickens and stuff?"

"Yes, Sir; got one chicken. But she's a good one."

"Well how about mineral resources? Any mica for example, or veins of silver and gold?"

The old man thought long and deep. The "coffee" was beginning to have its effect and our boy feared he might fade off to sleep while the moon was up. Accordingly, he turned his notice upon the eldest of the two sons, a stalwart-looking American-style old-fashioned farm boy whom no one in right mind would wish ever to irritate in any way whatever. There was potential here, a fellow with the juices in him to beget long lines of people down to the end of time.

"And what about you?"

"Sir?"

"Ever killed anybody?"

"Not yet."

"I suppose you're just waiting around for Ann, right?"

He blushed narrowly but deeply, the stain remaining but for moments on his Cauky face. "Yes, Sir. Him, too."

They all turned to "him," the second-eldest whose chest was perhaps even deeper than his twin's, his lungs heavier, and his head as hard-looking as a hickory nut grown to corresponding size. Which would get the girl? Not Hingis certainly, who had padded off to sleep a good quarter-hour earlier. Gladly would our boy have swapped this person (Hingis) for just a single chicken of ordinary size.

Their guests retreated off to their own places at shortly after three, but only then to come back a little later with half a dozen fellow villagers whose curiosity, one had to suppose, had become too much. They shook hands all around and after seating themselves (some on the floor) swilled off small draughts of cough medicine taken from the supplies. Those supplies and villagers, they formed only a very poor foundation for the new world Larry and Harry had in view. Would they, or not, disappoint those great men who had striven so hard and rescued so many, and done a lot of other things as well?

"We'll need to put up a wall," our boy said, directing the comment to Ann who to him looked more in season than he had been told.

"You'll never get these people to do anything," she said cheerfully. "Except drink whiskey."

"Oh they'll build it all right," Smith assured her. "We have ways."

"Anyway, it's too late for us."

"Too late? My God, we're going to have to put some fiber into you people!"

"We need it, that's for sure. Fiber."

They could hear someone scratching at the door, another delivery of junk mail that this time included a singing telegram from a collection service. They listened to the end and then, after trying unsuccessfully to recruit the singer to their cause, gave him an American coin that still had a sentimental value at least. In addition to people, they were going to need a much greater inventory of dogs to keep tax collectors, poll takers and Jehovah's Witnesses at bay. Meanwhile Smith, who had been thinking seriously about it, said:

"Dairy products, we could specialize in dairy products in the same way that certain old-world monasteries used to specialize in wine."

"Wine!" said one of the townspersons. "Yeah, let's do that."

"Butter and cheese; damnation, we could have us a thriving business out here and the IRS would never have to know."

"Wine and cheese. Shoot, yeah."

"I like a dab of butter now and again. On waffles, and stuff."

"Old-world monasteries! That's the ticket."

"But we can't do nothing without cows. You want butter? Then you want cows—that's just how it is."

There was truth in that. Our boy arose and after retrieving one of the escrubilators edging stealthily toward the door, convened a discussion about cows and their products. It was his understanding that such cows must needs be stolen, in view of how little funds they had.

"I guess we'll just have to … steal 'em," he said reluctantly. "From some other monastery nearby."

A farmer raised his hand. He had not spoken up until now, at which point he lost courage and opted to stay silent. A few moments having passed by, he again began to talk and again shut down. Finally:

"I know a fellow what's got a cow."

"Very good! OK, that's a start. Good to hear from you Willard; you ought to do that more often."

He grinned, Willard. They felt, all of them, that progress was being made. Spoke now our man, who couldn't allow too much silence to go by lest his leadership fall into abeyance.

"Wall first, cows second. Yes, and I have seen many fine rocks lying at hazard in this land, the best of materials for walls of that kind."

"Oh good, he's beginning to sound like his granddaddy."

"I got a wheelbarrow." (Having once begun to talk, the fellow showed signs of loving it too much.) "And my brother's son, he…"

"Good, good. Concrete is what we need. But I just don't see how we're to steal that."

"Concrete ha. Cement is just as good. And cheaper, too."

"Don't matter how cheap it is. If we're going to steal it I mean."

"Shoot yeah. If you have to steal, steal the best!"

They all laughed out loud, including even the nondescript woman who had an unlikable way of doing it.

"What's the difference actually? Between concrete and… What you said?"

"What's the difference between iron and steel?"

"Well for a start, your iron ingots are a whole lot different. Now you take your steel, that's what they use for certain kinds of things."

Our boy could feel a headache coming on. For one brief moment he was tempted to turn the authority over to Smith, and might actually have done so except for that man's underlying nature and genetic equipment. Instead he said:

"We'll call Larry."

They gathered around. The transmitter was weak and the capacitor of an obsolete manufacture; nevertheless they soon succeeded in reaching a ringing tone that suggested the radio waves were doing as they should, which is to say traveling at lightning speed over the vacant acres between them and him.

"Yes?"

Our boy jumped back. This was by no means Larry's voice, which always had given off a good rich baritone, mellifluent as a bassoon. It was, he knew, the ice cold voice of a government official who had been in too high a position for far too long.

"Could I speak to Larry please?" our pilgrim courteously inquired.

"And who might you be? And what is your location please?"

"Location?"

"Why yes; it's not a difficult question. And what exactly is your relationship with Mr. Schneider?"

"Schneider! In all this time, I never knew that name. Strange."

"You're not going to tell us are you? Location I mean?"

"Is he under arrest?"

"Arrest? We don't use that language anymore. No, these days we call it innovative hosting."

"Oh Lord."

"Is it Ohio, where you're at? Or California?"

"And what about the xylographer, did you take him, too?"

"Place was full of strange people. You in Montana?"

Functioning with extreme courtesy, our boy returned the speaker to its cradle and shut off the machine altogether. He hated to think about Harry and Barry, their hopes for the future, and the probable discontinuance of the movement itself.

"Well now!" he said expansively. "I think it's time we had a tour of our new home!" He looked meaningfully about the room, but especially at an anxious-looking individual of perhaps 70 years who seemed the perfect type of an old-style yeoman, as these people had once been called.

"Shore," the fellow said, staring down embarrassedly at the

floor. It was apparent he had never seen an escrubilator before and wanted to come no nearer than ten or fifteen feet to one.

The night was clear and the stars, of which there were a very great many, were blinking off and on in a pattern that seemed to be saying something. Or was it dust? He looked for, and uncovered, the only two-star constellation in existence, a gaudy array called Phlubius after a certain Greek entity who was much less famous than he had deserved. He could also see reminders of the faraway town—a violet glow prowling the western horizon like a cat. Calling the urchin to his side, he inquired abut it.

"Is that Dorisville?"

"Yes, Sir. But you don't never want to go there."

"Why is that?"

However the child had no more to say on that subject. Instead, turning in the direction of Pigeon Forge, headquarters of the most successful of the new religions, he made a sacred gesture with his left hand and right foot. Our man was flabbergasted.

"You don't actually believe in that stuff do you?"

"Well shoot yeah I believe it! Stands to reason."

"Gila Monsters?"

"You just don't get it, do you? They're good. Now you take your god, he don't even exist anymore!"

(Our leader was not accustomed to being thrown on the defensive by a trifling boy.) "Maybe not," he said, "maybe not. But He could if He wanted to."

"That's right, just keep it up. But don't blame me when you wake up in hell."

"Such nonsense." And then: "So how does a person join this outfit actually?"

They had come to the first of the two barns that either had been erected for the tourists or else had actually served at one time. Taking care not to step in the dreck, they entered the cavern-like structure that still smelled of the animals that putatively had boarded here at one time. It was true that such scents were commercially available now, as also the several denuded corncobs strewn about artistically on the earthen floor. Lifting the lantern high, our narrator inspected the quality of the barn itself, its rough-hewn timbers and ball-and-socket joints.

"Put us a machine gun right up there," he said, indicating the loft, "and we could hold out in here for days and days."

"We don't have the ammo."

"Is the other barn just as good?"

"You got any ammo?"

But the other barn was not nearly so good and moreover was listing to one side. A single shoat resided in the rearmost chamber where our boy had to put on his night goggles to find him. Could anything be more nostalgic than a forsaken barn, its tenants all long ago departed? Nothing. Apart from that, no one abided here except a few random crickets screaming for the people to leave them alone. Already it was nigh to four o'clock and the very last that any of them wished was to be exploring empty buildings when dawn with its rosy-hued associations came down upon them from out of the east.

The outlying fields! they extended to the river and back and had prefabricated haystacks placed here and there by an expert hand. And did they not also descry true pigs wandering at freedom while feasting on unharvested apples lying in the little bit of light? Not a bit of it, nor could one even so much as dream of apples left to rot in these starving times.

"Hello!" said Jones, viewing the whole extent of the orchard. "Good place for it, our new civilization."

"I don't see nothing," the urchin said.

"An opera house on every corner, observatories everywhere, more libraries than houses."

"My old granddaddy used to raise peas here. And okra as well."

"Yes, but that must have been long ago. When Sunset Carson was still alive."

The women had turned off and gone back, as was their wont. It left the men to talk of serious matters.

"Can't get anything done with a bunch of women about."

"That's for sure. Hey, where'd you get that tie? Is that silk?"

"It does look like silk, doesn't it? No, what I really wanted was gabardine."

"Goes good with your ensemble."

"Where do you get your things I wonder? I used to go to Regal Brothers but they're so dreadfully out of phase don't you see."

"I know! And they…" He stopped, bent down more closely to the ground, brought the lantern into play and then, suddenly, jumped back.

"Great God! What is that, a cobra?"

"Yes, Sir. Sure is."

"But they don't belong over here!"

"What, you thought diversity was just for folks? Actually, they're disproportionately underrepresented in this county."

The lantern they carried was a bulbous affair of about the size of a pumpkin with fourteen candles in it. (Unfortunately, one of those candles had tipped over and drowned to death in its own exudations.) Orange in color, it must have looked from a distance like a radioactive thing hovering about thirty inches off the cold hard ground. That was the way, certainly, it looked from close up as well. Continuing on with great care, they moved past a row of bee hives set on stilts.

"Ah!" the former entrepreneur said. "At least we'll have honey."

"Not really. Not 'less you want to go bald."

"Say what?"

"Got a virus in it, that honey does."

They went on, pushing past a silo where birds were dwelling, and thence to Willard's home, a frame structure that harkened back to the simple age. They waited with increasing impatience to be invited inside.

"Boy howdy, I sure could use a good strong cup of hot coffee just about now!" someone uttered in loud voice.

The next building on their route was a tumbledown structure that, to judge from it, had been used as a school house at some period. At this time it contained but a rotting harness and a few antique textbooks that had succumbed to the usual worms and mold. Our boy could not refrain from gathering up a geography text, a piquant document that portrayed the Hapsburg, Ottomite, Russian, Chinese, and Hohenzollern empires as still intact.

"Look at this," he said, speaking to the only other semi-educated man in the group. "They've got France colored green."

"And?"

"Supposed to be blue."

"OK fellow, tell you what—why don't you write 'em a letter and straighten 'em out?" He moved away.

Nor were they invited to enter the next home, a brick construction with all manner of potted flowers on the porch and an overweight wife in a robe standing in the door. They tipped their hats to her, those as had such apparel, and continued on past a log structure loaded down with smoked armadillos and a range of CCTV cameras directed at the doorway. It smelt in here of benzene and armadillo flitches imbued with smoke. There must have been good eating in those days—this is what all of them were thinking—and sweet honey available every day.

"Must have been good eating in those days," one of them said.

"No fiber, too much cholesterol."

"I tell you what Hugh, I don't give a blesséd hoot about fiber, just so long as I can have my cholesterol."

"Yeah, and look at the result."

"What's that? What'd you say just now?"

The recruits moved forward to separate the two men. To appease them further, our boy took out a cigarette, tore it in half, and gave one part to each fool. They had pretty well covered the fifteen acres, a five-sided territory that ended up in briars and a swiftly-flowing creek that, as they bent over it, was seen to be populated with irradiated pebbles and abnormal crawfish below the ice. It looked so much like water, that stream, that more than one of them was tempted to dunk his head into the matter and drink from it.

"Don't let him do it!"

That was when Hingis' escrubilator began to ring, a telemarketing call on behalf of an international consulting firm. Agitated by the noise, a large flock of birds had emerged from the silo and was in stage of disaggregating in the sky. Fifty million years ago a star had exploded, the evidence of it only just now drifting down to earth. How odd things were!

"Watch it! Sun's coming up."

They looked for it in various locations, although it was the man called Clarence who first pointed it out in the gap between two houses. (Never, never would anyone have imagined that this man, who seemed so good in so many ways, would prove to be a nicotine informant devoted to the state.) Accordingly, they trudged back to their individual homes and were able just in time to shut their doors before dawn could do its business and shower them with injurious waves. Ended thus their first night in the Node known later on as "Cobraville."

16

It was the passing of time that alerted our boy to the progress they had made. And now, instead of sleeping in one big room in view of one another, they had divided the place into one- and two-room apartments that gave free rein to their obnoxious qualities as sovereign human beings, something Larry had warned of in his writings. Lisa, to take but one sample, had put up lavender curtains whereas the nondescript woman had merely used bed linens to block off the single window that went with her room. Peering into Hingis' niche it could be seen, first, that he had somehow picked up a six-pack of beer from someplace and, secondly, that the cans were empty. As for Smith, he had done about as well as he could with the few books he had managed to bring along—some six or seven of them arrayed on top his chest of drawers in order of imprint information. Without actually setting foot in the other man's private quarters, our boy strove to read the titles, but managed to make out just Eratosthenes' name and no others. But where had the kid chosen to stay? He wasn't in the basement nor yet in the upstairs boudoir with its canopied bed. Nor had he hunkered down in the kitchen next to the old wood stove. Worse still was Penelope who after all this time had chosen to converse with Smith, that entrepreneurial man. This hurt. He had wanted, our boy, to inseminate her himself, and would definitely have done so had not he been so altogether overburdened with the privileges that weighed on him so much.

"I see you've been talking with Smith," he remarked the following night.

She admitted that she had.

"And I suppose you've had lots of boyfriends over the years."

"Some."

"What, you think men are attractive, or something?"

"Some of them."

That did it. Thenceforward he would forego any inclinations that ever had pointed him in her direction.

Two weeks now went by, a profitable time during which the apartments took on their final touches and everyone had at least a bed and bureau fashioned out of the materials at hand. Very little now remained of the barn that previously had provided a windbreak of sorts against northwesterly winds. He was pleased, our boy, and pleased further when he witnessed the nameless woman putting up canned fruits and armadillos in the pantry space.

Because their supplies, it is true, were running out. They had a hundredweight of rice, five loaves of hardtack, a few gallons of Wateraide, perhaps a dozen tins of marmalade and sardines and not much else. And they had the dog, who was proving useful against stragglers attempting to cross the property under cover of daylight. Standing off to one side, our boy remarked the moment a whole tribe of them, wanderers and flagellants and, he believed, devotees of the new confession, moved slowly and insolently across the perimeter, well aware that they were too many to be endangered by a dog or half-score of poorly armed farmers who had all gone inside and closed their doors.

"All right," our man had yelled out to them, "we'll let you through this time. But don't ever come back here again!"

He was answered by the foremost of them, a bearded fellow wearing a loaf-shaped hat with iconography all over it. "Excuse me," he retorted. "Actually we'll come here anytime we want. Yes? And what will you do about it?" (He aimed his staff at our man, who fell back three paces.)

"I'll plug you with my .357!"

The fellow laughed out loud and then drew a silver-plated instrument that even across the distance was to be seen as boasting at least two or three more calibers than our man's.

"OK, we'll let you through one more time. But that's all."

"No, actually we'll come through anytime we want."

"And don't be littering up the place with those candy wrappers!" He snorted then, our boy, and marched indignantly away.

Three nights later he called a meeting of Jones and three other persons and reached agreement on a curriculum for the churl. His own preference was for plumbing and escrubilators and other studies of a practical kind. It was Jones who made a better case for Military Science. Speaking of the history of that course of study, they both wanted the boy to concentrate on the earliest civilizations of all, recognizing, as they did, how many more people had suffered under the influence of the ancients than under those who had come along later on. Indeed they halted at the year 1300 for that reason, as also because it was then that Jones' knowledge began seriously to peter out. Sitting at attention on a three-legged stool, the churl listened keenly while at the same time Penelope cut his hair.

"You're the one," the pilgrim told him. "The one who must go out amongst the people and turn the world around."

The boy winced. It was a heavy duty to lay upon him, him with his narrow shoulders and punch bowl hair. On the other hand, he did have a certain kind of face. Bending low, our man tried to read the future in his eye but got no further than the cornea.

"My education is weak," our man went on, "but yours is weaker still."

"Yeah, but…!"

"Yes, yes, yes; you're good at scavenging and so on. But that wont take us far when it comes time to turn the world around."

The churl groaned and cast his eyes heavenward. He wasn't any more than about 90 pounds in weight and it was unfair, really, to set him up for the manifold trials, failures, efforts and finally, the death that lay between then and now.

"What a good country we once had! Time to be good again."

"Yeah, but...!"

"Did you know that in those days a man could support his whole family? That he could go fifty years with just one wife?"

"Bullshit."

"That water was so pure and plentiful, they used to have things living in it?"

The urchin turned back to his platter of red rice and beans. Slowly and slowly, he was acquiring the art of ignoring our man.

"That they didn't even have escrubilators in those times?"

He snorted out loud, the urchin. He was willing to listen to our man as long as our man was being funny. Having completed the beans, he then turned his notice upon the hot steeping mug of serotonin that had been set before him. It had a marshmallow in it and yet he was willing to delay that special gratification until the fluid itself was wholly consumed.

"That a boy your age could walk home alone at eight o'clock in the evening without anyone pouncing on him?"

"Yeah, right, sure. Keep it up."

"And could write his own name before he had finished fifth grade?"

"I can write my own name! Some of it."

"And were more interested, those little fellows, more interested in baseball than in rectal intercourse?"

"Don't knock it if you haven't tried it."

Our man watched silently as the urchin next brought out three medications in aspic and choked them down. The supervisor at once took up the empty box, reading that the pills were for integrity disorder and penile enlargement. Other pills were in his pencil box.

"Where'd you get these things!"

"Somewhere. Hey, lighten up man, OK?"

Days went by, and nights, and then our man summoned a convocation for midnight, the second such meeting since he'd succeeded himself to his current position. Democracy was no good any longer, neither here nor in the country at large.

"Doesn't work," said he, orating to the crowd. "And can't work when the people have fallen below a certain measure. That's why you have me."

The cheering stopped. One man was watching television on his wrist receiver while another had stretched out on the cold hard ground and seemed likely to fall off to sleep. The farmwives meantime had gathered in two separate knots and were gossiping happily about their trivia. Our boy could feel his gorge rising, an inherited characteristic of his.

"I'm not saying it'll be easy."

The tallest man in the crowd, the one in whom our man had vested his most exaggerated hopes, had turned away already and was trudging slowly homeward. Our boy counted just twenty-four subjects, all of them unproven and stupid except for himself and perhaps one or two others.

"You will notice," he went on, "that I have begun to carry this whip around."

"Yes, Sir. We was just talking about that, sure was." (The voice was frail and came from the back of the crowd.)

"You people. I have been here three months already and…"

His tongue fell out. He tried to sweep it up hurriedly and put it back where it belonged. Meantime the people were drifting back to their cozy, if dilapidated, homes and three-hundred-inch television sets. The whole world rested in the balance, the quality of the culture, the fate of the West. Suddenly, extracting his silver-plated revolver, he fired twice into the air, bringing their indifference to a stop.

"OK, that finishes it. The time has come to build our wall. You there, you with the boils, go and fetch your wheelbarrow. Now! And you over yonder, you're even worse. Come on back here right now and get to work!"

And yet they continued to disperse. Hingis turned and spat at them, casting an unlovely glob of expectorate to the ground. Put off balance by that, our novice said nothing at first. Until now, he had always thought an expectorate to be someone with an optimistic cast of mind. He decided to change his tack:

"What would Larry say? OK, I'll tell you. He would say that all he had ever wanted was to bring the people back to mediocrity again. And that's what I plan to do, too, even if I have to…" He raised his whip in one hand and ventilator in the other. It consoled him somewhat that the varlet had come to stand by his side, his primary support at this particular time.

"Let *me* have that gun."

Slowly he brought them back again. He was good, the scapegrace, with threats and guns and our man began now to see just how indispensable he might eventually turn out to be.

17

All night they worked, till the sound of thunder heralded the coming of the light. And even then they continued on for a considerable while. Sheltering under his blanket, our man shouted his orders, sometimes sending forth the rogue to do things to them. Penelope, it turned out, was a superior worker, as also for the most part the other females who were doing about as well as their bodily constitutions and paraphernalia allowed. Oddly, it were the old-time farmers who had mostly lost their traditional energies and stood forth as living disgraces to their ancestors. Hingis had disappeared.

Fortunately for their project, they had access to the debris field of a crashed meteorite, a fortuity that provided every sort of material, basaltic and otherwise, that lay about. Unfortunately, on the other hand, our man had been targeted by one of the new advertisements, a translucent image laudatory of a brand of fingernail polish. Hanging out over his eyes at a distance of about two inches, it would remain there in midair for the next three hours or so, nor could a person peer around it, as it were. Meantime the wall had arisen to a height of just seven inches and extended for a distance, when rounded off, of about thirty yards. He also had doubts, our man, about the mortar, a grainy confection devised by a louche-looking individual who grinned a lot and apparently preferred to do most anything except lift the heavy stones and set them into place. It was then that the sun at last severed its last connection to the horizon, an expected event that sent the people running for their dwellings.

He had intended, our man, to go to his accustomed space; instead, looking about at the Nodists, all of them coughing and complaining non-stop, he hefted up his escrubilator and after giving Penelope a last chance to join him, mounted to the second floor. It was darker here and more remote. A person could read in a purlieu like his and never mind that the roof had begun to sag again under the weight of sulfates and dead birds. A person could think, too, and that was what he mostly needed to do at this juncture in his career.

Having thought, he explored the storey at length, finding a trove of grocery coupons in one of the drawers and then, next, a family album dating back to middle twentieth-century years. He was of course reluctant to look into this lest it remind him how people used to be. Opening it anyway, he saw a healthy-looking youth (no piercings or earrings anywhere), looking pleasantly back at the camera. Or had some evil spirit invented these pictures in order to make today's people feel yet worse about themselves? Finally he viewed the family entire, a five-person institution standing proudly by an old Ford car.

He did find a few other items on that upper floor, none of them worth much discussion. He found a box of stick matches predating the development of escrubilator technology, a broom (its straw worn down to almost nothing), and in lieu of usable money, a cache of dollar bills placed just next to the naphthalene toilet. Found a radio that gave no noise, not until he hitched it to his escrubilator and was able to home in upon a cache of old programs originating in some of the big cities of those days. Inner Sanctum? What was that? And those old-style comedians with a sense of humor so dated one had necessarily to laugh at instead of with them.

That upper storey had one further virtue not yet described,

namely that it looked down upon the hamlet and even into some of the windows that faced in his direction. And yet the only person he could actually see was a heavyset woman watching television when she ought to be in bed. He wanted his people to be repopulating on a regular schedule followed by a good eight hours of uninterrupted rest. And then a hearty meal of whey and domestic wrens to supply the energy against the exertions yet to come.

His own bed was too short for his length and too wide for his width; even so, he climbed into it and by arranging himself diagonally was able to contrive a minimal comfort while at the same time keeping his eye on the window and doors. No one had actually threatened him as yet, although he knew enough about people to know that he could shortly expect it. Until then, he kept a gun under his pillow, a knife under the bed, a dog on the carpet and the miscreant at the door.

He woke once during the adjoining day and after rising and stretching and micturating, went and opened the curtain in order to surveil the outlying countryside. It astounded him to find a burly peasant in a red blouse cultivating his fields, as if the man cared nothing about the ions he was absorbing each moment he remained in the out-of-doors. And yet… Perhaps it were wise of him to die this way, performing once again the age-old labors of humanity's first few hundred thousand years. To be alive, to have been alive, it was all the same was it not? Never had he accepted the privileging of present time.

The hills were embossed in fog and smoke and the horizon was as vague and discontinuous as if it were no longer an actual thing but only a mention of the same. He had seen, had he, more confident boundaries on four-hundred-year-old maps. Saw, he thought, a goat or sheep, or some analogous creature working its way tremulously among the blank places in the scene. He saw where the district, represented in red, abutted upon a blue county identified in mile-high lettering that ran across the terrain. Suddenly just then the sun gave a shudder and was slow to come back on again.

Returning to bed, he gathered a volume from his small library and read again a few paragraphs from that good old text of his grandfather's in which the end of everything was optimistically foreseen. Next, he turned to a certain renowned Greek author who, though inferior to his grandparent, also had some things to say.

18

His authority had continued to expand and when he came downstairs next evening he was wearing a paisley robe put together from the tablecloth and two yards of white lace. His first impressions were positive, once it was shown to him that Clarence had come home with a pied cow and a two-gallon pail belonging to the neighboring people. Our man slapped him on the back, shook hands with him, and gave other signs of approval. Nor did it worry him greatly that Hingis had disappeared, probably forever, and definitely for good.

"Tonight," our man said, climbing to the podium, "I want to make the wall twice as high."

A groan went up. Still smiling, the supervisor lifted his escrubilator into view and allowed the villagers to gaze upon it. They, too, had similar equipment, but nothing remotely as up-to-date as this one, imported just two months earlier from the land of Gomer.

"Twice as high. And twice as long, too."

A spirit of heavy depression spread throughout the camp. He observed, our boy, that one of the men was screwing up the nerve to speak:

"Now just a damn minute! You come here, you tell us what to do, you…"

"Yes?"

The man weakened and looked away. "Nothing."

"And I want no entrances or exits in this wall of mine. Understand?"

"How come I ain't surprised?"

"What did you say this time?"

"Nothing." And then: "Hey, d'you think I could be the boss someday? Naw, I'm just kidding."

The breeze had lifted our boy's paisley robe and together with his long scarlet tongue he really was beginning to look like a prophet come to save this people in despite of themselves. The loneliness of it, and the burden; he must not allow himself to expose too much emotion at this time. Just then he noticed an airship hovering overhead, a flying apparatus engaged no doubt in taking photographs of their progress on the wall. Not that any great progress had been made, not with the people as handicapped as they were by the filmic advertisements dangling all times in front of their faces.

"Ignore them!" our man called, trying in vain to escape from the beer ad that for the past two days had interfered with his attention. And yet sometimes a person could see through these performances by focusing upon thin spots where the hologram had not altogether transmitted itself across the distance. Bending first in one direction and then another, our hero caught sight of a farm woman who apparently had done no work at all, not even so much as a little bit. Enraged, he strode to her and, bending in yet a third direction, required her to carry out ten pushups in full view of the airship overhead.

The night, at least, was good. He did so love it, knowing that the sun was wasting itself just now on Africa and Asia, far from the residue of the former West. He believed this: that as long as just one element still remained of it (i.e., element of The West), it might yet be possible to take back, as it were, those institutions that once, everything else notwithstanding... Naw, he was just dreaming once again.

His next job was to turn his notice upon the sky, a capacious zone filled with space junk and energy beams that he personally could not begin to understand. It soothed him to locate the eponymous Dog Star in its proper place, a conspicuous planet surrounded tonight by a smattering of little bright white shiny stars, or "puppies" rather, as he liked to call them. Meanwhile the wall was mounting higher every minute and he must begin to sort out those who would and would not be allowed to remain behind its confines. Retreating off to one side, he judged whether it was as solidly constructed as needs be, and whether the "mortar," they called it, would hold up under the pressures that might be brought against them. Already a CCTV camera had been embedded at about midlevel wherefore our hero, turning to face it, put on a modest and obedient expression of the sort that gives pleasure to elected people.

His escrubilator was with him and although the battery was weak, he judged it past time to try and bring himself into contact with one of the "Pennsylvania Nodes," as they were deceptively called. The distance was great, an entire seven hundred miles at the least, and the atmosphere tonight was cluttered with static waves and other energies working at cross purposes with each other. (Those beams and lengths, they were so many and occupied so many frequencies that it wasn't really possible any longer for a man to inhale without drawing in all sorts of stuff that he would have preferred to do without.) Twice he dialed the number and after working his way through a routing "tree," had then to sit quietly through a succession of obscene lyrics dating from the 2015s. Suddenly he lost connection and could hear instead a far-distant voice speaking, he thought, in Javanese.

He dialed again, nonplussed to see that the "tree" had reorganized itself in the interval and was beginning to ask about things that in earlier times had been considered private matters.

"No," he replied. "Mostly I just use a vending machine."

Came then a new piece of music, a highly scatological exercise that had caused the composer to be knighted both in England and in Spain. Our man was again on the verge of losing his connection, an irritation that he managed to forestall by whispering endearingly into the "ear" of the escrubilator, a shell-like appurtenance full of whorls.

"Hello!" he called, believing himself in contact with Node #523. (These numbers, too, were especially deceptive. He was reminded of the 101th Airborne Division.) "Can you hear me!"

"Why, yes. Is that our man on the other end?"

(As if there had ever been the first one hundred airborne divisions.)

"Oh gosh, I didn't think I was ever going to reach you."

"It's the music."

"Yes. And static."

"What?"

"Static."

"Can't hear you."

"The static! It won't let me say anything about the…"

"Can't hear you. The music."

From far away he could still hear the afterglow of that Javanese accent that, apparently, had become encoded in the air. Together with the music it formed a serious barrier to any sort of real discussion between the Nodes.

"We're about five percent finished with the wall," our boy reported, voice choked with pride.

"That's very good. We did ours three years ago."

"Yes, but ours is going to be twenty feel tall almost."

"So you say. But remember, they carry ladders nowadays much higher than that."

"And we've got a great iron pot in which to boil the oil."

"Careful that you don't fall in."

It was not his favorite among the Nodes, 523 was not. "And we've learnt to make bricks without straw."

"Basalt is better."

"We've got plenty of that, too, for Christ's sakes!"

"Good, very good. So why are you calling actually? You did know that they can trace these transmissions very easily now?"

"I just wanted to ask: Can you spare some ammunition?"

"Of course not. Why, are they already shooting at you?"

"Well what about food? My boys are watering for just a taste of old-fashioned spam."

"You ask about food when you're situated in the heart of armadillo country? Takes nerve, I'll say that."

"But what about women? Ours are mostly old and out of shape."

The man laughed. "Look, my friend, I happen to know you've got Lisa with you. OK, I tell you what, you send us Lisa and we'll send…"

"Never mind, OK, let's drop it."

"…fifteen of our very best. No, if you really want to help, you could fax us about a hundred thousand Yuan, if you got it."

"But we don't. Got it."

"Ha! My powers of prediction are getting better."

At this point our man attempted to break off conversation with the fellow, but only to find that the connection would not go away. Far in the distance he heard the nearly imperceptible voice of a well-known radio detective coming at him from the 1940s, he believed. Still striving to be courteous in all matters, our boy said this:

"Well. Reckon I'll hang up now."

"Yes, do."

The voice was not Javanese at all, as he now recognized, but rather a highly refined strain of static disguised as language. It dawned on him that the cries of the cicadas had their sources both on the connection and in the fields around him. That was when he observed one of the workers, a middle-aged man of no description, littering the landscape with a candy wrapper.

Exacerbated beyond endurance, our boy marched up to the individual, looked him in the eye and was about to levy a fine on him when new sounds began to emanate from the escrubilator he had left behind. He was tired, tired and hungry, tired, hungry and after observing Lisa for so many hours needed very badly to go to town.

19

The wall grew higher, but not by much. There was no question but that he needed more workers, more cattle too, and a good many other things as well. And then on Sunday while at his desk sketching the machicolations he intended for the wall, he heard a noise that at first he interpreted as that of a moth butting its head against the window pane. No, there had just now appeared a little round hole in that window, as also a very similar feature in the wall behind him on which he had mounted half a dozen framed portraits of Gail Russell in her various moods. Someone was shooting at him, no further doubt. Coming nearer he inspected the pane at length and then went to the wall and perceived what looked to be a leaden bullet lodged in the lathing.

Truth was, he had been to town and back and was not in the best condition for defending himself against those as wished to assassinate him. Instead he went to his desk, took out his vending machine receipt, and lay it away in the drawer along with other documents verifying his itemizations on this year's return. Suddenly he jumped back for the second time that night, astonished to see that the urchin had been lurking all this time in a corner of the room.

"What the…!"

"Willard. He's the one shooting at you."

"Oh?"

"Yeah. Said he was going to kill you, too."

"Oh, I doubt that'll happen. Not if I kill him first."

"Want me to do it?"

He summoned the boy nearer and looked at him. His face was so like a jack-o-lantern's that he had sometimes been dismissed as one. Not more than seventeen years in age, his hands were as big as a human being's.

"What is your story after all? You ran away from home?"

"Heck no! They did."

"Because of your behavior?"

The boy said nothing at first. And then, a minute having passed in extreme awkwardness: "We need more cows."

"Yes."

"That old son-of-a-bitch, he's got twenty of 'em. And two bulls."

"Who?"

"Casper and Pollux, that's what he calls 'em."

"No, no, not the bulls."

"Calls himself Bobby Earl. He ain't much. All we got to do is cut that wire and take over."

Our boy reflected upon those words.

"How many acres he got?"

"Eighty."

"And cows?"

"I told you once!"

"And two bulls."

"Yeah. We cut that wire and pretty soon his stock will come on over onto our land."

"And then we put the wire back up—is that what you're thinking?"

"Shoot no! We need that land."

"And what about the law?"

"That ain't no problem! Just give 'em one of the cows."

"Good Lord."

"Sure! That's the way you got to operate if…" (He came nearer, whispering passionately into the supervisor's and escrubilator's ears) "…if you want to turn the world around."

"Well isn't that what you want, too? Turn it around?"

"Hell yeah! That's why I linked up with…" (He pointed down through the flooring at the people down there.) "And I tell you another thing, between me and you—I wouldn't mind linking up with that, you know, the one in the…"

"Lisa? Leave her out of this."

"Aw, heck. Shoot! Everybody gets to link up with her except me. Me, I don't get to link up with nobody!"

"Save your energies for the wall."

"Wall shit; I can do a whole lot better things than that."

"I don't doubt it. OK, let me think about it."

The churl stood at attention by the desk, giving our narrator his chance to think about it. Even on a starvation diet the miscreant weighed almost a hundred and thirty pounds, not to point to the potential for a good deal more.

"Have you really? Killed somebody?"

"I can do welding," he said. "And drywall."

Our individual smiled, patted the boy on his head, and then went back to his papers, a routine that inspired the churl to return to his own corner and curl up in an ancient quilt that even at this distance smelled of mildew and linseed oil. He was a cautious man, the rogue (and our hero did now view him as a man), and never slept in the same location twice. It had meantime occurred to the captain of this place that, really, he ought to possess those twenty heads of cattle next door and take over the land as well, necessary crimes if he hoped to turn the world around. These ideas he wrote down for himself, using for that purpose the versos of a sheaf of papers whose rectos were covered already. Knowing that dawn would soon be on display, he had begun to experience that old familiar feeling in the back of his head, a spiritual illness in which the victim feels that the West is in worse condition even than yesterday.

Nevertheless he worked steadily for the remainder of the night and then went and plugged up the hole in the window pane with four or five bills of devalued currency. He was conspicuously visible both here and at his desk, a realization that encouraged him to button up the curtains in such a way as not to tempt the community's dissidents any further. It was a good desk, too, his, constituting perhaps the finest gift bequeathed him by its owners. The drawers moved in and out in a style that was virtually organic, making no noise. He had also been left with a good stock of ink and paper, an escrubilator directory, and a carbide lamp that, however, threw off more ejecta than was to be desired. Sitting there in dignity in his robe and pointed hat, his holster and underwear, he began to understand the pleasures of authority and its associated joys. And in short he had not realized how important he was, not until he had come, belatedly, into the sort of position that he had. Next, grabbing up the escrubilator, he dictated two directives and submitted one question to the butterfly person down below:

"Who's on guard?"

(He could hear the fellow rifling through his schedules.)

"Clarence."

"Very well. Carry on."

No one dared to disobey him. They might shoot at him, yes. But disobey? These thoughts were pleasant but could not hold back the sun which even now was sweeping over a ravaged horizon of abandoned cities full of viruses and broken buildings and, no doubt, the usual squads of treasure hunters combing the floors of the dried-up seas. It called to mind Old Testament days, which told of an enormous world with just five or six persons on it. Everything they did was of utmost importance.

"What a pity," he had said once when speaking to the mayor of his little town. "What a pity that we have all this destruction and disease and so many immigrants all about."

"Yes, terrible. And yet," he brightened, "it *is* good for the economy they say."

"Yes! And getting better every day," he wished later he had said, wishing he had said it while pointing to the devastation all about. As to his own little hamlet, he had improved it greatly, he believed, by requiring Christmas decorations to remain on display all year around. Suddenly on impulse he again plucked up his escrubilator, entered the name and description of an ancient girlfriend of his, and waited to be brought up-to-date on her activities.

He slept decently well for the first few hours and then came awake about the middle of the day in order to meet his bladder's demand. He disliked to be standing in an area of the room where sunlight could reach him; even so, he had to invest a minute or two searching for his day vision telescope. Next, he came to the window itself and positioned himself not ten inches from where the bullet had entered. His neighbor did certainly have cattle, even if our man was able to identify but sixteen of them from his vantage. There might be bulls, two in number, but he needed more evidence before committing to that. Searching further, he detected yet another farmstead a mile or two beyond, a prosperous-looking setup with a red barn and a great white three-storey home that might well serve as the armature for a turned-around world. And so, thinking of this and other matters, he climbed back into bed and covered up his head. It was pleasant to imagine that daylight was finished and that the moon and other stars were giving off the subdued light that made the world less unlovely than it was. The face of a woman, had you rather—be honest!—gaze upon it at midnight or under the sun? The question was preposterous of course and he wasted no further time on it.

Because at noontime a person can see every little flaw—enlarged pores, also here and there an unfortunate bristle, traces of sophistication and old age. Refusing to go on with such concepts, he bethought him of those one or two women he had known, good-looking people who were at their best just at midnight or slightly later. One had the eyes, one the nose, and the last one had the lips that, assembled into one person, would have sent the planet into a higher trajectory. Not so their other qualities called, respectively, greed, vanity, and extreme stupidity which, assembled into one person equipped with the composite face described above, would have provided all the materials needed for a modern celebrity indeed.

Thus our man, who at just after six emerged briefly from under his covers to welcome the coming of the night. There were some interesting clouds on the horizon, including a particularly dark one that looked like the Secretary of State in the Katresha Puta administration. Nor was he the only one to have seen it, to judge from the appalled silence that had settled over the community. Summoning his dog, our boy allowed him this one time to get into bed and burrow beneath the covers, where soon his master joined him.

He awoke once more at seven-forty to find that the ruffian had brought together a group of some of the more courageous villagers and already had sent one of the women forward to snip the fence that separated them from their neighbor's cattle, an episode remembered in history as The Electrocution of Betty Peal. He arrived just in time, our captain, to instruct the people in breaking down those wires with a wooden hoe handle that despised electricity and in fact was immune to it. The weeds were greener on the other side and they had only to stand back and count as one by one the calves and heifers trundled through the gap.

"I'm going to eat that one," the varlet said, pointing.

"That one? She's pregnant."

"Yeah!"

A light came on in the neighbor's house. It was a tall but

narrow construction such that anyone standing in the upstairs window would have a pretty good view both of the crowd down below and of his own abandoned fields. They listened attentively as with some considerable effort the fellow managed to leverage open his window and call down to them:

"Hey!"

"Well, hi there!" answered the farmer called Roger Peal. "How you been keeping?"

The householder carried a candle in one hand and in the other a long object that conformed to the size of a gun.

"Where's my cows!"

"Hm?"

"Cows! Goddamn it."

"Well, one of 'em's over there by the smokehouse. And that one"—he pointed—"that one's over yonder a piece. Don't know if you can see her from up where you are."

There was a long silence. Meantime the man's wife, a bony specter in a robe, curlers, and ghostly face, had come to stand by his side.

"We need those cows!"

"Well I reckon! I know how I would feel."

"And all these new people I'm always seeing over there. Maybe if you could just explain to me, Roger, what the hell is going on over there, maybe then we could reach an … accommodation. Know what I mean?"

"We don't need no stinking 'commodations!" the urchin said.

"We're keeping the land, too."

"Now just you hold on a minute! That land has been in my family for a hundred and twenty years!"

(The churl had dropped his trousers and was exposing his backsides to the man.)

"A hundred and twenty-*two*," his wife said. She was good at numbers apparently and our hero was beginning to see a possible use for her as a record-keeper, or mayhap official historian of turning the world around. He said:

"Send down your wife. We won't hurt her."

"Hell no you won't hurt her! Look, 'my friend,' I've got a .30-.06 pointed right at your left eye!"

They had to laugh at that, knowing, as they did, that our supervisor's escrubilator would have halted the missile in midair.

"And dog! I'll turn my dog loose on you!"

"Dog, you say. But remember we have a dog, too, and ours has been modified. Eats alligators, just to mention that one thing alone."

A murmur went through the crowd. He had never bothered, our man had not, to tell the people exactly how fearful his own dog really was. Far away they could hear an owl hooting, although one could not be sure whether it were a prototype or the genuine thing. They listened for, and then soon began to hear, the uncanny sound of true and artificial crickets blending into one distasteful song. It seemed almost certain now that the farm couple was coming down to discuss matters with the Nodists. For otherwise why would they have said they were?

He was a large sort of individual, gimpy, roseate, and expansive. His nose was blunt, his jaw beveled, his forehead cantilevered, and his wife spavined. And yet, in the very little time provided her, she had managed to free herself of her hair curlers (all save one), and to apply the usual chicory oils and rubefacients to her whitewashed face. Our hero bowed to her in his fashion and then attempted, unsuccessfully, to kiss her hand, the one with the Baretta in it.

"Now you listen here, my 'good Sir!'" she said. Her other hand had yet some other kind of weapon in it. Turning to her husband, our narrator then asked:

"That farm over yonder—do you know who owns it?"

"Old man Peterson? Of course I know who owns it."

"Old man Peterson owns it," the churl submitted. "That's

what I'm thinking."

"How many acres exactly does he have over there? He doesn't need all that."

"About 800. But he ain't selling—I can tell you that right now."

"That's all right; we aren't buying. Does he have any sons, or anything like that?"

"Not really. Got him a 'daughter-in-law,' if that's what she is."

"I see! 800 you say."

"Yeah. More like 900, if you include that training camp."

"Training camp?"

"Yeah. But they're gone now, most of 'em. Couldn't understand a word they were saying."

"Spanish?"

"I wouldn't know. Now if you'll just let me have my cows back, why I'll consider us fair and square. Deal?"

"You're craving your twenty cows and meanwhile you're living next to a scoundrel who has—what?—200 of 'em?"

"O he's got twice that. Maybe more."

"See? Hadn't you rather have 400 heads than just a score?"

"Well sure I would."

"Excellent!" Our hero shook with him exuberantly and then, coming nearer, actually embraced him in a momentary hug. Next, he passed him along to the other Nodists who embraced him also, and also shook.

"Together, there's nothing we can't do!"

"Hey!" the farmer reacted. "What's going on here?"

"Turn the world about!"

"And your wife, too. From this day forward, she'll be my first biographer!"

"We shall all go down in history!" Lisa said, causing the man to turn and look at her for a long while.

"The cream of the earth!"

"Shoot yeah. Nobody knows more about soybeans than this ole boy."

Showered with such compliments, the recruit could not but smile.

"I'll need a new outfit," the woman said. "If I'm going to be a biographer and what all."

They went forward. The ground was uneven here and the moon not powerful enough wholly to illustrate the way. It was a distance of perhaps 500 yards to the boundary and then a short stroll to Peterson's place, an impressive structure with double pane stained glass windows and three several chimneys resembling cathedral spires. He thought it incumbent upon him, our boy, to go to the door and call his name, but was surprised and disappointed to be preempted at the last moment by the butterfly man. He was the most impatient man in the whole sodality and one waited with foreboding to see what he would say.

Chimes could be heard from deep within the home. He would have been wrong, anyone who expected the squire himself to come to the door. Instead it was a postmodern teenaged youth hiding under the bill of a baseball cap. He said:

"Uhhh."

"Is your father at home?"

Suddenly there was the noise of a dog barking from the top of the stairs, a brief interruption that came to a halt as soon as Jones trained his escrubilator in that direction.

"I'll ask again: is your father at home?" (Already his patience was wearing thin.)

"Uhh. Home? Yeah. I guess. Whatever."

"Well bring him down here for God's sakes! What, do you sleep in that cap?"

The boy turned slowly and after starting out in different directions, began progressively to mount the staircase by taking two steps forward for each one back. He was wearing an earplug in one of his orifices and had a miniature television dangling in front of his larger eye, a vitrified organ destroyed by too much exercise. For a moment they thought he might slip and fall in the pills and capsules that lay about, but no, he was able to get past all that and proceed to his father's upstairs door.

They entered as a group. For a long time the new recruit, the farmer with the 20 cattle and the reticulated face, had been wanting to do this, which is to say disturb his neighbor's sleep and take possession not merely of his herd but his "daughter-in-law" as well. Accordingly, the others now hung back to give him his chance. Five seconds went by, a time of high tension at the conclusion of which they could hear doors opening, a woman screaming, an alarm system going off, a heavy acid band, and then the sound of a second dog (much smaller than the first) which had bravely chosen to make its exit at just this time.

"It's your choice," the butterfly man said. "Die. Or, you could join with us and turn the world around."

He was a phthisic sort, oval enough to recall a hard-boiled egg to mind. Truth was, the fellow was too heavy by far for a mattress that had been compressed down over the years to the approximate thickness of a book that held about 200 pages but lacked an index. As to the woman, she stood in the corner striving to cover her breasts behind the aubergine drapery bearing the likeness of a famous football coach. Two minutes more went by, a short time during which the churl had managed to open and explore each and every drawer in almost every piece of furniture the room contained. He had especially found some interesting-looking pieces of jewelry and what appeared to be a bundle of old love letters, to reckon by the out-of-date postage stamps.

"Die!" uttered the butterfly man. "Or, you could join us I guess. *Capisce?*"

"Die?"

"Absolutely."

The man blinked twice and began to pay closer attention to what was being said.

"I'm 76 years old! What do I care about dying?"

"We'll sic the boy on you."

He turned and studied the face of the churl.

"OK, what do you want?"

"Money, cows, etc. Carpet and drapes."

"Yeah, but the market's been bad, real bad. Most of my funds is locked up in decollateralized bismuth futures, and you know what that's like. Bismuth?"

"Bismuth is bad."

"Yes, and…" He stopped. Lisa had her back turned in his direction and, bending deeply, was going through the cedar chest. Seeing her like that, the rich farmer began patting his hair back into place and smoothing down his eyebrows with a moistened index finger. Arranging himself into a more dignified presentation, he began rocking back and forth, just like a hardboiled egg teetering on its point.

"First, we remove all those fences that sequester your lands, separating them from ours."

"Sure. Why the hell not?"

"And this house, it could easily hold six times as many people as just you and her."

"More."

They were getting along very well, it seemed to everyone. Standing back, they watched with fascination as this most hardboiled of all men struggled to get out of bed, an arduous endeavor that landed him finally on two thin legs no thicker than a hen's, an analogy that continued over to his feet as well.

"And hay. Shoot, I bet you got hay coming out your ears, what with all them barns of yours."

(Those feet had, each, three very large toes, also like a hen's. His shoes therefore were quite assuredly the oddest ever seen.)

"*My* barns? No, everything is yours now." And then: "If I could just have my letters back."

Seeing that all was proceeding happily, the assumed daughter-in-law now reappeared with a decanter of spirituous liquor along with glasses enough for all of them, excepting only the churl.

"Knew I wouldn't get none," he said.

"Notice how he gets those shoes on," said Jones then, speaking of the egg-shaped man. "One claw at a time."

"Yes. And latex instead of socks. Interesting."

The wine was good, pretty good, and soon had been drained to the lees. On this occasion our man was keen to see the sun, if only for a little while and only as to survey the new terrain that had been acquired with such facility. Even in the blackness he could see there were hills on the horizon (smoke coming off the summits), and either a river or ocean inlet sparkling in the distance.

"How much longer," he asked at large, "before the sun comes up?"

"Well, normally in about five minutes from now. 'Course, you could use your escrubilator on it."

He decided to do so. The daughter-in-law had meantime adduced a tray of little sandwiches from which the crusts had been removed. Sliced diagonally, those little treats were not so large that a person couldn't eat a dozen of them, which our captain chose to do. It was then the sun did come, a green and gold manifestation that seemed at first to be composed of sand, it was that grainy-looking.

"The sun!" someone yelled.

"But see how green it is!"

"Me, I'm looking at the cattle. Gosh, there must be hundreds of them out there. Notice how they have distributed themselves, so to speak, in order to maximize, one must suppose, the aesthetics of the scene."

"Oh boy, there he goes. Hit him."

"Hey, what's that little red cow doing? I never seen anything like that."

"That's a colt, you dolt! It often happens that your colts take on hues like that."

"Can I have him?" the urchin asked.

"'Have him'? Of course you can't have him! He belongs to the franchise now."

"These little sandwiches. Tasty little devils, ain't they?"

She ran for more.

"I knew I couldn't have him." (The varlet seemed to be talking to himself this time, making it difficult for anyone to overhear him.) "I still couldn't have one, not even if we had a thousand of them little red dolts. Oh, oh, they're listening to me."

Pleased by the vision, the acres and the cows, our hero now put the sun back down. It offered the people a five minute interval to get them back to their own apartments prior to the thing leaping back up again.

20

Good news for the Nodists—a fight had broken out in San Francisco between a gang of Gilians and two Millerite brigades. Instead of proceeding with their wall therefore, which in any case was obsolete by this time (owing to the new lands they had acquired), the chieftain had begun to propose to himself the much larger project of curtaining off the entire region from Richmond City in the east to the furthest western fragment of the former California along the sea. Yea, and then start anew, O Lord, right from the beginning once again!

It was a conceit that he was willing to share with none but the ruffian at this time.

"Can I have it?" the tyke asked.

"Which? East? Or west?"

"Let's flip for it."

Our man had to laugh. "You'll have to earn it."

"I already done that!"

"No, no, no; there's still lots to do."

"Well shit; let's get started then!"

They laughed, but the churl did not.

(This happened at just after three in the morning on September 16th, a foreboding time of year with winter threatening and many dark sulfide clouds running overhead. Strange was it, how that substance tended to organize itself into rectangular blocks, stratum after stratum of them penetrable by delta rays alone. Reaching as high as he could with the walking stick that he had discovered recently among his things, our boy attempted to touch the nearest of the layers, missing but by an inch or two. Much more pleasing to him was the sight of Skimpy Brown emptying of hay one of the barns they lately had won, great tawny-colored bundles larger than the Poofmobile parked behind the silo. This "Skimpy," wrongly so-called, was in fact a large man, appropriately morose, with a chin that came halfway down.)

"Good work!" our man called to him.

"Need more hay," the fellow called back.

"Oh?" He went to the person and after studying his uncommon face for a time, said: "And where do you propose we get it?"

(It was like a map of West Virginia, that face, taking into account the incarnadined nose, the mountains, and the warts lending character to his neck and wattle. Coming nearer, a person could also see in that visage the old colonial survey system that had formed the counties, most of them, in standard geometric shapes.)

"Where do you propose we get it?"

The man pointed, pointing into the eastern mists where rumor had it that several large and well-stocked barns were situated.

"But have you actually seen them, those barns, with your own..." (He had started to say with "your own two eyes?"), "...with your eye?"

"Yeah. And Hugh has seen 'em, too."

"Hugh? Hugh ain't worth shit!" the urchin submitted.

They agreed with that. Just then a woman came up, a humpbacked creature made even more so by the hod of wet mortar she was carrying on her back. She hadn't been told, apparently, that the wall was cancelled now and she was needed in the fields instead.

They collected in the moonlight, our supervisor, Skimpy, urchin, and the rather flighty man infected with the chromosomes of a Luna Moth (not "butterfly," as previously asserted). Skimpy had a shotgun and the ruffian, on this one occasion, had been allowed to carry our man's late model escrubilator, its snout pointing harmlessly to the sky.

"We'll pay for it, that hay," our pilgrim decided. "For the sake of good relations."

"Good relations shit! We'll just take it, is what we ought to do!"

There was something to that.

"How far have we come, do you think?"

"Mile. Maybe more."

"And the county, how wide is it actually?"

"Forty mile. Maybe less."

He made the calculation, a matter of plain simple arithmetic. "And so at current rate we'll control this whole county in about... What?"

"Year," the ruffian said.

"And how many counties are there?"

"Shit, I don't know! The whole damn country? Or just in ————?" (Without thinking, he had given away the name of the state.)

"Whole country. Except Massachusetts and stuff like that."

"Hell, I don't know."

"OK, we'll say a thousand, OK?"

"OK with me."

"OK with me, too! Shit."

"And let's say we've got one already, OK?"

"Aw for goodness sakes. All we got is one little teeny bit of it!"

"OK, we'll say we've got 5 percent of one county, right?"

"Doubt it. One percent. Maybe."

"OK, we'll say one percent then."

"OK. Now what was the point of all this exactly?"

They marched on. A crow had hidden behind one of the low-lying clouds and was vociferating in such a way as to reach the county's other 99 percent. Toads were calling and heat-seeking snails scampering across in front of them amongst occasional golf balls lost in the grass. Our man spotted a plaid-colored salamander and for a moment was almost tempted to chase after it, it was that pretty. It was a good world for reptiles and amphibians, poor for humans and plants. He saw, our man, a small band of wandering urbanites preceded by a man carrying a white flag. It was so stark and level, so level and so dreadful, that terrain. They passed a hanged man dangling from a former cell phone tower and then, next, the frozen corpse of a woman who, judging from her costume, had been sunbathing up until the final moment.

The more they traveled in an easterly direction, the more primitive the pottery shards and other indicators. Occupied mainly by city people, the region hadn't been able to accommodate itself to real conditions. "I kind of feel sorry for them," our man lied. And then, too, the tombstones were so rude, most of them inscribed with limericks and Gila Monsters.

Curvature of the earth! it had contracted so much these later years that they couldn't detect a human figure until they happened upon the actual person, in this case an aged farmer striving to get in some last minute cultivating before came winter and the sun. Our man went and stood next to him for a while.

"Winter's coming in," he said finally.

"Well sure it is!" And then, whispering half-audibly to himself: "Damned fool. Where do these people come from I wonder?"

"We're taking control here now. How many acres you got?"

"Taking control? Well I reckon that's just about the most ignorant thing I ever heard. When it comes to taking over, we're the ones that do that. You're the ones that get taken over, sure are."

Our boy laughed. "See that churl over there, the one with the instrument?"

"Oh, I seen him alright. Looks like one of those Mark IV models he's got there."

Our man jumped back. He hadn't expected such sophistication from so wizened a man

"We use them Mark IVs for spare parts."

"Can't be."

"And so I recommend you just get your little Cauk-white ass out of here, you read?"

"I've also got … this!" (He showed the .357 gun, yanking it abruptly from his short pants.) "And so you better mind how you talk to me!"

The farmer laughed. His paw, massive and devoid of nails, reached out suddenly and slapped the weapon from our boy's hand. Together they watched as it sank out of sight in the all-too-friable land.

"All right," our boy said. "OK, I won't use the gun on you. But I do have to have your land and cows."

"Do?"

"Why yes."

"And what would you do with 'em if you had 'em, hm? You don't look like the kind of person to me."

"Turn the world around."

The man jumped back.

"Say it again?"

"Turn the world around."

"Praise be to God, you finally got here! Martha! Come here and say hello to this man. Shit boy, we been waiting for you for so long. Ever since they took *Gunsmoke* off the air!"

They shook, searching each other for the underlying strength and masculinity. Having completed it, they shook again, whereupon the peasant took out a pint of corn whiskey and shared it with our man.

21

And so in the fullness of crime they acquired altogether some nine counties and parts of several others. Preferring to live in better dignity than others, our narrator by this time had taken up in a luxury hotel built to nineteenth-century standards, a "fortress," as it almost were, designed for hypochondriacs come to "take the waters" that still existed in those times. Later, with no water anywhere, the structure had been used to warehouse quarantined escrubilators and then, later still, as a flea market where the little creatures were trained and exhibited. Furbished, decorated, adorned with crown moldings and vending machines, the building had then been passed through the machinery of eminent domain and given to the members of the Committee along with their wives and lawyers.

Grown powerful, our narrator had become a different sort of man than herebefore. His hair was gone, much of it, and in its place one observed a lichen-like growth that ran down his neck and filled his sleeves. His tongue was just as long and almost as bright, and was continually dropping out at moments of anxiety. As to the man's eyes, they looked like "two fried eggs in a slop bucket," to use one of his grandmother's complaints.

Such was the condition of things when on March 7th the boy stood to deliver his inventory of Peluria, as the Committee for obvious reasons had chosen to name the new republic. He was at first greeted with applause, although this soon degenerated into coughs and foot shuffling and other staged activities of the kind. Beginning with the furthest of the new jurisdictions, he proceeded to describe them with all the familiarity of someone who might actually have been there and had seen them.

"Troezen County!" he said. "There's still about two thousand people there."

"Good soil, too," added one of the members.

"Say, isn't that the place where they have that real big old gulch that's full of fog and smoke?"

"It *is* big, that gulch, and deep. They say you can hear people down in the bottom, always moaning and screaming and such like."

Our speaker tried to call them to order. Somehow the varlet had penetrated the place and was sitting in the corner beneath the shelter of a baseball cap. The next county on our narrator's list had fallen into bad times, the combined result of an international coal salvaging operation and a strike force of environmentalists. They needed help, no question about it, and help, after all, was the Committee's preeminent obligation.

"Send 'em some money," Clarence said. "And then they'll get used to it and do whatever we say."

"Yeah! We can get it" (money) "from Enterprise County. They got too much anyhow."

They settled upon that solution, the churl casting his unauthorized vote as well.

"And then there's Washington County, named after a famous statue in Ne… Martin Luther King. High murder rate. I propose we send a few of our fellows to straighten things out."

"We already done that!"

"Yeah, and once you send 'em, they don't never come back."

"Oh really? Well let me choose the ones to send next time."

The meeting was falling apart among laughter and the sound of people tramping about the room. Spoke then a small man who had been sitting off to one side next to the punch bowl. The thing was almost empty and most of the cookies had likewise disappeared.

"I second the motion," he said.

"Which motion is that Rodney?"

He sat back down. There were others however willing to second it and before the pilgrim could bring things under control the men, thoroughly bored, had stood as of one accord and were filing out of the hall. He tried to call them back but, owing to his tongue, wasn't able just then to come out with tangible words.

"Ah me," said he, whispering to himself in a familiar voice, "this leaves me quite depressed." And then: "It's not my duty to turn out the lights, but guess who has to do it anyway."

The night was chill. Pressing at the window, he perceived an antelope, very probably the last of its kind, stepping delicately through the snow. Yes, and once the world had been full of such creatures, "wolves," so-called, and great whales leaping happily to harness for towing ships across the sea. These were the stories he used to hear. He also heard that water was cheap in those days and free of anti-depressants. That people could read and pairs of men and women would live together for long periods. That cold weather was sometimes interrupted by warm stretches.

He returned to his quarters. Sometimes he wondered if he really needed the whole fifth floor (37,000 square feet), when his constituents, most of them, had to settle for under 600, to believe the census report. Because if brought under attack, he would have a great many hiding places, that's why, and because he needed to overawe those who might otherwise wish to chase him down and do things to his person.

He had the largest desk in the nine counties, a thing so big and complicated that mice abided there in safety. He found photographs, ink and paper, escrubilator parts, and an unpublished manuscript called *Morning Crafts*. He liked to sit there behind this bulletproof piece of furniture and look down into the town where people were still behaving more or less as they always had. What would Larry say, who had wanted a more perfect system with libraries on every corner, every rooftop its telescope, and myriads of young people ensorcelled forever in the metaphysics of love? And so far as that goes, what would his grandfather have thought, who could have identified down below any number of people needing urgently to be punished? And finally, what did our own man think about it, who had conquered nine counties and wasn't certain what to do next?

The third drawer from the top on the right-hand side held his telescope, an antique instrument with fading powers that, however, remained good enough for the rather sizable city that lay some twenty miles to the north-northwest. Focusing upon it, he noted how it pulsed and glowed, as if some sort of effort might be going on. What, they wanted to restore civilization, is that what it was?

22

It was on a night pretty much like this one that Larry rejoined them. Never would they forget it, those who happened to be chasing bats with long-handled nets—the spectral scene of a tall man limping toward them through the snow. Believing themselves under attack, the hunters jumped up and down, pointed at the man, and right away began blowing on their horns. At first our man knew nothing about it, which is to say until the sound, gathering speed, came in through his partly-open window and smote him in the ear. His blankets were among the best in the world and he was loath always to get up and leave them; even so, he forced himself to do that and after catering to even more pressing needs, ran downstairs and called for the speediest horse in the Node's whole stable.

It was a short ride, but very, very cold. And then, too, he had come away without benefit of cloak, shoes, or escrubilator. So far as he knew, entire armies had invaded their little domain. Or, just as likely, someone had spotted a UFO. Or perhaps something else had happened. Given a choice of those alternatives, he had pretty well settled upon the last of them when he turned the corner and found a stranger on the ground and the churl on top of him.

It needed a long time to identify the man, apologize to him, and then bring the varlet under control and persuade him to return the money.

"Aw heck!" he said. "I don't never get to appropriate stuff."

He was in poor shape, the Founder, and was bleeding in at least two places on the forehead and nose. As for the money, it had been taken from a piece of canvas luggage that also had contained a great many documents, most of them now scattered about in a "debris field," if one wanted to speak of it like that. That was when our novice saw the cruel chain that yoked the old man's feet together, making it impossible for him to walk forward with anything other than the most trivial of steps.

"Outrageous!" our boy said. "What happened?"

What happened? Well, he had been arrested of course, given an attitude test, and then rendered to California where he was confined these last six months in one of the Innermost Sections of the Interior Department. All this was to be more fully revealed later on, together with other horrors having to do with certain re-educational protocols then in force.

"Did they beat you?"

"One gets used to it after a while."

"Oh God. And did they do anything to your mind?"

Declining to answer, he made an unavailing effort to rise and reach for his documents.

"Outrageous," our boy repeated to Clarence as they turned and began the long stroll back to their hotel.

"Someone will have to answer for this," Willard agreed. "Who is this fellow actually?"

"You're going to see some action now, now that's he's back with us once again."

"I dare say."

(Dawn was near and the town already was beginning to shut down, evidenced by the faraway street lights fading off to a wan pink glow. Soon the milkman would be making his route, this bravest of men who went about without an umbrella or anything else. The batsmen also were folding their nets and totaling their quarry—seven adult bats and an enormous songbird who had stayed behind.)

"Don't you think we ought to go back for that old man?" Clarence inquired.

"Ah!"

"And horse?"

In the event, they went back for both horse and man, which is not even to mention the documents. He had brought better than 2,000 Yuan with him, that old man, a smaller sum than if he hadn't had to pay for his escape. The sun meantime was moving toward its destination, a lodgment in the sky where it would remain stalwartly for the next few hours. Leaving Clarence and the others to run behind, our boy urged his mount forward and managed to enter the hotel on horseback before the rays could find him.

They gathered that evening in their usual place and lifted their mugs to the Founder. He had been seen by the nation's one doctor, a former barber with a supply of Band-Aids and Paxil. Having feasted on parsnips and batwings, he was in an expansive mood in spite of his past several years.

"Solzhenitsyn has nothing on me," he said. "OK, maybe a little bit."

They drank. His injuries had partly annealed by now and everyone there had hopes of detaching someday the chain that kept his feet so close together.

"Let the churl do it," someone recommended.

"Sure, let the churl do it, let the churl do it. I don't know why I ever signed up with you fellows in the first place!"

"You were starving, if you remember."

They drank. The time had come for more important business than the churl's, wherefore the Founder arose now and after tampering with the microphone, made ready to deliver the address they had been waiting for. But first the women, who left their places without demur and, smiling sweetly, headed for the exits. With serious business coming up, it wasn't right to have them worrying their sweet heads over such matters. They praised one woman in particular whose two hips were among the finest ever seen. Left to themselves, the men quickly came to agreement on which in fact was the finer of the pair. Spoke now the Founder:

"I have a dream. A dream that someday little white boys will lie down with silicone models and all God's children will gather on the left-hand side of the Bell Curve. I have a dream. I dream a bear is chasing me and my feet don't work."

Wild applause. Continuing on, he said:

"Look about you, all these acres. I ask you, who could ever have expected our boy to achieve so much, what? The last I remember him, he was just a pair of odd-looking ears with a long tongue sticking out between."

Laughter, some of it nervous and hesitant, greeted those words. No one smiled more happily than the novice, whose left hand began involuntarily to close about the .357.

"His dog was a more impressive creature than him!"

"Hear, hear!" someone said.

"Aw, he ain't so bad." It was the varlet. Our boy sought him out and tried with his facial expression to express his thanks. Still smiling benignly, he had managed to scroll up his tongue and force it back where it belonged.

"Look at him sitting over there. Thinks he's going to take over here, once my work is done. Don't you?"

The novice admitted it. "Well who else," he asked aloud with some asperity, "is better qualified after all?"

"We have the churl."

A riotous laughter filled the room, exciting the dogs and agitating the chandelier. He stood, the pilgrim, and was on the verge of leaving the place altogether when the Founder motioned him to be seated again. Someone brought a cup of punch and two cookies with caramel filling.

The Founder again went on:

"On my way to the forum this morning" (slight laughter) "I saw two derelicts squatting by the roadbed. Begging for coins. One had an accordion and the other somehow had come into a yoke of trained fleas, lethargic specimens barely able to carry out their little stunts and tricks. Know what I did?"

Two of the Nodists raised their hands.

"I harangued them, is what I did. 'If you don't find yourself some creative work,' I said. 'we're going to see to it, my boys and me, that you never eat again.' Remember Jamestown? 'He who does not work, neither does he eat?' That will be our policy from here on out."

He got a standing ovation for this, our boy joining in gladly.

"Prisoners are wonderful things, and we should hope for as many as possible. Cheap labor! Those who do not earn their room and board… Well! for them there'll be no board. Nor room either. Nor television or conjugal visits. Or library privileges."

"Hell no, we won't let 'em anywhere near that library!"

"They'll be begging to work."

"They don't work, they don't eat. And if they don't eat, they'll be entered in the register as having killed themselves."

"Right. Either we turn a profit off these people, or use 'em for medical research. My guess is that we'll soon have the most admirable highways (no litter) and reforested forests anywhere in the former America."

"Where is that library actually?"

It was the first order of business and the first, likewise, to receive unanimous consent. What an amazing development— the Founder had not been with them for more than a day and already they had taken the first steps on the path to social perfection.

"What other kinds of things should we be doing?" Clarence asked. (Once that man had lifted his hand, he refused to take it down.) "Like, for example, what other sorts of things?"

The Master laughed. "You're asking about our ultimate goal?"

"Yes we are," Smith said. "Matter of fact, we've been wondering about that for some very considerable time. Sir."

"Very well, I'll tell you, those of you capable of understanding. For example you, Smith, I'll explain everything to you. And him, the bearded fellow in the back row."

The novice was getting nervous. No one had served more diligently than he, and yet he had still not been selected up to this point. Hurriedly he moved to a position closer to the front and making himself as tall as he could, said: "We need people who have served the most diligently, those are the ones we need."

"Diligence?"

"Yes, Sir." He stood. "And I'm ready to take on any responsibilities you want to burden me with."

"I see. Yes all right, very well, you too."

Our bloke put on a bored expression, at the same time reaching out to keep himself from fainting. He could have named all manner of people who had not been appointed, even though he had.

The six men, all of them sound and true, retired gracefully to the upstairs room. It seemed prescient of history to have made available a round table of just the size, a pitcher of ale, and a fat candle of about six inches in height.

"Before that light burns out, we shall have accomplished a great deal," the Master said. "I feel sure of it."

"Yeah, I feel sure, too," the gaunt man said. "Pretty sure."

A moment passed by as Larry gazed down at the interior palm of his left hand, saying finally:

"The world, my friends, is full of universes, each of them full of yet other worlds. We know this from religion and physics both." And then: "Where does music come from?"

"Well, it…"

"Wrong. It comes to us, those who are prepared for it, like falling leaves in autumn, arriving from higher realms. Or this: a women who so loves her man that she'll be hung for him, or go willingly into a Soviet prison camp. It has happened. Where do soldiers come from? Or teachers and policeman who work ten times harder for one-tenth the reward? The beauty given us by Richard Wagner—whence comes that? Or certain landscapes that take your breath away. Or perfect souls seen in silhouette on the wall of Plato's cave? Do you see where this argument is leading?"

No one spoke.

"Because for us, we take our example not from this world, but that other, in hopes of entering it someday."

The candle had not burnt even so much as an inch—they were learning at breakneck speed. And then:

"It's too late for The West, but not so late, we may hope, for our little demesne of ten thousand souls."

But here Smith raised his hand. "More like 6,000 actually. Sir."

"Ah. Well, we'll have to address that. Ten thousand is so much better. Ten thousand can form a critical mass, whereas six cannot. As for twenty thousand and more—don't even speak to me of that. Abominations that drove the West insane. No my friends, I foresee a globe of a hundred thousand societies, each following a trajectory of its own, and each becoming more and more unique as time goes on. Diversity I call it."

"Well now that sounds real nice, Sir, but there's not a chance in hell they'd leave us alone, all these outsiders" (he pointed to them), "outsiders jealous of what we got."

"But we don't want them to leave us alone! Gracious. A healthy society should be at constant war, all the time, if it wishes to foster its best qualities. Life is sweeter when it's short. It simply brings nearer the time when we might step over the threshold to a better and stranger world. Yes, I've sometimes thought the great slaughterers might actually have been benefitting our species. Don't you remember how we fled from Tennessee, the bad weather, the danger of being recognized as Cauks? Not to mention my six bad months in the Innermost Department?"

There was truth in this. The men looked about at one another, finding that some had gone pale while others appeared appreciably more sanguine than even of just yesterday. Our bloke, knotted up with thoughts and ideas, poured himself another mug of ale. Smith, he noticed, had been writing down the Master's comments, materials toward the founding document known later on as The April Behest.

"Sir?" our man interjected. "I'd like to volunteer for the army."

"That's white of you, our boy. But you're far too young."

"Say what? I'm forty-five!"

"Far too young. No, we follow The Silver Shields, that awful group of Alexander's veterans who must be seventy and older. At that age, you see, they had so little to lose. Their children were gone and their wives were dead, and they were impatient to betake themselves into that other domain that we've been discussing here these past few minutes."

"Seventy years old!"

"Yes, and trained to an eighteen-year-old edge. No one could stand against them. Instead of old men sending the young to die, they did it the other way around."

"Seventy!"

The candle had burned down, but still had several inches of constitutional law to go.

"Education, Sir. You haven't said anything about that."

"My favorite concern. How many billions of Yuan, do you think, did the old country waste on this particular enterprise? To have seen them in action, you would have thought they believed everyone was equal. And because it was free, it was considered a punishment. Mental development? Don't make me cry. No, in our little republic education will be far more inaccessible than half a dozen cars and houses added up together. Rare and cherished, available only to the gifted and obsessives, people with outsized brains."

"But…"

"The others? Let them study the realities of the material world—that's what they care about after all—engineering, banking, plumbing and auto mechanics. Not that we can allow them to vote of course."

"They won't like that."

"They'll love it. Won't have to worry their little heads with ideas."

"And so all the power will be in the hands of a very few."

"Unlike now?"

The candle was continually diminishing and the level of the ale still sinking. The six men, or four rather, after Larry had excised two of them, had much to think about.

"We shall need to think about these matters," someone requested.

"Well, certainly!" the Master said. "I give you exactly … eight hours from today."

23

All day and for years to come, he tried to keep away from the sun. And yet, with May threatening and certain birds making a reappearance in the skies above, he rose up from his indentation in the bed and got into his socks. It was dark in the corridor and he needed several minutes to proceed down the two or three hundred yards adorned on both sides with blown-glass sculptures of some of the great men the prior age had ignored.

"Sir," he said, entering through the unlocked door, "dawn is near."

The Master turned and looked at him. His robe was saffron and bore a pattern on it of tiny brown bears with honey pots. The fire had meanwhile burned very low and the embers looked like embarrassed faces flushing on and off. The man had been reading, as evidenced by the pile of disorganized newspapers and the several upside-down books lying on the floor. Our boy made no effort to decipher the titles, knowing in advance that he wouldn't understand what they were all about. The things in that man's head! The books and titles!

"Sir?"

He had the best bed in the hotel, a full half-acre, as it almost seemed, with Lisa in it. Inspired just then by an impulse of some sort, the novice glanced to the ceiling where the painting of a huge God-like face was grinning down upon the sleeper.

But this was as nothing compared to the furniture, pieces so black and heavy and rudely wrought they might have been made just yesterday. And then, too, of course, there were those unseemly portraits on the wall.

"Sir?" our boy said, shaking the man as respectfully as he knew how. "Dawn is close by, and you wanted to see that city on the horizon."

"City."

"Yes, Sir. The one you want us to conquer for you."

"Ah yes. Well done. Truly." He turned and hid his face in one of the pillows. Again our boy nudged him on the shoulder.

"Sir?"

"Yes?"

"Time to get up."

"And leave my bed I suppose?"

"Yes, Sir. I did."

"So you say. Cold is it?"

"Fairly cold, yes, Sir. But not nearly as cold in here as outside where ice and snow cover the heath to a depth of six inches or more. I thought I saw a grouse frozen up to its knees in the stuff."

The man shivered violently and disappeared beneath the covers.

Came dawn and our man was still trying to cajole the Master out of doors. Life is hard on a person of that age, especially when his feet are held together with a corrugated chain. In fact it proved colder in the out-of-doors than either had imagined and they had not limped forward for more than twenty yards before they both began to weaken.

"Look at that sun. It's killing us of course."

"I know, I know. But some things just have to be done. If we want a critical mass that is."

"Yes, but you at least had your morning coffee."

"No, Sir, I did not! Not one drop! And I'm willing to swear to that."

"Very well. Hey! what's that wall sitting out in the middle of nowhere? Some damn fool put it there?"

"And we'll have coffee waiting for us when we get back."

They continued on. The snow had gelatinized and was pitted with thousands of little holes where the world's last generation of scorpions had sought refuge from the wind. Next, they ran up against a congestion of turtles seeking warmer weather, odd-looking creatures who had left their shells behind. By now the sun had arisen to a certain height, an expected event that caused the men to shelter their faces with their hands, or in the Master's case with a sheet of cardboard found blowing across the grounds. His neck was thin, putting his head at the mercy of the wind. There was no question but that they were aiming for a knoll positioned some eight feet in front of them, a significant distance in the circumstances of the times.

"Cream and sugar for me," the Master said, apropos of coffee.

"Yes, Sir. And you can have all you want, too."

Now they could see everything, across fields and meadows and finally the blue-green smudge where the pixels had bled into each other as it seemed. Mile-high snow spouts twisted this way and that and danced along the horizon. Taking his telescope, our boy inspected the faraway city that represented Larry's present interest and object of desire.

"The gate is open."

"Excellent! And?"

"Two guards. But they both look like puny men."

"You make me very happy."

"I seem to see evidences of an economy, a brick factory I believe." (He adjusted the scope.) "And suntan salon."

"I'll have that town by God. We're going to need an economy one of these days. Is there more?"

"No, Sir; just the usual line dancing. And upside-down cars."

They hastened back to the building and roused the people. Or roused rather the four "made men" in charge of policy.

Huddled over coffee in the darkened room, they drew up lists of people and then turned their attention to the town that for the good of civilization needed to be annexed to Peluria.

"I can put together at least 300 men," Clarence said.

"Super! And you have military experience do you?"

"Oh hell yeah. Spent six weeks in the brig."

"Anyway, their soldiers are mostly just women. According to what the churl reports."

Hearing that, the four men and their leader twisted up their faces and prepared to vomit.

"And so the blackguards defend themselves with women, I see. Really, we ought to slaughter every last stinking one of 'em!"

They voted on it. The churl's next report had to do with the enemy's weaponry, a sorry collection of shotguns and ill-fitting ordnance loaded with rabbit shot. They did have a Congreve rocket and a pruning hook.

"Wish we had an escrubilator," the fourth man said. He knew, of course, that all such weapons had been recalled several months ago, the result of a university study showing how they fomented a neurotic fastidiousness in black people and jumping ability in white.

"And so what do we have?"

"I was hoping you'd ask," the butterfly man said, rising from his chair and clearing his throat. Ordinarily a flighty man, he had come to the meeting in clothes and a three-cornered hat. "We have a .30-.30 hunting rifle and any number of high caliber revolvers capable of making holes in people. We have knives. And we have a 30-liter tank of laughing gas."

Lisa wrote it down. She had assumed a place just behind the Master and was taking down the minutes with efficiency and speed.

"Thirty liters. Very good. And you, 'our man,' what do you plan to contribute to our little project?"

"Well Sir, I've done a lot of reading. And so I thought I'd devote myself to the diplomatic side. Discussions and so forth."

"Discussions with a tongue like yours? No indeed, I want you to be our spoils person, who gathers up the good things and brings them back."

"Yes, I can do that."

"Me, I particularly like jewelry and old coins," the fourth man said.

But the time had come to move the table, owing to the movements of the sun. There were thin spots in the curtain and a palpable swatch of daylight crawling the perimeter of the floor. Suddenly:

"We attack tonight."

"What!"

"Good Lord!" the fourth man said. "Tonight?"

"Just so. While the gate is open and before the word gets out. Furthermore I..."

That was the instant Lisa fell face down on the floor and began thrashing about violently, the strangest thing that any of them had ever seen. Only the Master, who quickly took a little tool from out of his vest, was able to maintain any kind of equanimity.

"It happens," he said, removing her back panel and extracting a little hourglass of about the size of a human finger. Not more than three inches tall, the thing was filled with sand and served, they later learned, as one of the woman's gyroscopes. "Without it, she wouldn't be nearly so orgasmic," the Master explained.

"How orgasmic is she?"

"Women designed by men! One of the best achievements of the old country, you have to agree."

They patched her up quickly and, after some delay, put her clothes back on.

"My goodness," Clarence said. "I don't reckon I'll ever have one of those."

"Quite expensive really."

"Other people have one, but not me."

"Sounds like the churl doesn't he?"

"They do require a lot of upkeep."

"And so I won't never have one then?"

"Sorry."

24

They mustered in front of a hole in the ground where once it was thought water might be found. Comprising two dozen brave volunteers and 167 of the other kind, they formed up in rank and gave attention to Larry's brief but pungent oration in which he described what happens to cowards. (They had found no water in that place, but only a Bronze Age inhumation of two skeletons embracing passionately. Nostalgic for that era, it had affected our boy with particular severity.)

They were allowed, each of them, a cigarette and snifter of wine. Having just returned from one of his expeditions, the varlet possessed what probably was the very best weapon in the whole crowd, a tubelike device with a zooming scope and ammunition the size of beer cans. But better still was the grocery cart towed by Larry's orderly. It contained all manner of things, that conveyance, including medical supplies and, in case it came to bribery, several stacks of the newly-minted currency. Delighted with it, the nodists gathered around and began passing the stuff back and forth, especially the 27-Yuan note bearing the image of John Wilkes Booth. In accord with their values, the bills were of highly various dimension, all the way to the 1,219-Yuan Grand Paper Note of newspaper size. Embellished with the official 1832 portrait of Edgar Poe, it was hard to keep the wind from taking it away.

"Wonder what he's got in that little … doohickey?" Clarence then inquired.

"That is not," Larry said, "a doohickey, as you call it, but rather my personal etui."

"Wonder what's in it."

It was our bloke who was allowed finally to unzip the thing and look inside it. At once he saw quite a number of things, including perhaps fifteen keys along with a cork extractor and endoscopic device. He identified a punch for making holes in leather, a miniature stapler, and a gimmick for cutting glass. There was a tiny guillotine for abbreviating cigars, an old-fashioned butane lighter, tweezers, a leftover tube of sniffing glue, a plastic whistle from a box of Cracker Jack, and a directional compass that had no hand. He perceived a worn-out gadget capable of setting off a miscarriage at 150 yards, a Philip's Head screwdriver, and then once again that cork extractor. Of screws themselves, there were a good many of them. A child's protractor and pair of nose scissors with blunted points. A man of foresight, their leader had also brought along a gun. Standing in the wagon, he proceeded then to harangue his troops.

"We need that city," he said, "so we can teach democracy to them."

"But what if they don't want it?" someone asked.

"Ah. Well in a case like that, you must feel free to murder everyone in sight."

Cheering, very loud, proceeded from the throats of the seventy-year-olds who occupied the front ranks. One of these persons had actually dressed in a souvenir uniform dating from the Bolivian troubles. Suddenly just then a shot rang out, the starting signal that set them racing forward against the grain of the tundra.

Later on, thinking back on it, our boy mostly remembered the difficulty of that long march, the sand and snow, and all the little creatures migrating hurriedly across their path. They were being monitored by black birds in the sky—there was no question about that—as also by the two or three spies that, they later learned, had infiltrated the group. Our fellow nodded to the man with the chainsaw, a gloomy personality who had arrived three days earlier in hopes of harvesting the glands of the decedents. But even more grotesque than that were the half-score custom-built whores plodding forward loyally in their wake.

"Bang the drum slowly!" Larry insisted, turning upon them. "And bring the trombones to the fore!"

And so this then was how things turned out—the gate was guarded by an inebriated fellow in proper shoes of different colors, albeit one was twice as long as the other. Brushing him aside, they continued six abreast up to City Hall where they found a delegation of children waiting for them with flowers. Some of these were real, as also most of the flowers. At this point Larry strode out in front and began to parley with his equal number, a burly man whose own shoes were as incongruous as the woman's. They shook and then stood back to view one another.

"We're taking control here," Larry said.

"Why am I not surprised?"

Both men were southern, and both committed to the confessional style endemic to that region:

"I was doing all right, till my wife died."

"My old man! He just up and left us."

"Don't even know where my daughter is."

"Served six months for possession."

"Got arthritis in both hands."

"Any television producers in this town?"

"Not exactly. But we got a fellow who used to live in Hollywood."

"Well, bring him on out here by God, where we can see him!"

They remained in formation. The mayor had sent one of the

commissioners to fetch the Hollywood person, an interlude
that allowed the Nodists to evaluate the crowds standing quietly
at the curb. Easy was it to understand why they had chosen
to surrender. Our boy noticed a girl who had had to compete
so hard for attention in these crowded precincts that she had
almost certainly bankrupted herself on the procrustean shoes
and silver lipstick she was wearing. She smiled at him lewdly,
whereon he opened his mouth and let his tongue drop out.

Strange lot, the Hollywood man. Perhaps if he looked long
enough into his eyes, our traveler might understand what had
caused him to turn out as he had. Smith also stepped forward
and also looked, as did several others.

"Well?" the Master asked. "What are we to do with such
people?"

"Give him to the churl!" said the man called Wain, the hardest
and most unsympathetic character in all the nine counties.

Other voices came to his support. Reluctantly and not
without misgivings the Master called the boy forward and
turned the filth over to him.

"Do what you have to do," Larry said. "But do try to finish up
within an hour or two."

"Hour! No, Sir, I need a week, OK? OK, just let me have
five days, OK?" (He was almost too excited to make himself
understood.) "Just five? OK?"

"Well. Just make sure you clean up afterwards."

"Yes, Sir! I sure will. Shoot, I'll clean up so good you won't
believe it. Real clean. I'll wipe and shine and I'll even use a mop,
a wet one, and I'll…" etc., etc.

It was a good moment. Never in his life had the churl held
anyone so totally in the grip of his compassion. He herded the
man to one of the vacant buildings, entered with a flourish,
and closed the door. Most of the other buildings were vacant,
too, and it remained only to choose the one in which to set up
headquarters. Our novice stood by proudly as the members of

Larry's bodyguard now hoisted the newly-designed national flag, an enormous production comprising seven bolts of cloth, larger than a bed sheet but smaller than a tennis court. It did them good to see it and to understand for the first time how Larry had looked as a much younger man. A flag worth dying for, yea, but killing for was even better. Played they now the sacred anthem, an emotional piece taken, half of it, from Wagner. The night was brilliant with stars and neon, luminescent clouds overhead, hounds summoning from the hills, nightingales everywhere. The other half came from Mahler.

This done, the Nodists began to scatter, some of them looking for eatables and water, some for girls, and some for the gilt edge bonds that had lain untouched all these years in safe deposit boxes. Taking Smith with him, our man filed past a bingo parlor, a three-storey prison house for non-immigrants, a sleep therapist, and a surgeon's tent with a dripping kidney posted out front to call attention to the man's specialty. They continued past a video rental, three rock stars loitering in a doorway, a laboratory for overwriting tattoos, an arts and crafts shop full of women in sandals and jeans, an abandoned library, a bail bond raffle, two movie theaters showing pornographic films on emergency power, a squad of street whores striving to duplicate the clothing habits of high school girls, a litigation reduplication center, a self-defense workshop for Cauks, and finally a Gilian Temple with many examples of high-grade statuary of the Monster himself.

The hospital, when they came to it, offered a pathetic sight of patients lying two and three per bed. There were so many fascinating illnesses the new age had contrived. In the rear he spotted a group of authors who all looked just alike and then, nearer at hand, a row of youths who either suffered from a shrinking disease or, worse, had chosen to dress in trousers six times too large. But these were as nothing compared to the number of earwig and botfly infections, result of the truly horrifying increase in the demographics of these species. He especially feared "robber flies," so-called, who had learned to get inside a person's eyeball and make off with his vitreous solution. There wasn't a member of the Node who wasn't afflicted with at least one such annoyance.

"Yes," said Smith, "But we're supposed to be gathering up loot. Isn't that what we came for?"

"Need to find a gated community."

And did so, the two men hurrying forward and, ignoring the anti-Cauk signs, slipping through the bars. The area was occupied by Chinese, the most stubborn of people who even at this date had refused to give up on their preposterous writing system. Someone had set up a paper tiger in his front yard; avoiding this, they broke open a ground level apartment and went direct to the bedroom where they found a medley of golden coins, numerous black opals of uncommon size, and a Zoroastrian amulet inset with diamonds. Better still was the freezer—the combination was simple and they had little trouble getting it open—containing cold cash and a box of chocolate-covered oysters frozen as hard as the little cubes of water that… Water! He extracted the first one he came to and forced it into his already crowded mouth.

It really was water, as demonstrated by the way it proceeded immediately to those bodily tissues that stood most in need of it. The second cube was better yet. He handed one to the varlet who in his lewd way began immediately to try and make it last longer. The stuff was cold, but so too was the weather, and he was able to deposit the remaining cubes in his vest without danger of seeing them melt.

25

They assembled around midnight in the town's tallest building. Fires had broken out in the northeastern quarter where some of the lesser nodists had used the occasion to engage in bad behavior. The "fourth man" had apparently lost himself in these activities, and now the Council consisted of just three individuals, together of course with their triumphant leader. In celebration of these events, the women were preparing a brace of armadillos over a hickory flame and a tureen of saltwater eels poached in margarine.

"Well now!" the leader said, rubbing his hands together gleefully. "How many are we?"

Smith stood and after overcoming his nervousness, reported:

"Ten thousand, Sir. And maybe a little more."

"Fair enough. Let it be written that we now have all we need and never, never, never shall we ask for more."

He wrote it down, did Smith, entering the words one by one in the excessively neat little binder that he carried with him always. Having written, he repeated the decision aloud: "As of this date in time, we now have all we need."

"Date in time? Gimme a date, Smith, that's not in time."

"There may be such times," he answered thoughtfully, drawing on his pipe. "But then we'd have no way of knowing of it."

Larry broke in: "We remain small, a place where people know and are interested in each other. I realize, of course, that it's not good for the economy."

"Sir?" our novice spoke up. "We have seen what things are like when the economy is good."

Laughter.

"Yes, poverty is best. Well, not real poverty of course. Say rather like 1940 and thereabouts." And then, his eyes misting over: "My father toiled for forty cents an hour and he was a far better man than you or I. Anyway, we'll measure the world, not by prosperity, but the quality of men."

These were strange words, and our man began to feel strange just by listening to them.

"In other words," he added, "we care more about people than … stuff."

"You didn't like my original formulation? I thought I had expressed it clearly enough."

"And so we're going to have us a small world getting smaller, and good people getting always better."

"Jove! He says it better than I."

"And we're going to pursue our own…"

"Trajectory."

"…our own trajectory just as far as it will go."

"Yes, go on."

"Because we're the ones that care about diversity."

"He's got it. By Jove I think he's got it!"

Smith, not realizing that someday the words would be enshrined in the constitutions of a thousand nations, wrote it down. Taking momentary control of things, he dared to move the Master's coffee cup, who had had too much already, move it out of reach. This man had also been put in charge of educational issues, and gave his report like this:

"Sir, we've had only two applicants, and both have teaching certificates."

"Oh Lord. Well, keep on trying." And then turning to our novice:

"Revenue?"

"Yes Sir, we've decided against taxes. A government that's truly popular ought to operate on voluntary contributions only."

"Good! And where do we stand now on health and survival issues?"

"Well, it seemed right to us Sir, that people between 16 and 52 ought to get very good attention indeed."

"And the very young?"

"No, Sir. You just can't tell what sort of adults they might turn out to be."

The men looked about at each other. Never had so much progress been made in such short order. Fetching back his coffee, the Master, having arrived at the summit of his career, stood and pronounced a benediction that came, part of it, from religion, and the rest from modern physics. He was smiling. "Shall we," he asked, "go to the roof and look at our new possession?"

The night was wild with fires and the sound of screaming women. And if the hotel tilted somewhat toward the South (about 4 degrees actually), yet their educational system would soon have the engineers to set it right.

"You will have heard," their leader said, "that Barry's node has taken up a footing on the Canadian border and is expanding in our direction. Sweet, no? To have realized our most difficult ambitions? All those acres! Yea, and people, too. My dear friends, we have triumphed over the entire world!"

"How so, Sir?" (Entire world?)

"Well! Who's writing down the narration of all these events?"

"I am. Sir."

"And who always does the narration, if not the…"

They looked around at each other. The answer, as well they knew, was…

The winners.

TITO PERDUE was born in Chile and raised in Alabama, where he currently makes his home. He is the acclaimed author of six published novels.

ALSO BY TITO PERDUE

Lee

The New Austerities

Opportunities in Alabama Agriculture

The Sweet-Scented Manuscript

Fields of Asphodel

www.titoperdue.com

www.ninebandedbooks.com